THE
SOCIALITE'S
GUIDE
TO MURDER

THE SOCIALITE'S GUIDE TO MURDER

A PINNACLE HOTEL MYSTERY

S. K. Golden

CROOKED
LANE

NEW YORK

Copyright © 2023 by Sarah Golden

Published in the United States by Crooked Lane Books, an imprint of The Quick Brown Fox & Company LLC.

Crooked Lane Books and its logo are trademarks of The Quick Brown Fox & Company LLC.

Library of Congress Catalog-in-Publication data available upon request.

ISBN (hardcover): 978-1-63910-176-4
ISBN (paperback): 978-1-63910-478-9
ISBN (ebook): 978-1-63910-177-1

Cover design by Kashmira Sarode
Typography by Jerry Todd

Printed in the United States.

www.crookedlanebooks.com

Crooked Lane Books
34 West 27th St., 10th Floor
New York, NY 10001

First Edition: October 2022
Trade Paperback Edition: May 2023

10 9 8 7 6 5 4 3 2 1

For Paul.

Okay, okay. You were right.

Chapter 1

I was in the middle of my two o'clock appointment when a shadow fell over me.

"Mr. Peters," I said, "you're blocking my sun."

The bartender stepped to the side so my legs could continue tanning unencumbered, and I turned the page in my Agatha Christie novel. He hadn't set a drink down at my side, nor had he spoken a word or moved back to the bar, so I marked the page with my fingertip and looked at him over my cat-eye sunglasses. Dior, of course.

"Mr. Peters, how may I help you?"

"It's almost four, Miss Murphy."

Oh, right. The party. "Thank you ever so. I'd gotten lost in the book I was reading."

"It's not a problem, ma'am. Hope you have a swell time tonight."

I fished a dollar bill out of my straw tote and gave it to him with a smile.

"Thank you, Miss Murphy." He stuffed the green bill in his pocket and hurried back over to the bar, where patrons were waiting to order their next round of drinks.

I closed the book with a sigh and stood up. "Presley," I called. "Come on, love. Nap time is over."

Presley, a sweet Pomeranian mix whose mysterious father must've been a bear cub, looks like a teensy-weensy brown bear. He's the perfect size for my purse, and I keep his fur out of his eyes with bright-blue ribbons. He woke up from his doze on the lounger next to mine, yawned and stretched, and shook out his paws. I took off my floppy hat and put on a floral cover-up and sandals.

A woman at the bar raised her voice and caught the attention of both of us, Presley's furry little triangles turning toward the noise.

"I had it right here, I swear!" she was saying. "I don't understand what happened. Someone must have stolen it!"

"It's okay," Mr. Peters replied. "We can always bill your room, ma'am."

"No, no, no! This is not okay! Someone has stolen my purse! I thought the Pinnacle Hotel was supposed to be high-class! How can you advertise as a classy establishment when thieves are running about?"

I stuck Presley and my hat inside my tote bag and walked over to the bar, where the woman continued to be upset over her missing handbag and Mr. Peters's face got redder and redder the more she yelled.

"Excuse me." I came up to her side and offered a placating smile. "May I be of service?"

She looked me up and down. "I'm sorry, who are you?"

I held out my hand. "Evelyn Elizabeth Grace Murphy, the owner's daughter. I'm quite good at finding things."

She shook my hand but kept frowning. "My purse has been stolen. I need this reported right away. All my money was in that purse! My boarding pass, my passport! How will I get home?"

I nodded sympathetically. "I'm sure that's incredibly upsetting. We'll alert the proper authorities, won't we, Mr. Peters? But if you might indulge me, ma'am, where were you before you came over to the bar?"

"I was swimming. I hopped out to get a drink."

"And were you sitting anywhere before you swam?"

"Only for a minute. Right over there."

She pointed across the pool to a row of slatted white loungers, many of them occupied by sunbathing guests and a toddler who kept jumping from his father's stomach to his mother's back. Otherwise the rooftop was fairly quiet, with only a couple dozen guests enjoying the warmth of the sun. The scents of chlorine and suntan lotion and alcohol permeated the air as a handful of children did handstands in the shallow end.

I did the most sensible thing to do when an item goes missing: I retraced her steps. With my eyes on the ground, I left the bar area and weaved through flirtatious encounters, men looking for a refill, women searching for a dry place to sit. And there! Halfway between the bar and the row of white slatted loungers, a black purse lay on the concrete, partially concealed by a wayward towel.

I scooped it up, kicked the towel out of the way, and held it above my head.

The woman at the bar clapped her hands in delight. Mr. Peters's face was noticeably less red when I returned the missing item to the guest.

"You did it, Miss Murphy!" the woman said, flipping it open and riffling through it. "Everything's still here. Oh, thank goodness!"

Mr. Peters nodded. "Thank you, Miss Murphy."

"It's really no bother at all," I said. "Of course, each guest room does have its own safe. Or you could give your passport to the front desk for safekeeping. Then you wouldn't have to be so diligent in looking after your things."

The woman's expression changed from gratitude to annoyed, though I had absolutely no idea why.

I scratched Presley's ears and, with a wave, left before another meltdown occurred.

★   ★   ★

The lobby of the Pinnacle was bustling with new arrivals. Guests read newspapers while loitering on plush chairs. The shooting fountain reflected the glistening light of the massive crystal chandelier that hung by the entrance, the first thing people saw after a doorman welcomed them to the Pinnacle.

One woman walked past me wearing a mink coat, and I forgot what I was doing. Mink, in September? A bit gauche, but she did look fabulous. Her dapper companion in a three-piece seersucker suit tilted his fedora in my direction.

I walked over intricate yellow-and-red oriental rugs laid across the highly polished marble floor, nodded at the elevator operators as they filled up their lifts, and headed toward the Silver Room to see how preparations were coming along.

I adore parties. Planning them, mainly. I love to be involved in everything from the seating to the floral arrangements. And getting dressed up and having a drink while eavesdropping on all the newest gossip is my favorite activity. Being trapped in a big group is perhaps my least favorite part, but that is the price I must pay for being the only child of one of the world's wealthiest men. Luckily, tonight I wouldn't be alone. That was my secret for surviving socializing.

I set Presley down and let him wander around the ballroom while I got to work rearranging the flowers. The sprays were all wrong, stashed in back of the purple chrysanthemums instead of sprinkled throughout. And why *purple* chrysanthemums? This was the Silver Room. The florist normally went all white in here.

There was a crash behind me. Presley yipped, and a Scottish man swore.

"Miss Murphy!" Mr. Sharpe called from the back alcove of the Silver Room.

I stretched my lips into a smile and walked over to him. He was steadying a giant easel covered in a purple cloth. Ah, more purple. The artist has a theme in mind, then.

"Miss Murphy," he said, "your dafty dog got underfoot and knocked into me. I then knocked into a chair, and the chair knocked into this painting!"

I scooped Presley up from the floor. "Are you hurt, my baby? Did Mr. Sharpe step on you?"

He wagged his tail and licked my nose.

"Poor little baby. Mr. Sharpe is sorry. Aren't you, Mr. Sharpe?"

Mr. Sharpe was the Pinnacle's manager. Handsome for a man barreling toward fifty, he'd come with the purchase of the hotel as a low-level bellboy. Through the years, under Daddy's tutelage, he'd climbed to the top of the ranks. He's always impeccably dressed in the finest suits, he keeps his graying hair styled a bit like Elvis's boisterous do, and his voice is thick with a Scottish accent that his years spent living in the States haven't washed away.

"Miss Murphy, this is not a place for your dog. This artwork is priceless." He waved a hand toward the easel he'd steadied. "We do not wish to have an accident."

"Of course," I said, "but if that's the case, maybe don't have a chair so close to this display? If a dog could knock it over, imagine what a drunk guest could do."

Mr. Sharpe adjusted his tie with his left hand, cleared his throat. "Yes. I see your point. Perhaps we should move to standing room only. Bring out the tall tables for guests to eat canapés at?"

I nodded my head once. "Brilliant, Mr. Sharpe. As ever."

"Thank you for your . . . input, Miss Murphy. See you tonight."

I'd been dismissed, and before I'd had a chance to finish fixing the flowers. Oh well. More time to get ready. I bid him good-bye and went to see Judy.

Judy runs the Pinnacle's boutique, selling not only Pinnacle branded merchandise but a number of designer clothes. She also orders for me anything I see in a catalog that I want but can't travel to Paris for. Daddy tries his best, but he's overwhelmed on his own inside the women's section of a department store. Men can only handle so much, you know.

She came out from the back room with a shiny white box and set it on the counter with a smile.

I cooed at the beautiful sight in front of me. It was exactly what I wanted. "It's so creamy! You're the absolute *ginchiest*, Judy!"

"Oh." Judy blushed, pleased. "It's nothing. Happy to help."

CHAPTER 2

In my sanctuary of a room—an extensively girly suite, and I am not sorry for the pink carpets, the white furniture, the plethora of throw pillows, or the rose wallpaper—I washed off the suntan lotion with soap and cold cream and got ready for the party.

I'd slept in rollers the night before, and my floppy hat had kept most of the poolside breeze from my curls. Still, I wet them lightly and rebrushed, making sure a few hung over my right eye just so, and that they curled under and around my ears and neck, before setting it all with hairspray. It takes work to look like this. I'm naturally brunette, and keeping up the platinum blonde requires biweekly visits to the Pinnacle's salon. That's not even considering the countless hours spent curling it, or the trips to the salon twice a week to have the stylist wash and condition my hair. But what can I say? I want my hair to be soft and blonde at the same time, which is not a feat for the faint of heart. I don't bother dyeing my eyebrows—I rather like the color of them—but I do take great care to keep them shapely.

The second bedroom of my suite had long ago been converted into a closet. I kept my vanity in the middle of it so

I could be surrounded by all my acquisitions while getting ready for the day. There was no better source of peace than being in the middle of my well-organized purses and high heels and this season's dresses. I discarded my robe and put on a strapless pink long-line bra. A coordinating short pink girdle snapped into place underneath, and nylons the color of my skin with a delightfully risqué seam up the back snapped into that. Over everything, I put on a short crinoline petticoat. It was white, unfortunately, but it wasn't like anyone would see it but me. Still, I preferred it when everything matched, even my underthings. A few hearty spritzes of Chanel No. 5 and I was ready for my dress.

The gown I'd special ordered from France was a not-so-subtle nod to the one Lorelei Lee wears when she sings that diamonds are a girl's best friend—strapless, belted around the waist, and vibrantly pink. I sat at the vanity in the center of the room to apply my makeup. Foundation first, rouge second. A swipe of Vaseline along my cheekbones gave me a dewy, glowy look. Once satisfied, I applied a bit of Vaseline to my eyelids before sweeping on white, shimmery eyeshadow. Black eyeliner to make my lashes look thicker went on next, followed by white liner in the waterline to make my eyes look bigger.

Lips were the most important part of my routine. I lined them in a dark red before applying multiple coats of Guerlain's Rouge Diabolique, the brand and shade all the magazines said Marilyn Monroe used. A small dab of Vaseline to the center of my bottom lip acted as a highlight.

Finally, I applied my new automatic mascara—the brush inside the tube, ready to be applied the moment you pulled it out, will wonders never cease!—and fluttered my lashes to make sure they wouldn't smudge. My brown eyes stared back at me, dark and critical, and I winked.

Not bad, if I do say so myself. Not Marilyn Monroe, but close enough for the Pinnacle.

"Well, Presley?" I asked, applying a puff of powder to set the look.

He was asleep on his giant white pillow, a dark little speck in a sea of fluff, and he couldn't be bothered to wake up.

"Men," I huffed. They never appreciate a good thing when it's right in front of them.

There was a knock on my door, and I shot out of my seat, my hip knocking into my vanity and rattling every vial of perfume and makeup brush on the white wood. I couldn't open the door fast enough and squealed so loudly with delight that Presley roused from his sleep.

Henry Fox—*the* Henry Fox, star of the silver screen and debuting soon on Broadway—swept me up in a giant, twirling hug. Henry is my best friend. We share all the same tastes in everything important: food, music, and men. Henry set me down but held on to my waist, his bright-blue eyes looking me over appreciatively. "You're gorgeous, darling. Absolutely gorgeous. Give us a twirl."

We call each other darling all the time, only we pronounce it *dahling*. You're gorgeous, dahling. You're so talented, dahling. Pass the salt, dahling.

I giggled and did as he asked. The tea-length skirt tickled my calves when I spun.

"You're giving Miss Monroe herself a run for her money, darling."

"Oh, Henry. Thank you ever so. And you! You look rather dashing yourself!"

Henry has to be the best-looking man I've ever known. Tall and tan, with short brown hair and an easygoing smile that the press eats up. The black tux he wore was tailored to perfection. He was nothing short of stunning.

"Sorry I'm late, darling. I must admit I popped into the Silver Room and grabbed a drink."

"A drink already?" I playfully shook my head. "And you didn't bring one up for me. Tsk, tsk, Henry darling. Tsk, tsk!"

He chuckled. "I needed something to steady my nerves. It's not every day I get to walk into a crowded room with a girl like you on my arm. Besides, if it makes you feel better, it was about an hour ago. Grabbed a drink, got a sneak peek at the art, and picked up my tux from Judy."

"Were there many people there yet?"

"Very few," he assured me. "The artist himself wasn't even in attendance yet."

I walked back to my vanity and slid on the long pink gloves I'd purchased to match this dress. "Thank you for coming with me," I said. "Rumor has it the showing will be rather busy, and you know how I feel about crowds." Out of my jewelry box, I grabbed two bracelets, each with six strands of shimmering diamonds.

Girl's best friend and all that.

I held my wrists up to the light and admired the way the stones sparkled.

"Are you going to sing when we walk in?" Henry teased, offering me his elbow. "Steal all Bell's attention right from the get-go?"

I picked up my clutch, bid Presley good-bye, and took Henry's arm. The two of us walked side by side out my door and to the elevator. "Do you know the artist, then, Henry? Are you familiar with his work?"

"Yes and yes," he said. The elevator doors opened with a ding. "Unfortunately."

"Why unfortunately?"

Henry told the liftboy to bring us to the lobby, and the doors slid closed. "I take it you haven't had the distinct pleasure of meeting Billie Bell yet."

The elevator came to a stop after a few floors, opening up and letting in more people dressed to the nines. I smiled at them the way all good hosts should greet their guests, then continued whispering in Henry's ear. "That bad, huh?"

"He gives the Countess Dreadful a run for her money. It's no wonder they're such good friends."

I shrugged my bare shoulders. "She didn't have to pull too many strings. After all, Daddy is a lover of the arts, and Mr. Sharpe supports any parties that bring in money."

The elevator stopped at the lobby, and Henry and I followed the crowd to the Silver Room. We let the group enter before us and took a minute outside the doors to adjust our clothes. I licked my teeth to make sure there wasn't any lipstick residue, then flashed Henry a wide smile.

He double-checked my teeth and gave a nod. "Perfect. All set?"

I straightened his bow tie. "All set."

Once again he offered me his arm. I set my gloved hand on his elbow, and we made our grand entrance. The high, vaulted ceiling with multiple shimmering silver chandeliers running down its center highlighted the grandeur of the staircase leading into the room. Everyone below can see you when you arrive, which is why so many brides choose it for their wedding venue. The color scheme helps as well. Silver accents everywhere, the tables and chairs lined in it.

But Mr. Sharpe had done as he'd said he would. The chairs were removed and the tables changed. The new circular tables were smaller than their counterparts, but they were tall, coming up to chest height.

Paintings hung on the walls and on easels scattered among the guests. A few tables were covered in sketches and the floral arrangements I had done my best to fix. Waiters carrying trays of drinks and hors d'oeuvres snaked through the Who's Who of the New York Art Scene.

A bulb flash of a press camera went off, and I caught sight of the lone photographer allowed inside for the special occasion. Mr. Sharpe has a strict no-press rule that often takes me slipping a dollar bill in the hand of Presley's dog walker to bend. I smiled for the photographer and his bulky Graflex, and Henry and I slowed our steps to let him get a good picture of the two of us for page six, above the fold.

It's great fun when your date is a movie star.

It's good too, for my heart. I've had bad luck with men in the past. Rushed into things I shouldn't have because I wanted nothing more than to be someone's most important thing.

But other than Henry, no one had ever thought me important enough to stick around for very long.

Glasses shattered on the ground. I startled on the steps, gloved hand covering my heart, but it was only Malcolm Cooper. He'd dropped his entire tray of champagne glasses near the bottom of the stairs. He's a few years older than me, with slicked-back dark hair and the barest hint of stubble on his jaw. I told him once that growing a beard might make him look older, as he has a boyish sort of handsomeness about him.

But then he grew the beard, and I told him to shave it. He huffed, grumbled about women changing their minds as often as the sea changes tides, but came back to work the next day clean-shaven. Now he seems to alternate between clean and stubble, based on his work hours. I let him get away with it. At least he doesn't have a ducktail!

Mr. Cooper is Presley's dog walker. Bellboy extraordinaire, he picks up as many shifts as he can as a waiter too. And he'll do anything I ask if I have cash in hand. He's come in useful in many *Something is lost and must be found* situations.

"Come on, darling," Henry said. "I see the Count and Countess Dreadful beckoning us over."

CHAPTER 3

The headwaiter reprimanded Mr. Cooper while he cleaned up the spilled champagne. I gave him a sympathetic frown as I passed by. His gray eyes met mine, and he rolled them as the headwaiter continued his tirade. That was all it took to turn my sympathetic frown into a hidden giggle. Presley adores Mr. Cooper. The little bear cub is up and waiting at the door every morning for his favorite walker to arrive. And while Mr. Cooper acts as though he only walks my dog for the money, it's obvious to anyone he's as happy to see Presley as Presley is to see him.

"Miss Murphy," Count Drewry slurred, "and Mr. Fox, what a delight, as always." The count looks rather like Father Christmas. Ruby-red cheeks, button nose, massive white beard, and a jolly laugh audible even over the crowd around us.

And the crowd in the Silver Room was thick. I held on tighter to Henry.

Countess Drewry is a statuesque Italian woman. Her square, perfectly symmetrical face was framed by luscious dark curls, and her formfitting dress highlighted her fantastic figure. At least twenty years younger than the count, she'd borne him two children before the rumors of her particular extramarital activities started to swirl.

Gossip at the Pinnacle is a type of currency, one I am an expert in growing and trading. At first, I gave those rumors little heed. After all, most rumors are based on only a seed of truth and then exaggerated to suit the needs of the bored people who spread them. But then the countess met Henry and all pretenses of being faithful went out the window.

Poor thing. It didn't matter how hard she tried—and she did try hard—she would never, *ever* be Henry's type.

She air-kissed me twice before moving on to Henry, lingering a bit too long with her cheek against his.

"When did you arrive in town, Henry?" Countess Drewry sipped her drink. She licked the champagne off her lips with eye contact so intense it made Henry shift on his feet. "And for how long can we expect to have the pleasure of your company?"

Henry flashed his movie-star smile. "I only arrived a few hours ago. Had to make it in time to accompany my darling girl, after all." He raised my hand to his mouth and kissed it, glove and all. A flash came from behind, and I knew the photographer had gotten another great picture of the two of us. This one would be below the fold, maybe page eight. "I'll be in New York for some time. I've signed on to star in a new Broadway play."

The countess exclaimed, "Congratulations, how wonderful! You must save us seats for the opening night. Won't that be wonderful, my love?"

Count Drewry raised his glass in silent cheers before draining it all.

Mr. Cooper swept into our little circle with a new tray of champagne flutes. Merrily, the count traded his empty one for a full one. Henry and I took one as well.

"Thank you, Mr. Cooper," I said, pinching the stem in my fingertips. He nodded his head once. "Mr. Cooper is our own London transplant, you know," I told the Dreadfuls. "Moved across the pond about a year ago, isn't that right, Mr. Cooper?"

"That's right, Miss Murphy," he said, his accent on full display. He nodded again and then left in search of more guests who might need new drinks.

Countess Drewry looked me up and down from the corner of her eye, her mouth quirked to the side. "You seem to know the staff well, Miss Murphy."

"What else do you expect?" Henry butted in, coming to my rescue. "She is the Princess of the Pinnacle, after all."

The countess scoffed.

"He's only being a little facetious." I sipped my drink, bubbles tickling my throat. "My grandfather was twenty-sixth in line for the throne, and he had only Mom, no sons. Does that make me twenty-sixth now?" Another sip and then I smiled at the Dreadfuls. "Well, fingers crossed!"

The count choked on his drink, and the sound puffed my chest with pride.

Henry hid his grin with a sip of champagne. "Have you found any paintings to bid on, Countess? I know Billie Bell is a favorite of yours."

"He's marvelous, simply marvelous! I can't possibly pick only one, can I, darling?" She touched her husband's arm but didn't tear her attention away from Henry. "Shall I show you a few of my favorites? Of course, everyone is waiting on pins and needles for the big reveal."

"The big reveal?" I asked.

Countess Drewry finally broke intense eye contact with my date to stare at me in obvious disgust. "Don't you know? The big reveal! Mr. Bell has created a masterpiece. Everyone is calling it his greatest work of all time. He is revealing it here first in about an hour!"

She pointed across the room, over the heads of the growing crowd, to the large, purple curtain draped over a tall easel in the back alcove. The one Mr. Sharpe and Presley had almost knocked over.

Our head security guard, Phil Hall, stood in front of it, his hands clasped and a serene smile on his face directed at anyone who came too close.

"If he's revealing it here first, how can everyone be calling it his greatest work of all time?" I asked.

Countess Drewry pinched her mouth tight and stared me down. She reminded me of Nanny whenever I asked a particularly impossible question no one could answer without a trip to the library.

The count chuckled. "I suppose art people are often given to dramatics. Come, let me show you one of my favorites." He held out his elbow, and I took it with a nod and a smile. Henry offered the countess his arm, and the four of us made our way across the crowd to a landscape on the far wall.

It was one of those modern pieces, where instead of capturing what was actually being painted, the artist had attempted to capture the spirit of it. Colors that never appeared in nature splattered the painting. The dimensions of it were off, so it seemed more like a landscape found in a wonderland than on earth.

A man and a woman, neither of whom I'd met before, stood on either side of it. The man wore sunglasses, even though the sun was long set and we were inside, a vibrant purple tuxedo, and a white hat. He had the most spectacular handlebar mustache I had ever seen. It stretched halfway across his cheeks before it curled back under his nose, and the brown hair of it shone with something expensive.

"Billie Bell," the count said in a loud stage whisper. "And his assistant." He nodded at the woman. She was a pale little thing—five foot in heels was being generous—with flaming-red hair and thick Coke-bottle glasses. Her dress was bright yellow and fit badly, she wore no jewelry except four small silver rings across the fingers of her left hand, and she wilted like a dying flower under the gaze of the count. "I forget her name."

"Mr. Bell," I said, and held out my hand. "I'm Evelyn Elizabeth Grace Murphy. It's a pleasure to finally make your acquaintance, sir. Your work is unique."

He took my hand and kissed it. "As, you will find, am I." His accent was strange. Vaguely European, but slippery, hard to place. "Thank you for coming, Miss Murphy. Count Drewry. Oh, Countess! There you are!" He left his spot by the landscape to pull her into a full kiss on the mouth. She giggled and swatted him away. The count finished off his drink and deposited it on the tray of a passing waiter.

"Mr. Bell," Henry said, his jaw tight.

Billie Bell grinned. "Mr. Fox. What a delight! Last time I saw you, I believe you said . . . what was it you said? Ah, that I'd never work again, is that right? Well, here I am. Working. And in your girlfriend's very own hotel, as it were. Miss Murphy is your *girlfriend*, is she not?"

The way he said girlfriend was immediately alarming. For all intents and purposes, I was Henry's girlfriend. I was the girl he visited when he stayed in New York. I was the reason he didn't date girls in Los Angeles. It was important for Henry's career that the press continue to believe I was the reason he didn't go on dates with girls at all.

Henry didn't move a muscle save for his jaw, back and forth, the noise of his teeth crunching together so loud it banged around my ear canal. I moved from the count's side to Henry's, wrapping an arm around his back and resting my head on his shoulder. "You see, Mr. Bell, when two people are as happy as we are, what is the point of holding on to old grudges? They'd only slow us down."

Mr. Bell's dark eyes looked me up and down, as if he was only noticing me for the first time. He made a *humph* noise and turned away from the two of us. "Tilly," he said to his assistant, "please find Mr. Sharpe. I want to reveal the painting in fifteen minutes on the dot."

The redhead nodded demurely and took off like a flash.

Mr. Bell faced us again and, with a grin that twitched his spectacular mustache, said, "It's so hard to find good help these days, isn't it, Mr. Fox?"

To say I didn't know the full history between my Henry and this Billie Bell would be the understatement of the century. His question, so innocuous on the surface, sparked a rage in Henry I'd seen only in his movies. In seconds he was out of my arms and holding Bell by his tidy purple collar, a fist raised in the air. Gasping, I grabbed his elbow.

Phil Hall abandoned his spot in front of the covered painting and came running over. He tried to wedge his way between the two men, but Henry wouldn't give up space. "Mr. Fox, what's got into you?"

"Henry," I hissed. "Henry, enough!"

"You watch your mouth." The veins on Henry's neck were bulging. "You watch your mouth before I break every tooth in your head!"

Mr. Bell, bless him, managed an even cockier grin than the one before, even as his feet dangled inches off the ground. "Careful." He licked his lips. "I might like it."

Henry yanked back his arm as if to strike the man, even with me holding on to his elbow and Mr. Hall grabbing at his shoulders, but Mr. Sharpe arrived in the nick of time. He exclaimed, "Gentlemen, gentlemen!" and removed Henry's hands from Bell's jacket. "Whatever is the matter here? Mr. Fox, you are one of our most valued guests, but you can't be treating Mr. Bell like this. You know that."

Henry brushed off his clothes like he was wiping away crumbs, his jaw locked shut, his face scowling. Count and Countess Dreadful stood nearby with matching expressions of joy on their faces, as if this were a farce Henry was putting on for their own personal enjoyment.

Bell fixed his jacket and grinned, and I understood Henry's compulsion to break that man's mouth. There was something unsettlingly smug about his entire being.

"Mr. Bell," said Mr. Sharpe, "on behalf of the Pinnacle, I sincerely apologize for any inconvenience you may have suffered."

"No inconvenience," Bell replied. "We're old friends reminiscing. Isn't that right, Henry?"

Still Henry said nothing. I reached for the pendant of Saint Anthony around my neck but remembered, when there was nothing to hold, that I had taken it off for the evening. It didn't go with the *Gentlemen Prefer Blondes* homage I had been aiming for.

Mr. Sharpe put his hand on Henry's shoulder. "Come on, let me get you something to drink. Something stronger than champagne. Take a moment for level heads to prevail, shall we?"

Henry exhaled, still silent, still glaring at the artist. But he nodded and let the manager lead him out of the Silver Room.

Mr. Hall ran his big hand over his balding head. "I better get back to my station. You all right, Mr. Bell?"

"I'm fine, thank you, sir."

Mr. Hall nodded and scampered back to his station.

Tilly, the redheaded assistant, whispered something in Bell's ear. I twitched in surprise at the sight of her. When had she come back? She must've sneaked up in all the hubbub.

"Excellent," he said. "If you'll excuse me. I have something to attend to before the unveiling can get under way."

Chapter 4

Being alone with the Dreadfuls is not the most desirable of circumstances. The three of us stood side by side, still admiring the landscape of a bridge in wonderland.

"It's exquisite, isn't it?" Countess Drewry asked. "I could stare at this all day. The contrasting, vibrant colors. The rough texture, the heavy strokes of the brush. It balances both the masculine and the feminine in a breathtaking way. Don't you think, Miss Murphy?"

More people had found their way into the Silver Room before the grand unveiling. I could feel the pressure of them around me, building the way steam builds in a covered pot.

"Yes," I said, looking for an exit. "The pink parts are so creamy. Excuse me."

The nearest exit led to the tennis court and fresh air. I popped the door open with my hip and stepped outside. The sun had long ago set, but the lights of the city kept the stars hidden in the dark sky. I hugged myself and stared up to where I knew they were and thought about Mom. She was up there somewhere too, even if I couldn't see her.

The back exit opened, and Malcolm Cooper stepped outside. He pulled a cigarette and a Zippo lighter out of his pocket and offered me one.

"No, thank you, Mac." I smiled at him. "And you know you shouldn't either."

He lit up and took a deep puff. "Why not?"

"Because I don't like the way they taste."

His gray eyes sparkled. He dropped the burning cigarette and snuffed it under his heel. "That's a pretty good reason."

I giggled when he wrapped his arms around my waist, but the giggling faded when he pressed his lips to mine. There is something to be said about being kissed by a man who knows what he's doing.

It was a little like magic when warmth spread from the top of my head to the bottoms of my feet, curling my toes and melting away all the anxiety from the crowd. Mac is taller than me too. As a woman who stands at five foot ten inches barefoot, I appreciate that. I buried my hands in his hair and relaxed against him, let him work his magic.

Beyond being a dog walker extraordinaire, a bellboy, and a waiter, Mac is the sort of friend with whom I enjoy a casual bit of fun every once in a while. He's so charming and so good with Presley, and his eyes are so kind. And, as I've said before, he knows how to kiss a girl.

My only regret is that it took me close to ten months of knowing him to find out about this particular talent.

Someone screamed. The noise was far away enough that it didn't immediately draw me out of Mac's arms, but then it came again, a chorus of screams. I stopped kissing him.

He was covered in red lipstick.

"Oh, you're gonna wanna wipe up before you follow me."

"Follow you?" He wiped his mouth with the back of his hand, which only managed to smear the lipstick more. "Where are you going?"

I darted for the emergency exit and ran toward the sounds of chaos.

"Wait, Evelyn! *Evelyn!* At least give me a second before you scarper!"

I did not wait.

It didn't take long to figure out what all the fuss was about. The purple curtain was pulled back to reveal a giant, empty frame perched on an easel.

The Big Reveal had revealed a big robbery, and I hadn't even been there to see it.

Billie Bell had his fingers in his mouth and mascara-colored tears running down his cheeks as he stared at his empty easel. Tilly had collapsed, and a group of people stood around her, murmuring to themselves and drinking champagne. The thing about wealthy people is that they are so used to everyone around them catering to their every need, they are rubbish in a crisis that might require them to take care of someone else.

I shouldered my way through the onlookers and knelt down next to the unconscious assistant. Tilly had a pulse, confirming my suspicion that she'd fainted. Mr. Hall was missing. He must've gone to call the police.

Mac came in a few seconds later, his face mostly wiped clean.

"Get Mr. Sharpe," I told him. "There's been a robbery."

Chapter 5

It took hours for the police to interview everyone in attendance. After ninety minutes I'd taken off my shoes. Two hours in and I was sitting on the floor. They'd separated the guests into groups and were interviewing them in some sort of triaged pattern, where the wealthiest guests who weren't staying on the property got to leave first, followed by the ones who were staying, and so on. I supposed I was on the bottom rung because my father was the owner, so it didn't matter if I complained. Where else was I going to live?

The house in Aspen? The one in Paris? No, I was a Manhattan girl, through and through.

Mac sat down next to me and handed over a glass of water. "I sent up a bloke to take Presley for a walk," he said, "so you don't have to worry about him."

"Thank you, Mr. Cooper." If we hadn't been in public, I'd have kissed his cheek. But we were, and Henry was sitting on my other side, his head against the wall, his eyes closed and his mouth open.

Cross-country travel can make the best-looking of us appear as mere mortals.

A tall Black man in a well-tailored suit, a coordinating fedora, and a loose tie approached us with a notepad and pen in his hand. He was good-looking, midforties, and judging by the confidence exuded in every step he took, obviously in charge.

"Which one of you is"—he flipped through his notepad— "Miss Murphy?"

I stood up. "Yes, hello, nice to meet you." I offered him my hand.

He stared at it.

I cleared my throat and let my hands hang awkwardly at my sides. "I have some questions for you, Mr. . . . ?"

"Detective," he replied. "Detective Hodgson. And I'll be the one asking the questions."

I pressed my lips together and waited. Definitely the man in charge.

"I need your statement, where you were in the lead-up to the reveal." He scribbled something in his notepad, which I found to be rude, considering I had yet to say anything at all.

"Well, let's see. My date, Henry Fox"—I waved at my sleeping friend—"picked me up at my suite on the top floor. My father is *the owner,* in case you were not aware."

Detective Hodgson gave me a look of great disdain over his notepad.

"Right. We arrived at the party, talked with the Count and Countess Drewry for a while."

"I've heard from multiple attendees that Mr. Fox got into a physical altercation with the artist. Were you with him when that happened?"

"Yes. But it wasn't so much a physical altercation as it was a misunderstanding."

He wrote something down. "I see. A misunderstanding about what?"

"I'm not sure," I answered as honestly as I could. I didn't know what the history was between Henry and Billie Bell, but I intended to find out. "After their misunderstanding, Mr. Sharpe escorted Henry out to the hotel bar, I assume to settle hurt feelings. At that point, I went outside for some fresh air."

"And do you have anyone who can confirm that?"

My spine straightened at his accusing tone. Why on earth would I lie about something so small?

"Mr. Cooper." I waved at the man on my other side.

Mac climbed to his feet with a loud huffing noise.

"He went outside shortly after I did."

"And why did you go outside, Mr. Cooper? Weren't you working?"

Mac stuck his hand in his pocket and pulled out his cigarettes and a lighter. "Smoke break."

Detective Hodgson closed his notepad, nodding to himself. "That's as I thought, then. I'm going to have to ask the three of you not to leave the hotel for the time being."

"What?" Mac scoffed. "I don't live here. I live in Yonkers."

"Then I suggest you find a couch to sleep on," Detective Hodgson answered. "Out of this whole crowd, the only ones who are unaccounted for at the time of the robbery are you and Miss Murphy, Mr. Fox, Mr. Sharpe, and the Count and Countess Drewry. I'd like to keep you all in one place until I can get this sorted."

"Unaccounted for?" Mac said. "We told you where we were."

I scrunched my nose in thought. It's an annoying habit that I'm well aware of—it does absolutely nothing for my looks—but

I can't help it. Try as I might to fight it, if I don't scrunch my nose, it's hard to organize my thoughts. "You have a time the robbery took place, then?"

Detective Hodgson sniffed at me in lieu of answering my reasonable question. He nudged his foot against Henry's until he awoke with a start. "Mr. Fox," the detective said, "I need your statement. Miss Murphy, Mr. Cooper, you're free to go."

Henry yawned and rubbed his eyes. I took Mac by the arm and moved him away from the interview. "It's your lucky night," I whispered. "You're staying with me."

He perked up immediately. "Oh," he said. "Okay! I"—he patted his chest—"I can't say I'm surprised, but I am a little. I'm happy, don't get me wrong, chuffed—"

I pinched his side. "Stop it. I meant you'll take the couch. That detective knows more than he's letting on. So tonight, once the police clear out, I'll need your help to break into this room."

"This room?" Mac looked around the Silver Room as the two of us ascended the steps out. "Why?"

"To snoop, of course! Someone stole a painting in a crowded room with only two exits, one of which we were guarding, the other leading out into the very busy lobby. And I'd like to see if I can figure out how they did it."

CHAPTER 6

My alarm went off at 3:30 AM. The bed was empty, the spot by my feet that Presley normally occupied cold. I dressed in an all-black outfit of high-waisted sailor pants and a long-sleeved V-neck top and strolled out into my living room. Sure enough, Presley lay sleeping on Mac's chest.

I cleared my throat.

Mac did not stir, one leg hanging off the couch, one arm over his eyes. With a sigh, I stomped over to him and shook him awake.

"What?" he said. "Where? What?" He sat up, and Presley fell into his lap with a quiet yip. "Oh. Right." He rubbed the sleep out of his eyes. "Your bonkers plan."

"It's hardly *bonkers*. In fact, it's perfectly logical! If the police are so inept as to suspect *us*, of all people, of stealing one of those ugly kaleidoscopic landscapes, then we must find the real thief and clear our names. Don't you want to return to, what was it, Yonkers?"

He huffed, stretching his bare arms over his head. "Yeah, Yonkers. It's cold in here, Evelyn."

I could see the line of his bicep when he moved. I blinked and snatched Presley out of his lap.

"That's thanks to the new air conditioner installed on the top floor. Isn't it swell?" I kissed Presley's wet nose. "Do you want to find the real thief, sweet boy? Come on, let's get you in Mommy's bag."

"No. No." Mac was on his feet after a few more stretches. "We can't bring the dog."

"And why not?" I already had Presley's purse open on the counter, his little tail wagging at the sight of it. "He's a helper!"

"A helper?" Mac wiped his face with the palm of his hand, his stubble whispering at the connection. "Evelyn, we're going to break into a crime scene. You can't bring a dog into a crime scene."

"I can." I put Presley in his bag, slid it onto my shoulder. "I am. Look, I can even put flashlights in there with him! He'll keep them safe."

Mac opened his mouth, closed it, opened it again. "Safe from what? Evelyn, what if he barks? Or pees in the middle of the crime scene?"

I gasped. "Presley would never. He's a good boy, Mac."

"This is not up for discussion. If you want me to break into the Silver Room, you are leaving the dog here. That's it. I hate to give you an ultimatum, Evelyn, but it's me or the dog."

★ ★ ★

Less than ten minutes later, Mac was on his knees outside the back entrance to the Silver Room, a lockpick set in his hands. Presley watched him with great interest from the safety of the purse on my shoulder. I'd fished out one of the flashlights to give Mac the lighting he'd need to work his magic.

He grumbled the whole time. All twenty seconds it took to break into the crime scene.

I pulled the second flashlight out from underneath Presley's furry belly and handed it over to Mac with a wide smile. "See? He's a good helper."

Mac grumbled something else, but I slipped into the dark room unperturbed. All the paintings still hung on the walls, their unnatural colors amplified by the sharp beam of light from my torch. The alcove where the stolen painting was meant to be displayed was in the back corner of the room. There were three windows in the small corner, all big enough for a person to fit through. I handed my flashlight to Mac and opened them. Only one was locked.

"That's what you're thinking?" Mac asked. "Whoever took it went right out the window?"

"The only other thing they could have done would be walk past us. And, though we were preoccupied, we would have noticed a door opening."

"Unless they went out before we were out there."

Mac shined both lights on me as I pulled back the purple curtain covering the large easel and the now empty frame. I mimicked cutting out the landscape with my fingers. Frayed edges of torn canvas poked out in the upper right corner. Someone had cut it right out. The frame was at least four feet long and three and a half feet tall. This was no pocket-sized painting that had been taken.

I put the curtain back over the easel and frowned. "They could have waltzed right up the stairs. But how? With the room full of people, all of them watching? You'd need a big distraction to get the attention of Phil Hall, at the very least."

Mac handed me back my flashlight. "You mean a distraction like a fistfight in the middle of the room with the artist himself?"

I stared at him aghast. "How could you suggest Henry be the thief? He left the room empty-handed, escorted by our own Mr. Sharpe."

Mac shrugged and shined the light around the room, not looking at me anymore. "Maybe he was working with someone else. Some Hollywood insider. You know how those actors are."

"No, I do not. How are they, Mr. Cooper?"

"So it's Mr. Cooper now, is it? Now that your boyfriend is the best suspect for the theft."

I turned away from him, kept shining the light, hoped the beam would land on something useful. Something that would inspire a better idea. Henry couldn't be the thief. He was . . . well, he was *Henry*! He was good and funny and kind. Besides, good-looking movie stars didn't steal ghastly paintings. They just didn't!

Mac didn't share this view, apparently. He kept on and said, "Maybe he was preparing for a role, huh? You know, he's getting into the head of a master thief by pulling off a heist."

I shook my head. "It doesn't make sense. That isn't like Henry. And even if it was something he would do, he'd tell me. He tells me everything."

"Really? And do you tell him everything?"

I glared at him over my shoulder. "What's that supposed to mean?"

"Does he know you ducked out of the party to spend some time snogging me?"

I paced the length of the alcove, biting the inside of my cheek. "No," I said finally. "He doesn't."

"So maybe the two of you don't have the type of relationship you think you do."

At that, I couldn't help but chuckle.

"What?" Mac asked.

"You have no idea." I closed my eyes and tried to remember as best I could what the scene had looked like when Henry and Bell had their disagreement. Mr. Hall did leave his spot in front of the painting, but there were still over a hundred people in the room. Surely one of them would have noticed someone lifting up the purple curtain and cutting a painting out of a frame? Surely not every single set of eyes in the room had been directed at Henry and Bell?

But if it hadn't happened then, when could it have happened?

My nose wrinkled. "What if it was stolen before the party? I came down here after my appointment, and there were multiple members of the staff getting things ready. Even Mr. Sharpe himself. And Henry—" I clamped my mouth shut.

Mac pressed, "And Henry?"

It was suspicious of Henry to start a fight in the middle of the showing. It was even more suspicious that he'd been in the Silver Room alone an hour before he picked me up. But that didn't mean I figured him for a thief.

I squared my shoulders and glanced back at Mac. "Henry got a drink before picking me up, and he said there were people in here milling around. One of them could've snatched it." I shrugged. "Or it could have been stolen during the party. The only thing we know for sure is that it's missing. I'll talk to the artist tomorrow. See if he can shed any light on what happened."

"You'll have to talk to them today, you mean. It's late. I gotta clock in in two hours."

"Poor Mr. Cooper. Well, we'll let you get some rest." I scratched Presley's head. "Won't we, baby? Hopefully he finds a comfortable couch to sleep on, because he's not coming back to our room. No, he's not."

Mac sagged forward. "Aw, Evelyn. Don't be cross with me. I'm sorry I used logic and reason to show that your movie-star boyfriend moonlights as a criminal mastermind. I really am. Please? Please don't kick me out now."

He moved toward me slowly, and I pretended to ignore him, focusing all my attention on Presley. Mac opened his arms and raised his eyebrows as if to ask *May I?* I sighed my consent. He wrapped his arms around me and started to sway, the two of us dancing to silent music in the middle of the empty room.

Presley wagged his tail so hard it smacked the sides of his purse. Excuse me. The *three* of us dancing to silent music in the middle of the empty room.

"While I can agree with you that Henry's behavior is . . . suspicious, under the circumstances," I said, "I don't think he is the actual culprit. While we might not tell each other everything, I am a good judge of character. And I don't believe Henry is a thief."

Mac pulled me closer. "Let me guess. You're gonna prove it."

"That's right. I am." I kissed his cheek. His stubble scratched my lips. "Will you help me, in exchange for a nap on my couch?"

"You got yourself a deal, Miss Murphy."

CHAPTER 7

Mac slept on my couch for the remainder of the night. He even used my shower, though he had to wear the same uniform two days in a row, an experience I doubt he was unfamiliar with. He was awake before me and arrived with a freshly walked Presley and freshly brewed coffee while I made both of us an egg-in-a-hole. I don't need to cook, not when there is a staff of world-class chefs available to cater to my every whim twenty-four hours a day. But Nanny felt it important I be able to handle myself in the kitchen.

"Someday you might want to take care of someone," she said, "even if that someone is yourself. Cooking can be an act of love."

This morning, cooking was simply an act of not wanting the staff to know Mac had spent the night with me. Not *with* me, of course. In my room. On the couch. With a door separating us. But gossip spreads faster than truth, so it's best to limit outside sources.

"This is good, Evelyn," said Mac with his mouth full. "Oh, before I forget." He swallowed and pulled a note out of his jacket pocket. "Your criminal mastermind boyfriend requested I give this to you."

I snatched it out of his hand and read it quickly. I admit, there was a part of me that worried it was a damning confession scrawled in a hurry before he hightailed it out of New York. But it was only him asking me if I was free to swim with him this afternoon in the rooftop pool.

"Perfect," I said to Mac. "I'll need you to make sure the photographer gets to the roof without being stopped."

"Photographer? What, the pictures from last night aren't enough?"

I put our empty plates in the sink. I might cook, but the day maid can do my dishes. "After the hubbub of the robbery, I doubt Henry and I will make the paper. A shame. That dress was incredible."

"A knockout of a dress," Mac agreed. "I saw you in it and dropped my entire tray."

He makes me giggle with so little effort on his part. I smiled bright, my cheeks warm, and grabbed my purse off my vanity. "Here." I handed him a twenty-dollar bill. "For your help last night."

"Evelyn." Mac shook his head. "What are you doing?"

"What? Is it . . . is it not enough?"

"That's twenty dollars!"

I floundered with the cash in hand. "I don't understand. Do you not want my money?" He'd always taken every tip I'd ever given him before. I shrugged and pretended to put it back in my purse, but Mac took it before I had the chance.

"No, I want your money. But you're overpaying."

"Well. That's for last night, and for this afternoon. For your discretion in getting the press on property."

He grinned. "You're weaseling out of a second tip, eh?"

"Two birds, one stone, and all that."

Mac pocketed the money. He stared at me for a minute, that look in his eye that he gets when he's about to kiss me, but he shook his head and walked to my door. Then he turned around and came back. "Listen," he said. "What do you even see in this guy? He's only using you to get his picture in the paper."

"I don't think Henry Fox, *the movie star*, needs my help getting his name in the paper."

"He's B-list at best." Mac rubbed the back of his neck. "What is it? Is it his looks? His money?"

I cooed and set my hands on his shoulders. "Are you jealous, Mr. Cooper?"

"No," he said with a scoff. And then, quieter, "Maybe. So what if I am?"

I spared a few moments to ease his jealousy the way I liked best. He really *can* kiss a girl. Then, once he was fully at ease, I held up my pinkie finger.

Mac blinked at it a few times before coming back into his body.

"I'm going to tell you something," I said, "but you have to pinkie promise not to tell anyone."

He furrowed his brow but wrapped his pinkie around mine. Now, I wasn't about to tell him Henry's truth. That wasn't my place. But I decided, for the sake of Mac's feelings, I should tell him mine.

"Henry and I are not dating. It's all for the press. We get our picture taken together when he's here at the Pinnacle, and that way, when he's working, he doesn't have anyone hounding him to date the newest up-and-coming starlet. He's already connected to a hotel heiress, after all. As for me, well, I do so love to see myself in the paper."

A slow smile spread across Mac's handsome face. "So it's all for show?"

I nodded. "It's all for show. We are nothing more than friends." I squeezed his pinkie tighter. "You'll keep my secret, won't you?"

Mac squeezed back. "Of course. How else am I gonna get twenty-dollar tips?"

"I knew you only liked me for my money."

"No, I only like you for your father's money." He laughed when I swatted at his chest and ducked out of the way when I took a wider swing. "Gotta get to work now!"

I threw my slipper at him, but it hit the closing door instead. His laugh carried down the hall.

★   ★   ★

Sunday mornings are spent at the Pinnacle's salon, getting my hair touched up, my nails painted, and my feet massaged. They used to be spent at church, but the Pinnacle doesn't have its own chapel, and I can't be bothered to travel without good reason. I do wear the pendant of Saint Anthony my mother gave me around my neck, and often when I'm waiting for the dye to set, I'll close my eyes and say a prayer, but it's been years since I've heard a good Catholic homily.

My mother would be disappointed in me. It isn't my fault there's no chapel at the Pinnacle. If anything, she should be disappointed in Daddy for not making the space for one.

After the salon, I ventured out into the lobby and settled into my usual spot in front of the café, which has a marvelous view of the check-in counter. Mr. Burrows, a staff member who knows my preferences, brought me a cappuccino and a copy of the Sunday *Times* with a jerky nod of his head. He's a young man, younger than Mac. Skinny and pale, with big green eyes and thick glasses, blond hair styled in that unfortunate duckbill haircut, and even blonder eyebrows.

He's not an ugly man, not by a long shot, but he has one major flaw, aside from choice in hairstyles: his palms sweat. So much. I've never encountered anyone else who spends the majority of their time indoors having such a damp handshake, but alas, the newspaper felt soggy in my hand. I settled into my regular routine after making sure it was dated correctly: *September 7, 1958.* I read newspapers from all over the country—they're mailed to me from as far away as Los Angeles—but the local Sunday *Times* is always my favorite.

It was while watching the new arrivals over the top of the paper that I caught sight of Billie Bell sweeping across the room. He wore the most incredible gray coat I'd ever seen. It buttoned around his throat and hung to the floor, a train dragging behind him, making him look rather like an anamorphic slug with a human head.

"Mr. Bell!" I abandoned my drink and my paper in favor of chasing after him. "Mr. Bell! You're just the man I wanted to see."

Upon closer inspection, his coat was more like a cape, in that his arms were hidden somewhere inside. How could this be a practical garment for an artist? "I love what you're wearing," I said. "I've never seen anything like it! It's so way out."

"Our clothing is like art, you see," he said, slowing his pace so I could walk next to him in my heels. "It reflects to the world how we perceive ourselves." He stepped into the elevator.

For lack of a better plan, I followed him. "Oh." I looked down at my own outfit. A blue gingham silk shirttail blouse, belted around the small of my waist with a thick black belt, and mustard-colored pants. "I buy whatever has the prettiest ad in a magazine. Or whatever Marilyn Monroe wears. I love her sense of style."

"Fifth floor," he told the liftboy. "That's all well and good," he said as the elevator ascended. "But if you spend your life copying someone else's style, you'll never have your own. And then how can you be a true artist?"

"Guess it's a good thing I don't want to be an artist, then."

"What is it you want to be, Miss Murphy?" The elevator stopped. Mr. Bell walked out with me close behind. "You can't intend on staying the sheltered daughter of a wealthy man your whole life."

I smiled at him and batted my eyelashes. "Of course not! At some point, I'll transition into being the sheltered wife of a wealthy man. I wanted to talk to you, Mr. Bell, about the robbery last night."

Jingling came from somewhere inside his shapeless coat. I stared at his waist, wondering if he'd reveal a flap where his hand might appear, ready to unlock his hotel room. "Dreadful business," he said without producing a key. "Ugly, in fact. My greatest work, stolen before the public could behold it! I only hope the police can find it before it's too late."

"Too late?" My nose wrinkled. "What do you mean, too late?"

Mr. Bell glanced up and down the fifth-floor hallway. Once satisfied we were alone, he leaned toward me and spoke in a whisper. "Scoundrels will undoubtedly try to sell it on the black market. A stolen painting like that? It'll sell for double what I could have sold it for. Triple, even."

Mr. Bell had a small freckle above his right eyebrow that quivered with every word he spoke. "Once it's sold? It'll be gone, forever. Hidden in some gangster's basement, no doubt. A pity. A work as beautiful as that should have been in a museum, on display for all to see."

"A pity," I echoed. "I'm so sorry it was stolen, Mr. Bell. I really am."

The corners of his mouth twitched upward in what I assumed was his way of gracing me with a smile. "Thank you, Miss Murphy. Have a wonderful day."

"You too, Mr. Bell." I waited another moment, hoping to see his arm appear from under his coat. He raised his eyebrow, freckle steady, and I made my way to the lift. His right hand emerged, but from where I couldn't be certain. He unlocked his door and disappeared into his room, and I couldn't make heads or tails of his outerwear.

Artists.

CHAPTER 8

Wearing the exact high-waisted white bandeau bikini that Marilyn Monroe herself owns and my Dior cat-eye sunglasses, I walked into my two o'clock appointment with Presley in my arms. The dog started wiggling the moment he saw the pool. He loves a dip in the afternoon before his nap. I put him on his own four feet and he jumped right in, the guests in the pool giggling in delight.

"Darling," Henry greeted me. He walked over with a pink drink in each hand, wearing only blue swim trunks. He kissed me on the cheek and handed me a cold glass. "Come, have a seat with me. Let's dip our toes in the water."

He led me over to the stairs diagonally across from the decorative plants at the back end of the roof. I glanced in that area and thought I caught sight of Mac's green jacket, meaning he'd sneaked a photographer up there. I kicked off my heels and sat down on the stairs, put my legs into the pool up to my calves. Swimming after a trip to the salon was out of the question. Green hair was not fashionable, and I wasn't about to waste my full face of makeup. But the water was cool, the sun warm, and the drink tasted like strawberries. Presley swam over to us, his tongue hanging out of his mouth.

"What a good boy," I praised, but when I tried to pet him, he swam in the other direction.

Henry laughed. "Guess he's not ready for you yet, Mom."

"Guess not. Little stinker."

Henry put his arm around my back and snuggled close, the laugh still on his lips. I turned my face toward his and waited. After a second, he kissed my cheek and held it there for a moment. Satisfied the photographer had gotten a couple good shots of us, I decided to use this time to talk to Henry about the theft. He'd fallen asleep and I'd left the room before I could check in with him, and as much as I disagreed with Mac's criminal mastermind allegation, I couldn't deny the logic behind it.

"Bizarre what happened last night, wasn't it?" I studied his face and sipped my drink. "For something so large to be stolen so publicly with no witnesses."

He made a noise of agreement. "Tell me about it. The police have it handled, though. They'll find the painting soon enough."

"I can't understand why he's so popular," I said. "I thought his work was ghastly."

Henry laughed again. "This is why I love you, Evelyn. You have such excellent taste." He kissed my cheek again. Another picture? I held the pose for a moment before trying again.

"What is the story between you and him, Henry? I've never seen you so, so . . . well, so hot-tempered before. It was like being an extra in one of your movies."

"You'd never be an extra." He tucked a strand of hair behind my ear and stared at me straight in the eyes. We held that pose for a few extra seconds. "But there isn't much of a story to tell."

I scoffed. "Henry, you would have broken his nose if the security guard and Mr. Sharpe hadn't intervened."

He shrugged and sipped his drink without answering.

"Henry," I said, "why are you being so mysterious about this? You know you can tell me anything."

"I know I can." He patted my knee. "But there isn't anything to tell. Our personalities clash, that's all."

I opened my mouth to argue, but Mac approached us. He knelt down at my side and held out a tray with two new pink drinks on it. "Evelyn," he whispered, "take off your sunglasses so we can get a better picture of your face."

I felt it for the first time then. Completely out of the blue and totally unwelcome.

Mac took the empty glass from me and handed me a full one, his gray eyes sparkling in the afternoon sun, having delivered advice that would only help me. That wouldn't serve him at all. That he wasn't going to get tipped for.

A twist of the heart. An opening of a door. The revelation that my casual feelings for the friend I kissed sometimes were no longer casual.

Not at all.

Mac left us and I stared after him, mouth hanging open. Oh no. I *liked* him! *What do I do now?*

"Evelyn?" Henry prompted. "You want to take your sunglasses off?"

I moved them to the top of my head without thought.

"You all right, darling?"

"Yes." I faked a laugh and made sure my face was tilted toward the hidden photographer. Mac stood by the bushes and waved his hand. "Yes, I'm wonderful. Absolutely wonderful."

CHAPTER 9

Having more than casual feelings for Malcolm Cooper put a damper on all my plans. Indeed, on my entire day. I couldn't have feelings for him. He was my employee! My friend. What with Henry being across the country nine months of the year, Mac was the friend I spent the most time with.

What do I do now? He'd made it clear he was only kissing me to have a casual bit of fun. If I had feelings for him, would he be scared off? Would he stop walking Presley? Would he stop breaking into crime scenes for twenty dollars?

And *was* twenty dollars too much? I'd phone Daddy and ask, but he'd frown on the sleuthing bit.

Silly, stupid worries, all things considered. Somewhere in this very hotel, a criminal mastermind had stolen a giant landscape painting out from under the noses of well over one hundred people, including an armed security guard and the artist himself. I tried distracting myself with music and food. A waiter delivered the beef bourguignonne I'd ordered for Presley and me while Elvis's "Loving You" spun on the record player, but the gnawing unknowing wouldn't leave me alone.

I reread the same page in *Hickory Dickory Death* three times before I realized I hadn't retained any of it. Hercule Poirot would be so ashamed of me. I hadn't even figured out how the painting had been stolen, much less who had taken it. I'm normally so much better at finding things.

What I needed to do was hit the pavement. So to speak, of course. Talk to people. People like Mr. Bell's assistant.

I set the book down on the couch and nodded to myself, thinking it through. Assistants saw *everything*. She'd be able to shed some light on the situation, of that I was sure.

First things first, I needed her room number and a gift. A guest always brings a gift to their hostess, even one who doesn't know they're about to be a hostess. I could stop by the florist and pick up something pretty or—oh! I'd grab a nice bottle of wine from the kitchen. Try to loosen up the timid little thing and really get her talking.

Proud of my plan, I took the elevator down.

Mac was right where he should be, working as a bellboy, loading up luggage on a cart for guests checking in. The guests he was helping were three young and beautiful women, and he was saying something to them with a grin on his face that made them all giggle collectively.

I stopped in my tracks, every muscle in my body becoming taut. Something in the area behind my heart burned, sent fire up my throat. The problem with a man who knows how to kiss is that he's prone to practicing.

There is no worse feeling in the world than jealousy. Everything else I can handle. But jealousy? Where is the outlet for that? The worst moment came when Mac saw me. He waved at me over their pretty heads, and all three of them turned to look at what had taken his attention. My face flushed, and I turned on my heel and headed for the nearest escape route. I'd visit Tilly later.

I couldn't bear to wait for the elevator in his line of sight, so I took the stairs up to the first floor and decided to ring for the lift operator there. But halfway down the hall, I stumbled upon a dead body.

★   ★   ★

Mr. Bell could not have been dead long. I knelt down next to him and touched his neck in search of a pulse. His skin was still warm. He had a big, gaping wound on his back. The left side, under his ribs. The blood stained his slug coat and covered the carpet beneath him. His eyes were open and staring at me.

I closed mine, took a deep breath. I could still see her. In that dark alleyway, the walls of the building blocking out the lights from the Christmas decorations. The knife sticking out of her stomach. The blood on her chin, pouring out of her mouth.

There was nothing to be done for her now.

I made the sign of the cross and opened my eyes. I knocked on the door closest to us. When no one answered, I used a fist to pound away until it swung open.

A startled man in only his underwear opened the door, a curse dying on his mouth at the sight of me kneeling beside a still-bleeding corpse.

"Call Mr. Sharpe, the manager," I ordered. "Immediately. There's been a murder."

The stunned man left his door open while he made the call. I couldn't make out the words, but his voice changed from low

pitch to high and back again several times. Seconds after he dis-
connected, Mac came running around the corner.

He stopped on his tiptoes and windmilled his arms to keep
from falling on top of me. "Bloody hell—" Mac wiped his
mouth. "Evelyn, what . . . ?"

I didn't get the chance to answer. At that moment, Mr. Bell's
assistant Tilly came walking up, humming a tune. The tune
stopped on her lips when she saw her former employer splayed
out on the ground like a squished bug.

She dropped her purse and screamed.

Every door in the hall opened.

★　★　★

Detective Hodgson closed off the scene with a plethora of police
officers. The staff was instructed by Mr. Sharpe to keep the situation quiet to any guest not staying in the area of the murder.
Those who were staying in the area were given a night free in a
new room for the inconvenience.

"I've called your father already," Mr. Sharpe said. "But I
couldn't get a hold of him. I left a message with his secretary."

We stood off to the side as uniformed officers stood shoulder
to shoulder to block entry into the hallway. I was not permitted
to leave. No one was. Several guests wanted to check out but
were not allowed by the detective in charge. Everyone was a
suspect, he'd said, and couldn't leave until he'd taken a statement
and gotten up-to-date contact information.

An officer dressed in blues covered the corpse with a sheet,
the Pinnacle's logo stitched on the corner.

Mr. Sharpe adjusted his formfitting vest. "Terrible business."

Detective Hodgson approached us with his notepad and pen. "You're first on my list, Miss Murry."

"*Murphy*," I corrected. "Evelyn Elizabeth Grace Murphy. My father—"

"Owns the hotel. Yes, I remember. You were the one who discovered the body?"

"That's right."

He tapped his pen against his notebook. "And what were you doing in this part of the hotel?"

Not since I was a little girl had anyone asked me why I was in any place I wanted to be in my father's hotel. I still spent many weekends crashing weddings in the Silver and Gold Rooms. They have fantastic champagne. "I beg your pardon?"

"This section has nothing but guest rooms, does it not? And you live on the top floor, isn't that right? Now, why were you down here, among the rooms of the first-floor guests?"

"Miss Murphy has full access to every part of the Pinnacle," Mr. Sharpe answered. "A fact which she has taken full advantage of for close to two decades now."

"Yes, and I can hear how much you support that." Detective Hodgson's smile did not reach his eyes. "Please, excuse us, Mr. Sharpe. I need to talk to Miss Murry alone."

"*Murphy*," the manager and I said at the same time. I turned to Mr. Sharpe. "It's all right," I said. "I'll be fine. I have nothing to hide."

Mr. Sharpe adjusted his formfitting vest again, flashed Detective Hodgson a tight smile, and turned on his heel. We watched him approach the gathering crowd held off by police officers. Henry and Mac were at the forefront and stopped Mr. Sharpe when he tried to walk past.

Detective Hodgson tapped his pen on his notepad again, bringing my attention back to the matter at hand. "You're awfully calm for a woman of your age and station who has just discovered a dead body."

I raised my chin. "Mr. Bell is not the first body I've discovered."

The detective studied my face before checking his notepad. "I see," he said. "And how old were you when your mother was murdered?"

"Six."

"And was the murderer ever found?"

"I am not sure what my mother's case has to do with this one, but no. The murderer was never found. And it didn't take place on Pinnacle property, if that's your next question."

He scribbled away on his pad before clearing his throat. "Now, why were you down here? *Visiting* someone?" The way he asked the question was not subtle in its indication he thought me a bit of an outgoing sort.

"I don't care for your insinuations, sir," I replied. "But no, I was not *visiting* anyone. I was simply leaving the lobby to head back to my room. The elevators were taking too long, so I came here to the stairs."

Not quite a lie, but not quite the truth either.

"The stairs," he repeated as he wrote down what I'd said. "To your room. On the twenty-second floor. Because the elevators were taking too long."

I realized two things at once. First, how ridiculous my reasoning sounded. Lies were never my forte. Second, the expression on his face. Stern, judgmental, with a spark of cleverness in his dark eyes. He didn't seem like the type to smile much, but when he did, I'd wager, it must be quite the sight.

Exactly like my father.

"Please," I said. "I wasn't about to walk all twenty-two floors. But I wanted out of the crowded lobby. Easier to wait for the elevator on a less crowded floor than out in the hubbub of all the new arrivals."

"Hmm. I have heard that you're quite the . . . homebody," Detective Hodgson said. "So, while I gather I don't need to tell you this, since it's unlikely you'd do so on your own, do not leave the hotel."

I clutched the pendant of Saint Anthony around my neck in lieu of slapping him across the face. "How dare you! I—"

"You are the one who found the body. You do not seem to be in any sort of hysterical state the way most women of your age and status—or, frankly, anyone not in the police business—would be in after finding the corpse of an acquaintance. As it stands right now, you are my top suspect."

A suspect! Me? Saint Anthony twirled between my fingers, my breath so shallow I couldn't form words to defend myself. A murderer! Of all the ridiculous accusations! As similar as his manner was to Daddy's, at least my father always gave me the benefit of the doubt.

"For goodness' sake," I finally managed to gasp out, "me, a murderer?"

"Sir!" An out-of-breath police officer came running up to us. "Sir," he panted, "we've found it. We found the knife."

CHAPTER 10

The back half of the hallway housed twelve guest rooms. That meant twelve guests, plus a few spouses and children, were suddenly without their rooms. Those guests were blocking the exit, because that's where Mr. Sharpe stood attempting to deal with all of them. Detective Hodgson and his lieutenant had no trouble cutting through the crowd. They were out of the police block and toward whatever knife they'd found in seconds. I knew I needed to see it, but I couldn't, not without a distraction.

Henry swept me up in a hug before I could follow the detective. "Darling, are you all right?"

I kissed his cheek and let my lips linger to whisper, "Distraction," in his ear.

He understood at once. Henry set me on my feet and shoved me behind him when he turned around. "Mr. Sharpe!" he exclaimed, "I demand an explanation for this terrible circumstance you have allowed to happen. I am paying good money to be here and expect to not be murdered during my stay!"

The twelve angry guests cried in agreement. The policemen who remained were left to deal with the crowd and didn't notice when I grabbed Mac by the wrist and pulled him away. Together we trailed after the detective.

We caught up to him in the lobby. A team of cops were walking around him, all of them talking, but I couldn't hear what they were saying over the excited chatter of the guests and visitors. We knew by their direction that they were heading to the dumpsters.

"This way," Mac said. We doubled back through the lobby and pushed open the swinging doors into the kitchen.

It smelled heavenly. Like garlic and onions and fresh bread and everything good. Men in white hats of various heights were chopping and stirring and cursing in foreign languages. They called out greetings as Mac and I passed.

"Hello, Marco," I said to the head chef. He was easy to identify because he had the tallest hat and the bushiest eyebrows. The eyebrows aren't related to the tiers of chef seniority but are his most defining feature. "Good to see you. Dinner was lovely."

Past the gleaming stainless-steel counters and appliances, between counters stuffed with pantry goods, was a white door covered in scuff marks. Mac eased it open. We could hear voices in the alley on the other side.

He put his finger to his lips and whispered, "Shh," before beckoning me closer. I rolled my eyes. I didn't need him to tell me to shush when snooping.

The dumpster in the alley was to the left of the door. We couldn't see the police and they couldn't see us. If they looked closely, they'd see that the door wasn't completely closed, but our ears pressed into the empty space should be invisible.

Mac, though a little taller than me, was too close to my own height to find a comfortable eavesdropping position. I pushed him down to his knees. He glared at me the whole time, and struggled too, even as I put both hands on his shoulders.

He worked his mouth in silent words I couldn't make out and chose to ignore. I kept pushing him, getting a knee involved at one point, I am not ashamed to say. Eventually, he went down and listened at the bottom of the door while I held the middle.

"Still blood on the tip," Hodgson said. "No doubt it will match the victim's. And then, what's this? There's an engraving in the handle."

I stared down at Mac. He stared up at me. "Engraving," he mouthed. It was my turn to press a finger to my lips and "Shh" him.

He rolled his eyes.

"*PLH*," Detective Hodgson said. "Pull up our list of employees and guests. Let's talk to everyone with those initials."

PLH. PLH. Mac and I stared at each other again, and each of us whispered, "Phil," at the same moment.

"Did you hear that?" Detective Hodgson said. "Hey, that door is open."

Since I was still on my feet, I managed to run well before the detective swung the door open. Mac, on his knees, was not so lucky. Later, I would learn that Mac slammed the door closed seconds before the detective arrived. Since it was always locked to the outside, the detective was forced to knock. And knock he did. Pounded, more like. Until Mac, leaning against the doorframe, opened it up with a charming grin and a "How may I help you?"

★　★　★

I found Mr. Hall in his office. It was the first place to look—by far the most obvious—and the one I had thought the least likely. Considering there had been, not an hour earlier, a murder and he was head of security. He should've been helping the police at the crime scene or investigating on his own. But perhaps there was a jurisdiction reason he wasn't assisting. Maybe the police or Mr. Sharpe had excused him for the evening. It wasn't necessarily suspicious all on its own.

"Miss Murphy," he said, standing up behind his desk. His office was small—a glorified janitor's closet, with no windows to speak of, and a desk too big for the space. He looked all the more absurd for it. Mr. Hall wasn't a tall man, but he was stout. Wide and strong, with a round, friendly face and big brown eyes. He, like the desk, was too big for his office.

"Can I offer you a seat?" The only seat in the office was his, as there wasn't enough room for a second, so I shook my head and smiled.

"No, thank you. I won't be here long. I only wanted to ask you . . . do you have some sort of a keepsake knife? Maybe engraved with your initials?"

He smiled at me. "Yeah! I have a switchblade like that. Real classy. My brother gave it to me as a gift for being the best man at his wedding."

"Brilliant," I said. "May I see it?"

"Sure. It's, uh . . ." He looked around his desk, a frown furrowing his whole face. "I keep it right here." He indicated the empty spot next to a pencil jar wrapped in a decal of an American flag. "I like to display it, you know. Conversation starter. I—that's very strange."

I pressed my lips together and bent closer to the desk. There was no dust in the empty oval-shaped space but plenty around it, so the knife must have been removed recently. "Can you tell me, Mr. Hall, have you had anybody visit you in your office? Anyone besides me, I mean? In the last twenty-four hours or so?"

He ran a hand over his balding head. "I've had just about everyone in here since then, ma'am. What with the painting going missing. And on my watch too. It's been a long weekend."

"I see," I said. "Thank you for entertaining me, Mr. Hall. I do hope your weekend gets better."

They arrested Phil Hall that night.

CHAPTER 11

Mac paced the length of my living room and back again. Presley hopped behind Mac's heels with every quick step, hoping for his nighttime walk. I watched with a hand over my mouth, doing my best to look sheepish and not at all like I was enjoying the display.

Difficult, considering I was enjoying it very much. After all, it was only a few hours ago that he'd been flirting with three beautiful guests directly in front of my face.

"First off, you left me!" Mac exclaimed out of nowhere.

"Oh, we're talking now. I see. Go on."

"You left me in the kitchen!"

"I did," I admitted, peering up at him from under my lashes. He hadn't stopped pacing. "I left you. It was terribly selfish of me."

"Yes." He stopped pacing long enough to wag his finger at me. "Yes, it was. He caught me there, and he had the nerve to question me! Like I didn't belong in my own kitchen."

"Well," I said, "it's the Pinnacle's kitchen. And you aren't employed as kitchen staff."

Again he wagged his finger. "I work as a waiter. I have every right to be in that kitchen if I feel like it. I told him as much."

He crossed his arms tight over his chest, narrowed his eyes. "I didn't tell him you were with me, if that's what you were worried about."

I shrugged. "Not worried. I actually do have the right to be wherever I please. But"—I left my seat and stood before him, wrapped my arms around his neck—"I am sorry I left you. I was in such a hurry, you see, to talk to Mr. Hall. It was brave of you to stall the detective for me."

Mac sniffed and uncrossed his arms, set his hands on my waist. "It *was* brave of me. You're welcome."

"You're so good to me. However can I repay you?"

The corner of his mouth twitched. "I can think of one way."

"Oh? Whatever could it be?" I tilted my face toward his, brought my lips only inches from his mouth. And then, staring right into his gray eyes, I whispered, "Maybe those girls from earlier can help you."

His pucker turned into a self-deprecating grin.

I twirled out of his hold and grabbed Presley's leash. "After you're done walking Presley, of course."

He hung his head. "You," he said, "are something else, Evelyn."

I hooked the leash to Presley's sparkling blue collar and handed it to Mac. "Why, thank you ever so. Toodle-oo," I said when he walked out the door. Waiting a moment to make sure he wasn't about to come back and sneak in a kiss—and feeling a little disappointed that he didn't do exactly that—I sat down on my couch and reflected on the day's events.

Of course Phil Hall wasn't the real killer. No one with a lick of sense would commit a murder with a weapon with their own initials engraved in the handle. It did work out for me, however, as I was no longer the top suspect in Mr. Bell's death.

I doubted Mr. Hall was behind the theft either, but Detective Hodgson was of a different mind, having arrested him for both crimes. Mac had overheard the working theory: Hall had stolen the painting, Bell had figured it out, and when Bell confronted him, they'd ended up in an altercation that took Bell's life. But it made no sense to me.

How *could* Hall have stolen the painting? The only possible moment for the theft to have occurred was when Henry and Billie Bell had their misunderstanding. But Mr. Hall left his station and tried to put a stop to the fight. How could he have stolen the painting if he wasn't near the painting? That suggested he had an accomplice. But who?

Who could still be wandering the halls of my hotel, a murderer? A thief? This was my spot in the world, *my home*! My mother had been killed outside the hotel, and her killer had never been found. Ever since then, the only place I'd ever felt truly safe was inside the walls of the Pinnacle. And I would not let some backstabbing so-and-so muck about in it and ruin it for me.

My eyes drifted to *Hickory Dickory Death*. Hercule Poirot would've figured this out already. He'd be smiling at me from underneath his spectacular mustache, urging me on. Telling me to use my little gray cells. I could make the hotel safe once again.

The only question was: Who *had* killed Billie Bell?

Oh, and *why*. Two questions.

And who had stolen the painting? And how?

Four questions.

Four questions remained, and it was up to me to answer them, or else I might never feel comfortable again.

★ ★ ★

I took a good long soak in the porcelain claw-foot tub that sat in the center of my bathroom. My bathroom, like the rest of my suite, was primarily pink, but gold details shined up the place. From the feet on the tub to the spouts on the sink and the sconces on either side of the four-foot-wide mirror, everything was gold and girly. I filled the bath all the way up, added lavender-scented oil and enough bubbles to hide beneath, smeared a mask on my face, and put my hair in curlers. After discovering a dead body in my very own hotel, I deserved a bit of pampering.

The water was warm, but I felt cold all over. Goose bumps had broken out on my arms and shoulders and the back of my neck.

Someone had died. In *my* hotel. And I was the one who had found them.

With my foot, I cranked the hot water lever, slid down until my shoulders were covered. Ducked down until the water swished in my ears and I could hear the pulse of it filling the tub around me. But the white noise allowed my thoughts to drift, back to Bell. Back to my mother. To unsolved murders and what happened in the aftermath. The Pinnacle was supposed to be safe. Free from murder, at the very least. But Bell, with his ridiculous mustache, had ruined that. Now there was a murderer on the loose in the one place in New York that was mine.

At this rate, I'd never settle down. I sat up, dried my hands, and grabbed my book. I read three more chapters of *Hickory Dickory Death* by candlelight before my eyelids grew heavy from fatigue. Sleeping in the bathtub is terrible for the skin; dries it all out and makes it pruney.

It was time to go to bed. I drained the bubble bath, dried the back of my head before tying on a polka-dot scarf as a turban, and wrapped myself in a towel.

Someone wolf-whistled when I opened the bathroom door. The towel almost fell when I jumped. I clutched it by the seams, barely preserving my modesty. Mac was lying on my couch, hands behind his head and his shoes off, the traitor Presley asleep on his stomach.

"That color looks brilliant on you, doll," he said.

My face was still covered in clay.

"And your hair. Love it." He winked at me. "Marilyn would be proud."

Oh, and the curlers too! Those pretty girls he was talking to earlier in the day would probably never be caught dead looking like this in front of a man.

"You," I said, "are *not* sleeping on my couch again."

"You want me in bed? Wonderful. I like the curlers; keep them in—"

"Mac!" I stomped my foot. "It is late, and I need my beauty sleep. What I don't need is you in here, making a mess of things."

"Making a mess of what, exactly?"

I gestured to his shoes on the floor.

"Come on, Evelyn. It's two o'clock in the morning! I'd get to Yonkers and have to turn around and come right back."

"Yes." I tightened the towel over my chest. "Like normal. Like everyday, ordinary New Yorkers who have to commute for work."

"Evelyn, there was a *murder.*"

"I know that, Malcolm. And you don't see me sleeping on someone else's couch because of it!"

"You live here!"

Presley licked Mac's face in a lazy attempt to get the humans to be quiet.

Mac sighed and scratched him behind the ears. "Listen, Evelyn, it's one more night. I'll get out of here quiet as a mouse in the morning, walk this little monster. Take my shoes with me. You won't even know I stayed here."

"Again," I said. "Stayed here two nights in a row."

"Right. Again. You dig?"

I huffed. "Do I *dig*? Honestly, Malcolm Cooper, why do I put up with you?"

He grinned. "Presley won't let anybody else walk him."

The towel slid. Holding tight, I tapped my thigh and whistled. Presley wagged his tail but stayed on Mac's chest. Mac grinned at me. "Come on, baby," I called. "Come to Mommy."

Presley did not. Mac's grin grew.

"Your accent sounds ridiculous when you try to use words like *you dig*," I said, before slamming my bedroom door. Mac's laugh followed me.

Traitors, the both of them.

CHAPTER 12

Every Monday morning, I wake up promptly at seven AM and, after having breakfast with Presley, head to the Pinnacle's tennis court and get in a lesson with our on-staff pro. But on this particular Monday morning, I woke up in a fog and stared at the ticking hands on the clock face until it clicked to 10:18.

What happened?

I hadn't felt like this since my twenty-first birthday, when I had overindulged at Mac's insistence.

Ugh. Mac. Sleeping on my couch with my dog like he owned the place. The nerve of the man.

I kicked my legs free from the blankets and struggled to sit upright. But I hadn't had anything to drink. There had been a theft and a murder, and apparently the late nights had caught up with me. Still. I do hate to miss an appointment. Very unprofessional.

I found Presley in his fluffy white pillow. The couch looked unrumpled, and as Mac had promised, both he and his shoes were nowhere to be found.

"Did he feed you?" I asked my dog. "Get you walked?"

Presley kept sleeping.

"Good. Good. Excellent." I sniffed and looked around the penthouse. It always seemed so big, first thing in the morning. Like it had grown on me overnight. The city skyline shone at me from my sliding-glass balcony doors, the tops of the trees in the park beginning to fade to fall colors.

I shrugged out of my robe and walked back into the bedroom. Nothing to do but be late for my tennis lesson. The penthouse would sort itself out by the time I got back.

★ ★ ★

The phone rang. I slipped on my white tennies and answered with a happy "Hello!"

"Miss Murphy?" The voice on the line cleared their throat. "It's, uh, it's Peters. From the pool."

"How do you do, Mr. Peters?"

He cleared his throat again. "I got a call up here. Well, I think everybody got the call, actually. Security is scrambling without Hall."

"Oh," I said, confused. "Um. Okay."

"Anyway, I thought I should tell you."

I waited for him to continue, but the only thing that came through the line was his breathing. Had something happened to Daddy? My chest was tight, twisting in knots. Was that the call that had come in? But surely the person who informed me of my father's troubles wouldn't be the rooftop pool bartender. Surely, at the very least, Mr. Sharpe himself would knock on my door.

"Mr. Peters?" I wrapped my fingers in the spiraled cord of the phone. "Whatever is the matter?"

"A little girl is missing," he said at last. "The diplomat's daughter from France. She's been gone for about thirty minutes. And you, Miss Murphy, you're so good at finding lost things—I thought you'd like to know."

I exhaled in relief, the nervous knot in my chest dissipating. Daddy was fine, then.

"You were right, Mr. Peters. I do want to know. Thirty minutes, you say? Where was the last place she was seen?"

"In the lobby. Her parents were grabbing a bite at the café. They left her by the fish tank."

I grabbed the nearest memo pad and pen and jotted down what little information he'd given me. "And how old is she?"

"I think they said eight. But it might have been nine. Definitely it was younger than ten."

I sighed, shook my head, and scribbled *8–10*. "Thank you, Mr. Peters. I'll start looking right away."

★　★　★

There are advantages to living in the same hotel for seventeen years. Chief among them, I know every nook and hiding space an eight-year-old—or nine-year-old, definitely less than ten-year-old—girl might sneak into. Of course, that's only if the girl is missing because she wants to be and not because of something more sinister.

First things first: rule out the probable and then worry about the improbable.

I went to the lobby, Presley's purse on my arm, and stopped where the missing girl was last seen. The fish tanks. The café was stationed behind them, with plenty of seating to the side. Lots of guests and visitors alike were having coffee and chatting.

But a little girl would've taken no interest in that. What she would have noticed from that spot were the service elevators. A little girl looking to hide from her parents would find them irresistible.

I sure had when I was her age, whatever that age might be.

Staff members in green uniforms greeted me as I walked by. No one tried to stop me from stepping into the service elevator and going down. In fact, the maid vacating it held it open until I was inside, thereby eliminating the need for the employee-only key. A little girl who was prone to sneaking would've had no trouble slipping in behind a distracted worker.

It's cold below ground, except in one corner, where the heat from the boiler rolls out in waves. There is a false wall nearby, with a hidden door that opens into a dark, cozy space the old owners used to store black-market goods. Ah, the Roaring Twenties. It was also where I used to hide from Nanny when I was a little girl and needed a break from grown-ups telling me what to do.

She never did find out about it.

I'm not sure how many people know it exists, actually. As a child I assumed I was the only one in the world who knew about the hidden room, but that can't possibly be true. You have the architect who designed it, the workers who built it, and the gangsters who used it. I'm sure Daddy has all the blueprints somewhere.

The wallpaper changes over the hidden door. A little off-center, an inch and a half away from perfection, only noticeable if you're paying attention. It opened with a push and a creak, and the light from the boiler room cast a giant shadow of the little girl against the barren walls.

"Hello," I said with a smile. "My name is Evelyn. This is my dog, Presley." I've found when dealing with children it's best to lead with Presley. He is positively irresistible. "May we sit with you?" I put him down, and he scampered toward the child like I knew he would. Presley loves being adored.

The little girl cooed when she saw the puppy-sized bear cub, and I climbed in behind him, shutting the secret door. She was still in hiding after all, and it would be rude to give her location away now.

She was a pretty little thing, blonde curls and green eyes, an expensive dress. "How did you find me?" Her English was superb, though from her accent, it was obvious French was her first language. "I thought this was the best spot."

"Oh, it sure is." I settled into a seat across from her. Presley climbed into her lap and busied himself licking her face. She giggled and scratched behind his ears. "I used to come here when I was your age. See?" I pointed to scratches on the wall. "*EEGM1*. That's me."

"EEGM1?" She rubbed her nose against Presley's. "That's a strange name."

"Evelyn Elizabeth Grace Murphy. The first." I smiled. "My father bought the Pinnacle when I was four."

Presley curled up in her lap the way a cat naps in the sun, and she giggled again. "I'm Amelia," she said. "You have a lovely home."

"Thank you, Miss Amelia. I'd love to show you around," I said. "We have our own sweet shop. Do you like candy, Amelia?"

She tore her attention away from Presley to look at me. "Yes! Chocolate is my favorite. And marshmallows!"

"Oh, me too! You have exceptionally good taste, Amelia."

She smiled bright. "Thank you. I like your dog. And your necklace. May I see it?"

I touched the silver pendant hanging around my neck. "Oh, of course." I unhooked the chain and handed it over. "That's Saint Anthony. My mother gave it to me on my sixth birthday. Do you know what Anthony is the patron saint of?"

She shook her head, her little fingers tracing the pattern of the haloed man holding a small child.

"Lost things," I replied. "Mom always said I was good at finding lost things. Saint Anthony helps me, you see. Like when I was looking for you." I added a teasing note to my tone. "I prayed: *Tony, Tony, Tony, something's lost and must be found!* And then I found you!"

She giggled and handed the necklace back. "I don't feel lost." She sounded much older than she looked. "I only like to be by myself sometimes."

I clasped the last gift my mother ever gave me around my neck and leaned against the cool wall of the hidden room. "Your parents are looking for you." I said. "They're worried."

Amelia scoffed. "Not my parents."

That was not the answer I was expecting. "I beg your pardon?"

She sighed. "Well, she is my mother. But *he* is not my father."

He being the French diplomat. I stretched out my legs, sensing we were going to be confined in the small space for longer than anticipated. Presley looked at me curiously, but when I didn't stand, he went back to relaxing in Amelia's lap.

"I see." I fiddled with the hem of my tennis skirt. "He's your stepfather?"

She nodded once and scratched Presley under his chin.

"Is he . . . is he mean to you, Amelia? In any way?"

"No." She was quiet, her full attention on the small dog in her lap. "No," she said again. "In fact, he is very kind. But he isn't . . ." She trailed off, and even in the low light of the hidden room, the tears on her cheeks were visible.

"Oh, I see. No matter how nice he is, it doesn't make up for the fact that he isn't your father, is that right?"

She wiped her face dry and whispered, "Yes."

"Miss Amelia, you and I have more in common than our exceptionally good tastes. My mother passed away when I was six years old. My father, he's always been busy with his work. All his different business dealings. You can't expect a man like that to spend all his time raising me. So he hired a nanny to take care of me. Nanny lived with me in this hotel for years and years, and she was absolutely wonderful. Simply the *best* nanny any girl could ever ask for. But she wasn't my mom. I loved to hide here for a little while. Just to get some time to myself, and maybe, if she was upset for a few minutes—well, maybe she deserved that for not being Mom."

Amelia picked up Presley and hugged him like a teddy bear. The dog wagged his tail and licked her nose. She buried her face in his furry little back. "I miss Daddy sometimes."

I nodded in understanding and felt the bond between us form across the decades that divided us. Whether you're less-than-ten or twenty-one, the pain of losing a parent at a young age never really goes away.

"I tell you what," I said, "when you're ready, why don't I take you to the sweet shop, hmm? I know the woman who runs it, and she'll give us all the chocolate and marshmallows we can eat!"

"Really?"

"Really!"

She set Presley down on his own four feet and stood up. "I'm ready, Miss Evelyn."

The sweet shop off the lobby was a massive hit, not only with Amelia but with people walking by on their way to Central Park. The window display was visible from the street, candies and cookies and cakes filling the brightly lit, golden-trimmed window. Amelia squealed and spoke in rapid French, devouring all she could grab.

Her relieved parents swept into the sweet shop, and Amelia, covered in sticky goodness, hugged them tight. I recognized them from the day of the art showing. She'd been the woman wearing a mink coat, and he had tipped his hat at me. They were less fashionably dressed now, thank goodness, as getting marshmallow out of fur would require an emergency trip to a dry cleaner.

Holding Presley in the crook of my right arm, I popped a chocolate in my mouth and allowed an indulgent smile. I'd done that; I'd brought them back together. And while it was only a matter of knowing all the best hiding spots in the place I'd lived in since I was four years old, her stepfather clasped my hand in his and her mother kissed me on both cheeks.

"I'm on the top floor," I told Amelia before they could take her away. "Room twenty-two seventeen. Feel free to visit Presley whenever you want."

She wrapped her sticky hands around me in a big hug. "Thank you, Miss Evelyn!"

I hugged her back and whispered in her ear, "And remember, no one knows about that secret hiding spot but you and me."

She held out one shiny pinkie and said, "Pinkie promise."

I grimaced and kept my hands to myself. "Pinkie promise."

"No," she giggled, "you can't say a pinkie promise. You have to *do* a pinkie promise."

Still grimacing, I wrapped my pinkie around her sticky one. We kissed our own thumbs.

Amelia released me, leaving behind a marshmallow residue. "I'll see you soon, Miss Evelyn. Bye, Presley!" She scratched his ears and he licked her face. Her mother took one hand, her stepfather the other, and off the three of them went. A perfect New York postcard of a family in a fairy-tale candy store.

CHAPTER 13

Giving up on tennis for the day, I returned to my room and got ready for my standing lunch date with Presley. I applied a light dusting of talcum powder and slipped on a sweet pink girdle and matching bullet bra, clipped on nude panty hose. My dress was made of pink silk shantung. White pearlized buttons went up from my belly button to the column of my throat and clasped the sleeves closed above my elbows. I wore pearl drop earrings and a two-strand bracelet covered in pearls but kept my pendant of Saint Anthony on, tucking it under the fold of my collar so it hung between the buttons. The matching pink belt accentuated the exaggerated waist the girdle supplied me.

I switched out Presley's regular purse for a white one so it would match my high heels. I considered a pair of white gloves, but searching for Amelia had made me ravenous, and the gloves would only slow me down.

Presley and I took lunch at the Pinnacle Bistro. Black, white, and red is its color scheme, and signed pictures of celebrities who at one time or another pulled up a seat and ate at one of its square tables cover the walls. It overlooks the busy street, with partial views of the Park beyond. The silverware wrapped in white cotton is expensive. So is the food, with the towering double-patty cheeseburger the bistro is known for being one of the most pricey in town. But the burger itself, covered in onion rings and dripping in cheddar cheese, was worth the price of every bite—monetarily and calorically.

Presley had his own chair, a bowl of water, and a plate of beef. He was the perfect dining companion while I tried to piece together the puzzle of Mr. Bell's untimely death. It was hard not to think of my mother. Every time I pictured Bell's body in the hallway, it morphed into the memory of my mother in the alleyway. The two blended together in my mind's eye until it was difficult to separate the two of them.

"Ah," said a familiar voice, "I'm surprised to see you out of your room. Thought after your eventful night, you'd be sleeping the day away."

Henry grabbed a chair from a nearby table. The metal legs scratched along the linoleum floor so loud Presley tucked his head down and everyone in the bistro stared at him. Even passersby outside the windows heard and stared. He set the chair between me and Presley and sat down with a quiet huff, immediately grabbing a fistful of french fries off my plate.

My mouth fell open. Henry? Eating a side dish that wasn't steamed veggies? What on earth! But people were still staring, so I kissed his cheek. He let me, but his mouth was set in a deep, serious frown.

"Darling?" I questioned. "Is everything all right?"

"No, everything is not all right." He stabbed a fry into a smear of ketchup. "I thought we had an understanding."

Presley licked his plate clean until it rattled on the tabletop. I slid it away from him and smiled at my newest companion, so far a less perfect one than my dog.

"I'm not sure I catch your meaning."

He leaned in close, one hand on the back of my chair, and whispered, "I know that boy spent the night with you."

His revelation caught me by complete surprise. "Boy? You mean Mac?" I laughed. "That's nothing."

"Nothing? He was seen leaving your room in a disheveled mess this morning. Shirt untucked, pants unbuttoned. Rumors like that, Evelyn, travel fast."

"I see." I pushed my plate toward Presley, having lost my appetite. Mac must have overslept too and missed his morning shower. Unfortunately, that meant the maids must have been on duty by the time he vacated my suite. "It looks worse than it is. He was here late because of the murder. I let him sleep on my couch since he walks Presley at night and in the morning. It was really nothing."

Henry shook his head and heaved a giant sigh. "Doesn't matter if it's nothing. People are talking. That's what matters. I can't have it look like you cheated on me. And I certainly can't have it look like my steady girl is *easy*. Not now, when I'm about to open this play."

I wrapped my hand around his forearm. "I'm so sorry, Henry. If there's anything I can do, I'll do it."

"Just stay away from him for a while."

My fingers twitched on his skin.

Henry furrowed his brow, stared me down with harsh judgment in his eyes. "Surely you can do that. He's a bellhop, for Pete's sake!"

"Of course." I smiled. "Of course, he's nothing. He's no one. He only helps with Presley is all."

"So get someone else to walk the little bear." Henry scratched Presley behind the ears. He wagged his tail and licked Henry's wrist in response.

"Presley doesn't like anyone else," I said. "He'll sit and refuse a walk from anyone but me or Mac."

Henry took my hand off his forearm and held it in his own. "That's an idea, then. You walk your dog. For a week, maybe two. Until this stupid rumor is put to bed. We don't need this press, Evelyn. It's bad for us both."

"You're being ridiculous. You're behaving like a jealous lover. I told you this rumor holds no weight. It isn't true. And Mr. Cooper is vital to my everyday routine. I can't fire him."

"Why not?" Henry scoffed. "You're the one who is being ridiculous. You said it yourself. He's nothing. He's no one. He's a bellhop and a dog walker. For the sake of our arrangement, you need to cut him out of your daily routine. You will do that for me, won't you, darling?"

Around the bistro, the other diners were busy with their own meals and conversations. Yet I still felt eyes on me, though I couldn't tell from where the audience was coming. "You're my best friend, Henry. My very best friend. I'll relieve Mr. Cooper of his duties for the time being. But only for a week."

Henry smiled his movie-star smile. "Two weeks. Please."

I rolled my eyes. "Fine. Two weeks. And then I'll need my dog walker again. Honestly, you're making me wake up at six AM to walk this dog. I hope you're proud of yourself."

He kissed the back of my hand. "I owe you one, darling."

"I believe this makes us even, actually. You did create a distraction for me last night."

"Ah, yes." He grinned. "That was some spectacular work on my part. Did you get what you needed?"

"Maybe. Right now everything is still very confusing. I was surprised by how fast you got to the scene last night, Henry. Grateful, of course, but surprised. I think you were the only guest not staying on that floor to make an appearance."

He took another bite of fries. "I was with Mr. Sharpe when the call came in. I was talking to him about my *friend of Evelyn* discount. Somehow it hadn't been applied to my room."

I grimaced. "Sorry about that."

"It's fixed now. How are you, darling? I know you live for books about this kind of stuff, but finding a dead body like that must've been hard on you."

My heart melted. It was sweet of him to worry about me. "I confess it has brought up memories of my mother. And I'm incredibly annoyed that someone would dare sully the sanctity of my home by committing a murder in it. But I'm fine. Really. Thank you for asking."

"Glad to hear it, darling. I must get going, though. The stage waits for no one. You can call me at the theater if you need me, you know that, don't you? Otherwise, I'll see you later?"

"Of course."

He kissed my cheek in good-bye and then was off like a man leading a parade, head held high and waving at passersby. Presley had cleared off my plate too and was having his fill of water from his bowl. I sighed. "I guess we're on our own for the time being, baby."

No matter. Mac had started working at the Pinnacle a year ago. I'd gotten into plenty of adventures without him. I could handle this bit of investigatory work on my own. After all, he was just a bellhop.

CHAPTER 14

"There you are!" a young girl singsonged. "I've been look-ing absolutely everywhere!"

Amelia hopped into Henry's recently vacated seat. "My love," she said, scratching Presley's chin. "My little love. Did you miss me?"

"How would he have had a chance?" I asked with a sur-prised laugh. "My dear Miss Amelia, didn't we just return you to your parents?"

She shrugged, still scratching the hairs on Presley's little chin. "They are both on the phone *busy with business*, so I went to visit your room. But you weren't there, so I played the eleva-tor game."

"The elevator game? What's that?"

She grinned. "The elevator game is this fun game I invented where I take the elevator to the lobby and then run to the third floor and hop in the same elevator and ask to go to the fifth floor. And then I run out of the fifth floor all the way to the eighth floor and take the same elevator to the lobby. I choose a different floor each time, but I always use the same elevator. It's fun. I've seen the entire hotel like that, and the liftboy loves it, I can tell."

I grinned back. "I bet. Have you seen anything interesting playing the elevator game?"

Amelia plucked Presley out of his chair and put him in her lap. My dog did not mind in the slightest. "Not today," she said. "I did yesterday, though! I saw a man dressed like a slug. I thought that in America you saved fancy dress for the end of October, so I followed him a while."

My nose scrunched up. The man dressed like a slug had to have been Billie Bell. Cautiously, I asked, "Did the man dressed like a slug do . . . anything interesting?"

She popped a fry in her mouth and shook her head. "No, he was very boring. But this short woman with bright-red hair came up to him and started yelling at him."

His assistant? That timid little thing who had stood meekly by at the party? Yelling in a hallway?

"What was she yelling?"

Amelia shrugged. "Something like 'How could you?' or 'Why did you?' I don't remember. They went into a hotel room, and I tried to listen, but they were too far away from the door for me to understand what they were saying."

At that, I had to laugh. What a precocious little child. She reminded me much of myself, so much so I felt I understood Nanny for the first time, and missed her something terrible.

I hadn't talked to the assistant yet about the missing painting, and that was something I needed to remedy as soon as possible.

"It's getting a bit late in the day," I told Amelia. "Let's get you back to your room."

She sighed but acquiesced, and the three of us walked to the bank of elevators. "Remember," I told her before she walked into the nearest one, "you are always welcome to come over and play with Presley. He adores you."

Amelia wrapped her arms around my hips in a big hug. "See you soon, Evelyn!"

"Take her to her room," I told the liftboy. "Do not allow her to get off on any floor but her own."

She let go of me with a grumble but told the operator her room number. It was the one directly across from my room. I filed that away for later and waved good-bye.

Something glittered in a nearby potted plant. Odd. I approached it with a furrowed brow, Presley's head popping out of his purse, his tail hitting the sides and bumping into me.

"Car keys," I said, fishing the things out of the soil. "What a place to lose these, huh, boy?"

He tried to lick them, but I moved them away from his face with a giggle.

The line at the check-in counter was immense. This was both not surprising, as the Pinnacle is a staple of New York society—one murder wasn't about to change that—and infuriating. I didn't want to wait forever behind guests checking in to get Tilly's room number, but I didn't want to go all the way back up to my room and phone the front desk either. First, because I had keys I needed to turn in so whoever lost them could be reunited with them, and second, because that would involve even more walking and my toes already hurt, but I wasn't about to change shoes. They made the entire outfit!

If only I hadn't told Henry I'd steer clear of Mac. My half-eaten cheeseburger and french fries sat heavy in my stomach.

Mac would be able to find Tilly's room number in seconds, and him snooping behind the check-in desk would look normal. Part of his job, after all, is ferrying bags and deliveries from the lobby to the correct room.

While both the check-in and concierge counters were busy, the mail desk had not a soul before it.

I sauntered over. Mr. Burrows was the clerk on duty. Perfect.

"Good afternoon, Mr. Burrows. I found these." The keys clanged when I handed them over. "And I'm here to pick up a very important package." I placed Presley's purse on top of the counter.

Presley popped his paws on the front of the bag, and Mr. Burrows flinched like my little bear was a full-grown polar.

"Important package?" He tossed the missing keys in a cardboard box labeled *L&F* and fumbled through a binder in front of him. "I don't have anything noted here. I'll have to check the back room."

I smiled. "That's fine. Presley and I will wait. Won't we, baby?"

He wagged his little tail and let out a happy yip that caused Mr. Burrows to all but jump out of his skin. He dabbed at his forehead, mumbled something incomprehensible, and disappeared into the back room.

Since Mr. Burrows was the only one manning the mail counter and every employee at the check-in counter was busy with guests, I slid into the empty station. He'd left the binder behind. I glanced to my left—check-in counter still busy and paying me no attention—and to my right—the door to the back room still shut—and flipped through the binder. I couldn't remember Tilly's last name. Darn. What was it? Had I ever been told it?

I skimmed, looking for any woman's name starting with a *T*. I realized my search was foolhardy in a single flip of the page. If she hadn't ordered anything to be delivered, she wouldn't be in the bell services list. I needed to get to the check-in counter.

Two palms smacked on the mail desk. The binder flew out of my hands and fell between my feet. Presley yipped and jumped out of his bag, covering Mac's laughing face in kisses.

I gulped in air to steady my racing heart. "You frightened me something awful! Where did you even come from?"

"Over there." He waved at the lobby behind us. "What are you doing back there? Snooping?"

"What else would I be doing back here? Working?" I retrieved the binder and flipped through a few more pointless pages.

Mac gave Presley a kiss on his snout and then stuck him back in the purse. "What do you need? You know I can get you whatever you want."

"Can't ask you for help," I said. "Apparently, you overslept this morning, and someone saw you leaving my suite *disheveled*."

He ran a hand through his hair. "You heard about that, huh?"

"I hear about everything, Mac. The problem is that Henry heard. And he's not happy."

The door opened and Mr. Burrows walked out. He froze when he saw me behind the desk and stared at my shoes when he said, "So sorry, ma'am. I didn't find anything for you."

"Well, I'll have a look!" Mac exclaimed. He cleared the desk in one jump. "Come on, Miss Murphy. Maybe you'll find it. You're so good at finding things. You watch the dog, Chuck." He ushered me into the bell services storage room with a hand on the small of my back, Mr. Burrows sputtering behind us. Mac shut the door and turned on me. "What was that? *Henry* isn't happy? Who cares what Henry thinks?"

Hands on my hips, I spun around in a circle, taking in the room. It was organized chaos, with shelves upon shelves of tagged luggage needing to be delivered, either to guest rooms or to the airport. Then there was the mail, sorted in boxes and bins, going to employees or guests or back out again.

"I care what Henry thinks," I said. "He is my very best friend. Oh, and my boyfriend."

Mac mimicked my posture, both hands on his hips, and frowned at me. "You told me the truth about that, remember? So if there isn't a man with a camera around, what does it matter if we spend time together?"

"Don't be ridiculous. You know how rumors work. Speaking of work, don't you need to get to it?" I spun around again, gesturing at the chaos with my pointed elbows. "Lots of very important suitcases and packages need to get delivered, Mr. Cooper. Too many, I think, for us to have any adventures together."

He slumped forward ever so slightly. "What are you saying, Evelyn?"

"I'm saying that I won't be needing your services for the foreseeable future. No dog walking and no lock picking. You understand, don't you?"

"No," he said. "No, I don't. You're gonna let your fake boyfriend keep you from being seen with me? Are you that ashamed of me?"

I felt my resolve waning. He looked so sad, so pathetic. I wanted to scoop him up in a hug and show him how little I cared what people might say about the two of us. But the truth was, I did care. At least as far as Henry was concerned.

"Of course I'm not ashamed of you. But I need at least two weeks for this rumor to die. We can do that, can't we? Two weeks?"

Mac bit his bottom lip, blinked up at the ceiling.

I waited for what felt like an eternity for him to answer, and when he didn't, I crossed my arms over my chest. "Two weeks gives you an awful lot of time to play with the pretty guests. Or the pretty maids—I know that's how you usually spend your time."

He shook his head. "Ridiculous," he said.

"What is?"

"*You* are. You're ridiculous. Everything I do for you, and you . . ."

His tone was exceptionally rude. I crossed the little distance between us so I could give him a proper glare. "I what, Mr. Cooper?"

"Mr. Cooper," he repeated with a huff. "Fine. Fine. This is what you want, innit? Then that's what will happen. You're in charge, anyway, aren't you? *Miss Murphy*."

I tugged on the necklace my mother had given me. "Come on, Mac! Don't be so rude."

"Rude? Me?" He pointed at his face with both index fingers. "I am so sorry, Miss Murphy! Let me prostrate myself before you to demonstrate my overwhelming sorrow at having been rude to you. Me, a dodgy employee, and you, the owner's posh daughter."

Mac moved backward in an attempt to bow low in the space. I shoved him, but my thumb was still hooked around the silver chain. It snapped and fell to the ground, the charm of Saint Anthony rolling under Mac's foot.

"Don't move, don't move!" I dove to my knees and fumbled for the small silver pendant. "Don't move. Oh, don't crush it!"

Mac moved his weight to the outsides of his feet, balancing precariously above me. "Hurry, ugh, Evelyn—!"

"I got it! I got it!" I pressed the pendant in my palm, closing my eyes in relief. "Thank God. That was a close one."

"It's okay? I didn't hurt it?"

Plucking up my courage, I twirled the pendant in my fingers, looking at it from every angle. "It's fine." I smiled up at Mac. "Completely perfect. Here"—I held up my empty hand—"help me—oh, oh no."

My hair got stuck in the zipper of his pants.

Mac tugged on my hand, and I cried out. "Stop! Stop, I'm stuck!"

"Where?" He swore and let go of me. "Hold on, let me try." He fiddled with my trapped hair, somehow only making me more trapped. Mac let out a noise that sounded like a suppressed laugh. I tried to glare up at him, but I couldn't move my head.

"This isn't funny!"

"No, not at all." He unzipped his pants, and the movement released some of the pressure but didn't untangle me. "I can see it. I can see the knot. I need one second. Or maybe some scissors."

The gasp that left me scratched my throat. "Don't you dare, Malcolm Cooper!"

He made that noise again—a high-pitched suppressed laugh—and said, "I won't. I won't. Hold on. Two more seconds."

It hurt worse, springing tears to my eyes before he finally got it loose. "There! All set."

I grabbed on to his knee with one hand, touched my head with the other, my mother's pendant cool on my sore scalp.

He smiled down at me. "You all right?"

The door opened. Mr. Burrows and several check-in employees stood behind him. Mac and I stared at each other, openmouthed, before staring over at them. The three women of the group burst into fits of giggles, while the two men who weren't Mr. Burrows let out whistles.

I struggled to my feet, mouth moving, but words refused to come out.

Mac *tsk*ed. "Good luck handling this new rumor, Miss Murphy."

Head held high and mouth firmly closed, I strolled out of the room. I collected Presley, still in his purse, while Mr. Burrows apologized profusely behind me.

"Please, Miss Murphy," he said, "if there's anything I can do!"

That stopped me in my tracks. "Actually, I'm hoping to call on Tilly . . . you know, the assistant of Mr. Bell? I don't know where her room is, though, and the line is so long."

He pushed up his glasses with his index finger. "You're in luck, Miss Murphy. I helped move Miss Bourke into her new room this morning. She had a lot of paintings with her. It took quite a while. Shall I take you there?"

I smiled, ignoring Mac as he left the mail room. "That would be wonderful. Thank you ever so."

Chapter 15

The door to room 703 opened shortly after Mr. Burrows knocked. Tilly, the tiny red-haired assistant, opened the door with a meek squeak at the sight of me.

"Miss Murphy," she said. Her high-pitched voice was tinged with a Welsh accent as adorable as she was. "Mr. Burrows. Good to see you again."

Mr. Burrows shifted on his feet. "Miss Murphy here wanted to call on you, ma'am, and since I knew what room you were in . . ."

I realized we should've called ahead. Ghastly manners on my part. I'd even forgotten the wine!

I smiled to soften the awkwardness. "I do apologize for dropping in like this. I only wanted to see how you are doing."

"Of course, it's no bother. Please, come in. I'm sorry for the mess. I've been . . . well, I've been a mess myself."

I squeezed her elbow and offered a reassuring smile. "That's understandable, Miss Bourke. I must apologize for not visiting sooner."

"I moved into this room this morning. I couldn't go back to the other one. Not after . . ." Her sentence trailed off, her mouth a deep frown. "Mr. Burrows, I'm sorry. I don't have any cash."

The poor fellow's glasses fogged up.

"Good thing I do," I said, and slipped a dollar bill into his hand. "Thank you again, Mr. Burrows."

"Anytime, Miss Murphy." He nodded his head. "Miss Bourke."

Tilly stood back and let me into her room. It wasn't messy so much as cluttered. All of Bell's paintings had been moved into her room. They were stacked in scattered piles across the floor, many of the piles covered in tarps. The kaleidoscopic painting the Dreadfuls had forced me to admire was one of the uncovered ones, unfortunately.

"I don't know what I'm going to do with all these. Please, sit." She motioned at the chairs around a small table, the only empty spot in the room other than the twin bed. Her row of silver rings glistened in the lamplight. She had good taste in jewelry, I'd give her that. "I've got to start calling galleries and see if they will sell any for me."

I set Presley's purse on a tabletop covered in black-and-white sketches, careful not to bend a page. When I sat, the wooden chair creaked beneath me, which I found incredibly impolite of it, considering I'd eaten only half that cheeseburger.

I forced a friendly smile and once again lamented having forgotten to bring wine. "Did Mr. Bell have any beneficiaries?"

"A sister." She sat down, only to stand immediately back up again. "Do you want room service? I could call for tea?"

"I'm fine, thank you. I suppose it will be up to the sister what happens to the paintings."

She sighed. "I suppose you're right. And in the meantime, I'll be babysitting them. A shame."

Presley licked my fingers. "Pardon? What's a shame?"

She jumped like I'd yelled. Poor dear. She really was a mess. "Only that he was struck down so soon into his career. He was gonna be somebody, Miss Murphy. He was so talented." Her lips trembled and her eyes watered. She tried to continue speaking but fell into hysterics. I reached out and clasped her shoulder, shushing her quietly.

"It's all right, dear. It's all right. I am so, so sorry for your loss."

Tilly grabbed a handful of tissues with her left hand and dried her face. "Please forgive me."

"There is nothing to forgive." I squeezed her shoulder once more before letting go. "You and Mr. Bell were close?"

She sniffed. "It's more than that. I know he was a hard man to be around. I know that he was rough around the edges and had more enemies than friends. But that's because he was a genius. An artistic mastermind. All geniuses are difficult, you know?" Tilly blew her nose, loud and wet. "Look at Degas, for instance. He scarred some of his subjects, and I don't mean emotionally. Billie was special. He was gifted. He was, he was"—the tears started up again—"wonderful!"

"Sweet thing," I said. "You loved him, didn't you?"

She nodded ferociously, let out a wailing, keening noise that made Presley bark and hide in his purse. I grabbed more tissues and dried her face. "There, there. It's awful, what happened. But I'm confident the killer will be found."

Tilly blew her nose again. "What do you mean? I was under the impression the killer had already been found and arrested. What's his name, the security guard?"

"Phil Hall," I said. "Yes. He was arrested. But I don't believe he was the real killer. I also don't believe he stole your painting.

Which reminds me, I was confused about something, and I hoped I could pick your brain?"

"Of course."

I fixed the blue bow between Presley's ears, giving myself a moment to figure out how to phrase the question. "Is there any chance . . ." I began, meeting her eyes. Her glasses were somehow thicker than Mr. Burrows's, a feat I would have thought impossible. "Any chance at all that the painting was stolen before the party?"

"No." Her high-pitched voice was hoarse now, and stuffy, as if she had a bad cold that scratched her throat and clogged her nose. "No, we carried it down ourselves."

"I see. And was it covered when you carried it down?"

"Well. Yes." She threw away the old tissues and grabbed a few fresh ones. "We covered it in the room before we took it down."

"And did you check underneath the covering once it was in the Silver Room?"

Tilly bit her lip in thought. "I don't remember," she said. "But it doesn't matter. We carried it down, as I said, and it was framed. So if the frame was empty, we would have felt that. Our fingers would have gone through the opening, covered or not."

My nose wrinkled. I smoothed it out with my thumb and smiled at her. "I'd heard from a friend that you and Mr. Bell had gotten into a bit of an argument the day he died."

"Oh." She shivered. "I—oh, Miss Murphy, I'm so ashamed of my behavior. It's only, I caught him . . . at least, I thought I caught him. In a precarious situation. With a beautiful woman. He said they were talking, only talking, she was interested in buying a painting. But they were standing so close together, whispering in each other's ears, and she's so tall and so beautiful. Like you, Miss Murphy, only a darker coloring."

A tall, beautiful woman interested in buying Mr. Bell's art? Had to be Countess Dreadful.

"We talked about it over drinks. Up at the rooftop bar. We made up. He swore to me that it was strictly professional, and I believed him. I believed him so much I gave him my key and sent him to my room to wait for me while I paid our tab. If only I'd have gone with him, Miss Murphy. Or I'd have gone first! He never would've been in that hallway if it wasn't for me!"

She fell into hysterics again.

"Miss Bourke, the hallway wasn't the issue. Whoever killed Mr. Bell would've killed him no matter where he was or who he was with. The only thing you did was keep yourself alive. If you'd been there too, we'd be looking at a double murder."

Tilly sniffled. "I suppose that's true. It doesn't lessen the guilt I feel, though."

"No, I'd imagine it wouldn't. I am so sorry for your loss."

She smiled at me, poor thing, her eyes all red and puffy.

"Thank you for talking with me. I really appreciate it." I patted the top of her head when I stood up and tucked Presley's purse under my arm. "You can stay here as long as you need, okay? On me."

Tilly jumped to her feet and wrapped me in a hug. "Thank you, Miss Murphy!"

"Please." I rubbed her back. "It's Evelyn."

She let go of me and smiled, her face flushed with embarrassment. "I'm sorry about—my emotions have been all over the place, and I'm not usually so . . . this way."

"Truly, think nothing of it," I said. "It's to be expected, given the circumstance. I'll be seeing you, Tilly. Yeah?"

"Yes." She nodded and smiled. "Yes, you sure will. Evelyn."

And with that I took Presley and left the room, feeling confused but positive. I'd get to the bottom of this, one way or another.

CHAPTER 16

When I returned to my apartment, I was greeted with a familiar sound. Florence's off-key hum was louder than the water running in the sink as she washed my dishes. Twenty years older than me, with graying brunette hair, bright amber eyes, and a comely face, Florence had been my day maid for well over a decade. She hummed every day and never once held a tune, but otherwise she was a perfect employee.

"Good afternoon!" she said when she saw me. "And to you too, Mr. Presley."

I set his purse on the floor and he hopped out, then gave himself a good shake before trotting over to his bowl for a drink.

She turned off the sink and wiped her hands on her apron. "How are you, Miss Murphy? Do you need fresh sheets?"

My cheeks warmed. I cleared my throat and forced myself to meet her gaze. She'd been my maid for years and had never caused any trouble before now. But still, her assumption that I'd need fresh sheets after the rumor of Mac's late-morning appearance, not to mention our recent discovery in the holding room, roused my suspicions.

"Florence," I said, "I have to ask you a question."

She straightened her apron. "Yes, ma'am? Anything you need, I can help."

The warmth of my cheeks spread all the way to my hairline. Why was this so hard to say? Because it wasn't at all true, but I wanted it to be? Did I want it to be? Mac was casual about everything, me included. And I didn't want to be someone's casual nighttime activity.

"A rumor got started today. A rumor that Mr. Cooper spent the night with me. Do you know anything about that?"

Florence bowed her head. "I have heard that. Didn't believe it, of course. Not you, Miss Murphy. Not with someone like him. I know how devoted you are to Mr. Fox."

I chewed my bottom lip while I studied her. Contrite and honest, as Florence had always been. "Please, let me apologize," I said. "I shouldn't have suspected you. You've been so good to me all these years, I don't know why I . . ."

"Think nothing of it, Miss Murphy. I'm the likeliest of suspects, of course, being the one in your room the most. But I didn't see Mr. Cooper this morning. I didn't start on this floor until an hour ago."

"Why's that?"

"The *police*." She dropped her voice to a conspiratorial whisper, leaned in close. "Held us up, asking us questions. All about Mr. Hall and where we were last night. If we saw anything suspicious. Of course, the only thing suspicious I saw they dismissed as silly."

Presley walked between my feet, tail wagging. I obeyed his silent command and picked him up. "And what did you see that was suspicious? If you don't mind me asking, of course."

She shrugged both shoulders. "A table across from where the body was found. It was off-center."

My nose wrinkled. "Show me."

★ ★ ★

The police presence was gone, but guests had not been allowed back yet, leaving Florence, Presley, and me rather alone with the ghost of Mr. Bell.

Not that I believe in ghosts, but there was something of his presence in the brightly lit place where he'd met his grisly end. Perhaps it was only the blood staining the carpet. Perhaps it was the memory of finding the body. Whatever the reason, there was a chill in the air that made me hold Presley a little closer.

"See how between the doors, there are those decorative tables?" Florence gestured at the objects in question with all ten fingers. "And on each end, there's a vase? We work very hard at keeping fresh flowers in every vase on every floor."

The tables were a light cedar. Each one was centered between guests' rooms, each with a delicate yellow table runner, each with vases on both ends filled with fresh flowers.

"But this one," she said, and walked over to the table directly across from the bloodstain, "it was pushed over. Like this." She shoved the table closer to the door on the left-hand side. "See?"

I stood back and admired it. It was off-center, as she said, but only when you took in the whole of the hall did you notice it was different from all the other tables. "Maybe a guest bumped into it by accident? Or maybe even in a struggle between Bell and his killer?"

Florence shook her head. "No, it must've been intentional. The tables don't look like much, but they're heavy. They take your full weight to move them."

"Huh." My nose wrinkled as I stared at the table. I didn't understand the significance, only that it *was* significant. "Well. It certainly is unusual, isn't it?"

Florence centered the table again. "You think it's silly, don't you, Miss Murphy? Something only a maid would notice. That's what the policeman told me."

"I don't think it's silly at all," I said. "After the weekend we've had, what with a theft and a murder, it seems like all unusual things should be considered. Let me know if you think of anything else."

"Of course, Miss Murphy. And will you be needing your sheets changed?"

I sighed. "Yes, please."

CHAPTER 17

Florence left me in the hall where Mr. Bell died to finish cleaning my room. I waited until she turned the corner before setting Presley down.

"What do you think?" I asked him. "A suspicious table?"

He smelled the bloodstain, sneezed, and then darted away from it. I stared at the table for a moment before deciding to push it myself. It was heavy, and it took both hands and all my attention to move it. "Hmm," I said. "She was right about that." I pushed the table back and then stared at the bloodstain, hands on my hips and nose wrinkling.

"So, I found him here."

I drew his location in the air with my finger. "And the wound was here." In my mind's eye, I could see the gaping hole in the left side of his back. "Square in the kidney. Whoever hit him was either lucky or knew what they were doing."

I pretended to hold a knife in my hand. "How did they do it, Presley? Overhand?" I held my fist up like a knife was jutting out of it, brought it down into an imaginary back. "If they did it overhand, they would have to have been much shorter than Bell. Or standing while he was on the floor." I knelt down next to the bloodstain. "No. There wasn't a sign of struggle, beyond the table being moved. Whoever got him surprised him."

Underhand, then. With my pretend knife, I jutted my fist upward into that same imaginary back. It felt strange, going from my right hand to the back's left side. But then again, I'd never killed anyone before. A lot of it would depend on how they were standing when the conflict began. Maybe he was turning, or the attacker was turning, or maybe the attacker was a short left-handed attacker who had surprised him and gotten him overhand. Or a tall right-handed attacker who came up behind him and struck him underhand without Bell ever knowing.

I tried to imagine how Mr. Hall would have done it. Mr. Hall was not the quiet type. Bell would've heard him coming. Words would've been exchanged. I couldn't imagine that anything Bell said to Mr. Hall would have made him angry enough to kill.

Henry, on the other hand, with the way he behaved at the party—I'd never seen him that angry. I'd never seen him get physical with anyone like that outside of a movie. Could he have done it? He was rather tall, and he would've been light on his feet. He could've come up behind Bell and surprised him.

But Henry was as likely to be a murderer as he was to be a thief. I didn't believe him capable. Maybe he would've broken Bell's nose in a crowded room over a rude barb, but coming up behind him and stabbing him in the back?

Still. I should probably confirm his alibi with Mr. Sharpe. That would definitely prove his innocence.

I stood up and wiped my hands clean of imaginary murder weapons. "I don't know, Presley. Guessing the angle of the deadly strike by memory is proving not to be a natural talent of mine."

He wound between my feet until I held him, then licked my chin.

"I bet you're ready for your walk now, aren't you, baby?"

His tail wagged so hard his entire little body wiggled in my arms.

I laughed. "Okay, okay. Let's go for a walk."

I turned and almost ran face first into a maid.

My heart jumped into my throat, strangling the scream that threatened to spill. "Goodness gracious!" I laughed at myself. "I didn't hear you."

She was a pretty little thing. Younger than me by a few years, a late teenager. Heart-shaped face, dark-brown hair, gray eyes. Those gray eyes narrowed and held me still, pierced me so thoroughly I thought of Billie Bell's ghost haunting the hallway.

But there is no such thing as ghosts. There are only maids who walk on tiptoes.

"Stay away." The maid's accent was British. "I don't care who you think you are. You stay away."

I covered my heart. "I beg your pardon?"

"You heard me." Her lips twisted into a sneer. "He is not your plaything."

"Plaything?" I looked over my shoulder at the bloodstain on the floor and the suspicious table. Then I turned back to this maid and returned her glare. "This is very serious, and I can assure you, I am taking it seriously. Have a good day."

I brushed past her, my shoulder bumping into hers. And yes, I'm not ashamed to admit, there was some relief in feeling her corporeal form. Not a ghost. Just a mouthy, quiet-stepping maid.

Presley's baby-blue leash was tucked away in a pocket of his purse. I pulled it out and clipped it on him well before the two of us stepped foot outside. The lobby was crowded with guests returning from sightseeing, people checking in fresh from the airport, and others stopping by for dinner at one of our world-class restaurants. The doorman saw me approach and held one of the front doors open for me with a smile and a tip of his hat.

I smiled back, held Presley's purse closer to me. It was just a walk around the Park. The Park was only across the street. But it was dark out already, the streets busy with people. Maybe all Presley needed was a stop outside around back, in the same area where Mac and I had taken a break during the art show.

So, with a friendly wave at the doorman, I turned around and walked toward the Silver Room. That proved to be a mistake. There was some sort of banquet being held. Why anyone would hold a banquet on a random Monday in the middle of September was beyond me, but nevertheless, wending my way through the crowd with my dog proved difficult. He was not the accessory of an incognito outfit.

Backing out of there as quietly as possible, I hovered in the hallway, unsure of what to do. Presley licked my hand that held his straps.

"I'm sorry, baby. You're being so patient."

I missed Mac. But after the *moment* we'd had in the mail room, I couldn't face him and ask him for his help, even if Henry hadn't made me promise. What I needed was someone else, someone to replace Mac. Because I clearly was not cut out for this. This walking thing. At night. Alone. Outside the Pinnacle.

Nodding to myself, I made up my mind. I walked into the nearest elevator and headed for the roof.

★ ★ ★

"It would only be for two weeks," I told Mr. Peters. Presley waited like the good boy he was in his purse on the rooftop pool bar. Mr. Peters dried a glass while swaying side to side behind the bar. There was no music playing. The pool was busy with guests enjoying their nighttime swims. "I'd pay you handsomely for your troubles. And Presley is a good boy. Plus he knows you from our afternoon appointments. Don't you, baby?"

Presley didn't answer, but he kept waiting like a good boy, which was close enough.

Mr. Peters frowned, started rocking on the balls of his feet. Back and forth, back and forth. "I really can't leave my shift."

"Of course," I said, "I'm not asking you to stop working. What I'm saying is, take a break for a bit. Ten, fifteen minutes. You'll make five dollars. And then you can come back. I'm sure one of your fellow bartenders can fill in for you for a few minutes while you help Presley out. And, like I said, it's only for two weeks."

He fumbled the glass. "Five dollars?"

"Five dollars a day," I said. "I'll need you to walk him twice a day for two weeks. What do you say, Mr. Peters? Please? Won't you please help me?" I leaned forward on the bar, poked out my bottom lip, batted my eyelashes. More often than not there are two things men can't resist: an easy buck and a pretty woman.

He sighed. "All right, Miss Murphy. You talked me into it."

I clapped my hands in delight. "Wonderful. Oh! While I'm here. Do you remember . . . that artist who was killed? He had a drink here right before he was murdered."

Mr. Peters nodded. "Yeah, sure. He and that little red-headed broad sat over there." He pointed at a little table away from the bar with a view of Central Park.

"Did you notice anything about them?"

"Besides the fact that they were lousy tippers?"

I suppressed a chuckle. "Yes. Were they arguing? Were they laughing? Touching?"

"Ah. Yeah. They were all over each other. Playing footsie under the table and holding hands and kissing. Luckily they kept it at that, since we get kids up here."

I stared at the table in question and took in the view of it all, Central Park beyond it, the pool before it. Right now it was filled with families of all shapes and sizes. I could see what Mr. Peters meant. It would be awkward to be too lovey-dovey up here.

"Do you remember when they left? Who left first or if they left together?"

"He left first. I remember because I thought I might actually get a decent tip out of her, but she was even more of a cheapskate."

"Thank you, Mr. Peters. For the information and for the dog walking. Here! Presley's leash." I pulled Presley out of his purse and handed him, leash and all, across the bar. "I'll be in my room. Knock when you get back. See you!" I kissed Presley's soft head and grabbed his empty bag, waving at Mr. Peters as I went.

There. Problem solved. And information acquired. All in all, a solid decision by *moi*.

CHAPTER 18

It was still pretty early in the evening when Presley returned safe and sound. He'd refused to walk, Mr. Peters said, and forced the bartender to carry him to the park and back. He'd still managed to do his business, but he'd snipped at Mr. Peters's ankles twice.

I paid him in cash and bid him good-bye, told him tomorrow I'd have a key.

After washing my face with soap and cold cream and dressing for bed in pink silk pajamas and bunny slippers, I called the front desk and asked to speak to Mac.

"He isn't available right now," the friendly female voice of the phone operator said. "May I take a message, Miss Murphy?"

"Yes, will you please send him to my room when he's available?"

A sound like a muffled giggle hit my ear. I blushed and cleared my throat. "I have some . . . dog walking, um, questions for him, and . . . anyway. Yes. Thank you." I hung up and blew out a loud breath through puffed cheeks.

This wasn't any good. I couldn't even speak to Mac in person without the gossip train leaving the station. Poor Henry. All

I had done was make the situation worse after he asked me to give Mac a break.

I'd have to make it up to him somehow. Maybe a big, public spectacle?

"What do you think, Presley? How can I embarrass myself for Henry's benefit?"

Would a big, flashy gift be too much? Would that only confirm the suspicions of those spreading rumors? *Look at her, giving him a present out of guilt and shame. Like that'll make up for the heartache!* Or would it quell them? *Aw, look at that! She loves him so much—she's so thoughtful!*

I flopped down on my couch. "Only one way to find out, I guess. I'll buy him a present and see what happens."

Even if it did only confirm things for certain people, Henry deserved a gift. He was a good friend. He put up with a lot. And he made sure I made it into the paper, above the fold, where I belonged.

I'd finished two more chapters in *Hickory Dickory Death* before there was a knock on the door. Presley sniffed into his pillow but made no other move to defend his home. Up to me, then. The person knocked once more before the door swung open. Mac stood there with a small grin and the key held up in his fingers.

"You rang, Miss Murphy?"

Leaving the book open on the couch, I walked over to Mac. "I needed this back." I plucked the key right out of his hand. "Thank you."

Mac's lips twitched. "You needed it back? Why?"

"Mr. Peters is going to be walking Presley."

"Peters?" Mac's incredulous question came out in a much too loud voice. I shushed him and pulled him inside, shutting the door. "*Peters*? That good-for-nothing—he's not gonna do it right, Evelyn, and you know it."

I planted a fist on my hip. "Not gonna do it right? What is there to do wrong? Take Presley to the park, pick up his little doo-doos. It isn't exactly brain surgery, Mac. I think Mr. Peters will be quite sufficient. He already took Presley for his nighttime walk."

"He already . . ." Mac's words trailed off into a scoff. "You replaced me in a day? A single day?"

"What was I supposed to do? Walk him myself? I tried that. It was so dark out, and there were so many people!"

He pressed the pads of his fingers up and down his brow. "Stupid."

My mouth fell open. "Stupid? How *dare* you? I am many things, Malcolm Cooper, but stupid is not one of them."

Mac glared at me. "I'm not calling you stupid. *I'm* stupid. Here I thought, all this time, we were friends. But I was fooling myself."

The accusation struck me like an arrow through the throat or a knife in the back. The Pinnacle was so big. The Pinnacle was my entire world. But it wasn't quite big enough that I could fill it up with a never-ending group of friends with whom to spend my time. I had Mac and I had Henry. I couldn't lose either one. Not without losing half my heart.

"Of course we're friends. Of course." I held his wrists in each hand, stepped closer into his personal space. Mac blinked rapidly and looked everywhere but at my face. That didn't stop me from rubbing the tip of my nose against his. He smelled like cigarette smoke and cologne. Citrus and smoke. The woodsy, lemon and vanilla blend in Chanel Poor Monsieur, the gift I'd given him two months ago on his birthday. "I'm so sorry, Mac. We are

friends. But this is Henry's career. It's only for two weeks." I
rubbed my nose over his again. "Maybe three, after that scene in
the mail room."

He chuckled, and his breath was warm against my mouth.
"Yeah," he said. "Fair point."

I dropped his right wrist to place my hand against his cheek.
His stubble tickled my palm. "We're always gonna be friends,
Mac. You can't be my dog walker for a few days. That's all."

He met my gaze for the first time since I'd taken the key
from him. His soft gray eyes had a ring of sky blue around the
pupil. He whispered, "That's all?"

Nodding, I replied, "That's all."

He kissed me, and I kissed him back.

After a minute, he let me go and said, "But what if that isn't all?"

I licked my lips. "I beg your pardon?"

"Let's say, for the sake of argument, he did steal that painting. Or, even worse, he did kill Bell—"

"He isn't—"

"I know, I know." He kissed my forehead. "But he made his
dislike of Bell obvious, so I'm playing devil's advocate. Maybe
he doesn't want to keep us apart because of his career. Maybe he
wants to keep us apart so I can't keep you safe."

I huffed. "Keep me safe? From who?"

"From him," he said. "If he is the killer, Evelyn, you gotta be
careful. You can't be alone with him. Promise me. I know he's
your friend, but it doesn't hurt anything to be careful. Please.
Promise me."

He held up his pinkie finger.

I sighed, rolled my eyes. But Mac had a point. I didn't think
Henry was the killer, I really, truly didn't, but I could also be a

bit more careful. After all, we didn't have to be alone to get our picture taken for the paper.

"Fine." I wrapped my finger around his and squeezed. "Besides, just because you can't hang out in my room doesn't mean you can't call me. You do have phones in Yonkers, don't you?"

"Yeah," he laughed. "Yeah, I got a phone in Yonkers. I don't get home until late."

I shrugged. "Phone rings all hours."

Mac held my face with both hands, bent his head down until he was staring at me eye to eye again. My pulse buzzed in my ears, goose bumps prickled my arms. I parted my lips and waited for the kiss that my entire being demanded.

But instead of kissing me, he said, "All right. Three weeks. I'll keep schtum," and it was almost as good.

Relief that he understood, that he was on my side, filled me up from the bottom of my feet to the top of my head. I couldn't stop smiling. "Thank you, Mac."

"Hey." He bopped my nose. "You owe me one."

"That's a deal. Any favor you want."

Mac whistled low and long. "*Any* favor?"

I giggled, lightly slapped his chest. "Within reason."

He grasped the hand that hit him and didn't let go. "So not any favor. Okay, okay. As long as we're on the same page." He squeezed my fingers. "I've got to head home. But, uh, I'll ring you? You'll be up?"

"Yeah," I said. "I'll be up."

Mac kissed me good-bye. And like he said he would, he called me when he got home.

"You're up, then?" His voice was groggy over the receiver. The sound tickled my ear, sent tingles down the back of my neck.

I rubbed away the goose bumps. "Mm-hmm. I'm in bed reading. Where are you?"

"Kitchen." His mouth was full. "Only got the one phone in my apartment."

"Aw, that's too bad. I have three."

He repeated "I have three" in a high-pitched, garbled voice that made me laugh.

"What are you eating?"

"Some tinned veg. Toast."

Presley jumped up on my bed and trotted over to my side. Immediately he flopped down and rolled onto his back, tongue lolling and tail wagging, until I had no choice but to give him the tummy rub he so desperately required. "Sounds, um, delicious."

He gave a muffled laugh, and the goose bumps on the back of my neck returned. "Not all of us have access to twenty-four-hour-a-day room service," he said. "What did you have for dinner?"

My hand froze on top of Presley's soft stomach. "Um. Hmm. I think I forgot to eat."

"You think you forgot?"

"I definitely forgot."

Mac huffed. "How can you forget to eat?"

"I was upset!" I said. "We were fighting, and Henry was cross with me. I needed someone to walk Presley. Eating slipped my mind. Hold on. I'll grab something and be right back." I hopped out of bed, much to Presley's displeasure, ran to the kitchen, and grabbed an apple out of the fruit bowl Florence kept stocked for me. Then I ran back and picked the receiver up before climbing into bed. "I've got an apple now."

"That's a healthy meal," Mac said. "You were that upset about me that you forgot dinner?"

"No," I said. "Not only about you. I was *busy* is all. Collecting alibis. No need to feel so special about it."

He laughed. "Never. What alibis were you collecting?"

"Only Tilly Bourke's, the assistant. And Henry's. Henry was with Mr. Sharpe at the time of the murder, and Tilly was on the rooftop, paying off her and Mr. Bell's tab."

"You sure about those?"

"Mostly sure," I said. "I confirmed Tilly's alibi with Mr. Peters, and tomorrow I'll confirm Henry's with Mr. Sharpe. And then that will leave . . . oh, I didn't tell you this! But Tilly let it slip that Countess Dreadful was carrying on with Mr. Bell."

"So? She carries on with everyone."

"Fair point," I said, "but if he broke things off with her so Tilly would take him back, that's a motive for murder."

Mac exhaled so loudly I could almost feel his breath through the phone. "I suppose. But if I was a betting man—and I assure you I am a law-abiding man and would never condone such unlawful behavior—all my money would be on Henry Fox."

"I'll take that action. What do you say? Twenty dollars to the victor?"

"That depends on who your money is on."

"Can I bet anyone but Henry?"

Mac laughed. "That hardly seems fair, but I'll allow it. Since it is Henry. Without a doubt."

I took a crunchy bite of my apple. "Mac," I said, after swallowing, "I don't like it when we have our disagreements."

"Fortunately, we don't have very many. Or else you'd never eat and you'd fade away, like when you turn a line sideways."

Presley curled up at my hip. "Turn a line sideways?"

"It's a math joke." He yawned. "Sorry. Too late in the day for math jokes."

"Any time of day is too late for math jokes. Get some sleep, Mac. I'll see you tomorrow."

"Give Presley a kiss for me."

I smiled, buried my fingers in my little bear's fur. "I will."

CHAPTER 19

The next morning, after Presley returned from his morning walk with Mr. Peters—which, I was told, was again not so much of a walk as it was a carry—I called Daddy's assistant to relay my plans of a present for Henry.

The assistant agreed to placing the order but insisted the gift remain in my name. When I argued back, the assistant offered to pull Daddy out of a meeting and let me talk to him about it. I decided it best not to bother Daddy while he was working and accepted the compromise.

Assured the delivery would arrive this afternoon after Henry was back from rehearsal, I dressed in an adorable green wiggle dress with an off-the-shoulder sweetheart neckline and three-quarter-length sleeves. The merry widow corselet underneath gave me a positively darling figure in the dress. But the best part of my ensemble was my Juliette cap and black veil. Judy had picked this outfit out all by herself, earning at least a ten-dollar tip for her extraordinary taste. I pulled on black wrist gloves, checked my red lipstick in the mirror, and deemed myself ready for an in-person meeting with Mr. Sharpe in order to inform his office of the arrival of Henry's gift.

I could have called his office instead, but I wanted to con-firm Henry's alibi in person.

To get information out of someone, it's best to be face-to-face. You can see their posture, where they look, the way they open their mouths before they speak. A small movement of the face betrays more honesty than full sentences ever can. People don't seem to notice that I'm watching them. They dismiss me as being unimportant, unworthy of scrutiny. They bring me around for a bit of fun, then let me go without consequence or guilt, because it's not like I'll leave the Pinnacle to track them down.

Right now, for the very first time, that was for the best, and I could use it to my advantage. If I was investigating someone for murder, it would be good if they didn't think much of me.

I left a message for Henry and gave our favorite photographer a time. Then, with Presley in his purse under my arm, I headed for the elevator. We were not the only top-floor guests waiting for a lift.

Countess Dreadful pressed the down button and glared at me when I had the audacity to stand beside her.

"The Pinnacle is not what it used to be," she told me. "I hope your father knows."

"Used to be?" I couldn't help but smile. "Daddy's owned it for seventeen years. Did you spend a lot of time at the Pinnacle before then, Countess?"

She sniffed and looked away. Everyone knows the countess didn't come from money. She married the count because she was young and beautiful and driven. She wanted a rich husband, and she snagged one. Something I fully support, of course, except when the participant acts like their past never happened. She should embrace it! Teach young girls how to follow her example! From a no one to a countess—that's a rags-to-riches story people would pay to read about.

"You know, rumor has it the hotel used to be owned by gangsters moving alcohol during Prohibition. You wouldn't know anything about that, would you, Countess?"

"Don't be ridiculous," she replied. "Or is that too much to ask of you, you silly girl?"

The lift opened, and the operator asked us what floor. We both requested the lobby at the same time. We then both glared at each other.

I had a feeling that in another life, the two of us would have been friends. I quickly shook that feeling off. The ride to the lobby was silent.

The countess and I walked in step out of the elevator. This caused the poor liftboy to get shoved to the side by Countess Dreadful's pointy elbow. To his credit, he took it to the gut with a very graceful grunt.

The manager's office is behind the check-in counter. I headed in that direction. So did the countess.

We were both on our way to see Mr. Sharpe, then. But I would do everything in my power to get there first.

I picked up the pace.

So did she.

I couldn't shake her from my side. She went to elbow me in the gut, but I sidestepped, avoiding the sharp point but walking right into a luggage cart. The metal struck my shins and knocked me off-balance. The luggage fell underneath me, clattering to the ground. I didn't have a chance to scream. I landed hard on my knees.

Presley hopped out of his purse to lick my jaw while a crowd gathered around the mess I'd made.

"So sorry," I said, standing with a wince. "I wasn't looking where I was going."

Countess Dreadful rounded the corner and walked into the manager's office with a pretty little wave.

There was no doubt now. We'd definitely been friends in a former life.

Mr. Sharpe's secretary wouldn't let me past her desk.

"He's in a meeting." The older woman, her gray hair in a severe bun, looked at me over her navy blue winged top glasses. "He'll be done in a second."

It was no use reminding her who my father was. She already knew and wasn't impressed. I could wait like any other guest of the hotel. I took a seat and adjusted my veil, which had gone askew in my fall, and informed her of Henry's upcoming delivery.

"Very well." The secretary pushed her glasses up her nose with one finger and resumed typing away at the typewriter. Presley was fascinated by the paper moving each time it let out a *ding*.

Countess Dreadful waltzed out of the office with her head held high.

"I'll take care of that right away," Mr. Sharpe said in his thick Scottish accent. "I am so sorry. And of course, on behalf of the Pinnacle, your stay will be complimentary."

She offered him her perfectly manicured hand. He stared at it, took hold of it, and instead of kissing it in the way she obviously intended, moved it up and down between them.

"Thank you, Mr. Sharpe," she said. "I'll be in my room."

Countess Dreadful stuck her tongue out at me when her face was no longer in Mr. Sharpe's direct line of sight.

My mouth fell open.

She grinned and practically skipped out of the room.

"Miss Murphy," Mr. Sharpe greeted me, sliding his receptionist a note. "If you need to talk to me, it'll have to be on the go." He patted his vest with both hands, nodded his chin at the door. "Well?"

I held my breath and gathered my wits. After all the hubbub with the countess, I'd quite forgotten what I was trying to get out of Mr. Sharpe. Oh! Right. His alibi and any updates on the murder case. Funny how a little not-so-friendly rivalry wipes a recent murder out of one's mind.

"Thank you, Mr. Sharpe. I'd love to walk with you. It'll be my exercise for the day." I tucked Presley's purse under my arm and walked with him in stride. "And how are you doing, Mr. Sharpe? Everything smooth now that Mr. Hall was arrested?"

He huffed. "Hardly. Was there something in particular you needed, Miss Murphy?"

A brush-off so quick into the conversation! No matter. I could outtalk any man, of that I was sure. "I still can't believe it was our very own Mr. Hall. I never even saw him interact with Mr. Bell. Did they have a fight?"

Mr. Sharpe shrugged. "Not that I'm aware of."

"Obviously, Mr. Bell was not a pleasant person. I'm sure you remember the fight you broke up between him and my Henry. And Henry is such a sweetheart! To provoke him to such a thing!"

He cleared his throat. "Yes. I remember. Mr. Bell did not have many friends. Though his art did have a lot of fans. Miss Bourke is having quite the time getting everything sorted, the poor lass."

"Yes, I visited her. I told her she could stay as long as she needed and I would cover it."

He pursed his lips and held open the door for the stairwell. "Thank you for letting me know."

I chose to ignore his sarcasm. "You're very welcome. But, as I was saying . . ." Wearing heels and walking upstairs while carrying a dog in a purse is close to my natural state. However, I held Mr. Sharpe's arm as we ascended in an attempt to lower his defenses. Throw him off-balance, so to speak. And my shins still hurt from the fall I'd taken over the luggage cart in the lobby. "Mr. Hall was always nice to me. And so level-headed with the other employees. It's hard to picture him snapping. Did you ever witness such a thing?"

"Can't say I did," he said. "What's more, he'd only ever been written up once, months ago."

My nose wrinkled. "What for?"

Mr. Sharpe looked down at me in that stern way of his. "Now, you know that's confidential, Miss Murphy."

I nodded my head but started going over Mr. Sharpe's schedule in my thoughts. He'd be out of his office tonight, creating the perfect snooping opportunity. I happened to know an excellent lockpick.

"I hope when we called about Mr. Bell's untimely demise, you weren't in the middle of something important?"

"More important than a murdered guest? Hardly. I was signing forms my secretary had left on my desk."

I missed a step. Mr. Sharpe caught me by the elbow and steadied me. "Are you all right, Miss Murphy?"

"Quite fine, thank you. Wasn't paying attention to where I was going. So you were signing forms? That's all?"

His brows furrowed, a lock of silvering hair falling into the middle of his forehead. Mr. Sharpe pushed it off his tan face. "That is all. Do you have any more questions for me, Miss Murphy?"

I shook my head and thought of Mac collecting his winnings, pictured my elegant Henry in handcuffs.

We walked onto the third floor, and I removed my arm from his elbow. "Thank you for talking with me, Mr. Sharpe. I do hope you have a wonderful day."

"You as well, Miss Murphy."

I pressed the button for the lift and was waiting for the poor, abused operator to open the doors when the thought struck me. What was Mr. Sharpe doing on the third floor anyway? I turned around to ask him, or at least see for myself, but he was gone. I hadn't heard a knock, or a door open, or a voice bid him welcome.

Where had he disappeared to? What's more, *how* in the world had he disappeared?

CHAPTER 20

The lift took me back down to the lobby. I needed to find Mac and quietly make plans for getting into Sharpe's office. He was game for everything and anything, as long as he got a few bucks out of it. Breaking into his boss's office might take substantially more of a tip than normal, but I was prepared to pay anything to have my questions answered.

Mr. Hall hadn't kill Bell, of that I was sure, but if his only three incidents the entire time he worked at the Pinnacle had been

3. a murder,
2. a stolen painting,
and 1. a write-up,

then it seemed imperative to know what exactly was in that write-up.

Mac was outside, unloading luggage out of the back of a taxi. He was glistening in the sunlight, his expression focused on his work, the veins in his hairy forearms bulging while he handled heavy suitcases. I toyed with the pendant of Saint Anthony as I approached. He cut a lean figure in his green uniform. I thought of Henry in swim trunks and wondered what Mac would look like wearing them.

The front stairs were always busy, and today was no exception. I'd have to be cautious so as not to draw attention to myself. I sidestepped a couple arguing loudly in a foreign language, refused to make eye contact with any of the valets. At the foot of the stairs, I cleared my throat.

Mac loaded the last piece of luggage onto a rolling cart. He wiped the sweat off his brow and smiled at me. "Thought we couldn't be seen together."

"I'm being sneaky," I reassured him. "But I require your assistance to get into Mr. Sharpe's office. Tonight."

He raised both eyebrows. "You don't say."

"Carefully make your way to my apartment at the end of your shift, please. And I do mean carefully."

He winked. "I'm always careful."

I rolled my eyes. *Boys.*

A police car pulled up behind the taxi. Mac closed the trunk and began the arduous process of pushing the luggage up the ramp. I waited to see what the police were going to do. It was none other than Detective Hodgson who stepped out of the passenger side.

"Detective!" I waved. "What a pleasure. What brings you back to the Pinnacle?"

He gave me a look—too tired to be a glare, but nevertheless not a friendly glance—and walked up the stairs. I matched his stride and kept smiling. "Surely we haven't had another murder."

"No," he said, "no murders. Just another theft."

"A theft? I haven't heard of anything."

"I didn't realize you were the be-all, end-all of crime at the Pinnacle."

The doorman held the door open for us with a tip of his hat. Detective Hodgson picked up his pace, but I would not be deterred.

Pretending to stumble at the entrance did the trick.

He reacted on instinct and reached out to steady me. I smiled gratefully and slid my hand through his arm. He stared at me, confused, but when I started walking, so did he.

"I can only wonder what was stolen. You know, we had a bit of a hubbub about six months ago. A maid stole cash out of a guest's safe. But she was caught, confessed to everything, and gave the money back. No reason to go to the police."

He shook his head but didn't voice his disagreement.

"Poor thing's mother was sick, she saw the money, and, well." I patted his arm. "I'm sure you know all about people giving in to temptation."

Detective Hodgson grunted. I took that as a good sign.

"What was stolen, I wonder? Certainly not something as big as the painting, or else I would have heard about that! But if it was from a guest room, that should be handled internally. Don't you agree?"

He stopped walking, pulling me to a halt. With two fingers, he removed my hand from his arm like it was covered in a contagious disease.

"Look, *Miss Marple*, I do not have time for this. You think you're clever. You're not. If you were, you'd be steering clear of that boy you got big eyes for."

Big eyes? Boy? I blinked my big eyes at him, my hand hovering in the space between us like it didn't know what to do now that it had been rebuffed. Men never had a problem escorting me anywhere.

And who on earth called someone Miss Marple as if it were an insult? There had never been a better compliment!

"What big-eyed boy?"

"No, not a . . ." He pinched the bridge of his nose between his thumb and forefinger. "You and Cooper."

"Cooper?" I repeated. "You mean Mac? Whatever are you talking about, Detective?"

"That boy has a criminal record," he said. "Discovered it when we were looking into the art theft. And then the murder. It stretches all the way from London. Breaking and entering, petty theft, grand theft. You name it, that boy has stolen it."

Mac? A thief? The news caught me off guard, my balance swaying. And then I came back to center. *Of course* he'd been a thief in a former life. Who else could pick any lock? Who would do anything for a tip? Who never batted an eye when I wanted to snoop around?

I shrugged. "He isn't the same person as he was in London. Mac is reformed. He's a model employee and a fine young man."

Detective Hodgson shook his head. "The countess had a diamond necklace stolen out of her room. Your Mr. Cooper was seen on the top floor on the night in question. With his criminal record, he's the best suspect we've got."

At that my mouth fell open, and my previously useless hand covered it.

"You're a bigger fool than I thought if you don't wise up, Miss Murphy," he said. "That boy is using you. Through and through, once a thief, always a thief. You'd do well to cut ties with him this second and never look back."

"Mac isn't using me." An excellent lockpick, sure. A good kisser, yes. A former thief, why not? But using me? Pretending with me? Not a chance. "He isn't. He's my friend. And he didn't steal that necklace."

"Then you are as stupid as they say you are."

He could've slapped me. It would've had the same effect. I was frozen in place, my face on fire. The detective shook his head and walked away.

I fulfill a certain expectation for others. I understand that. They see me, the spoiled heiress with a small dog in her purse and diamonds on her wrist, and they assume I'm vapid and silly. I use this to my advantage. After all, the best place to hide is in plain sight. But to be called stupid to my face? That was a new one.

I didn't like it. Not one bit.

★   ★   ★

Presley and I arrived on the top floor as Detective Hodgson was being let into the count and countess's suite down the hall. He didn't even look my way. I bristled at that. Who did he think he was? Calling me stupid and then ignoring my pointed glare? The *absolute* nerve.

We walked into our apartment, and I set Presley's purse on the floor. He hopped out and trotted to the kitchen while I paced the width of my living room, thinking about Mac. Thinking about the way he had paced the same path only two days prior when I left him alone in the Pinnacle's kitchen.

Mac stealing a diamond necklace? And doing what with it? If he was hard up for money, wouldn't he come to me? I kept his palm well greased. I knew he didn't live large, but he wasn't exactly starving either.

Although he'd been eating tinned veggies last night. Ick.

A knock from the door stopped me in my tracks. Detective Hodgson, come to call me more names? Mr. Sharpe, to inform me of Mac's arrest? Oh, Mac. I couldn't let him be arrested! No matter what he'd had to resort to in his life before coming to New York, I felt certain he wouldn't steal anything now. Not without me directly telling him to, anyway.

Not that we had ever stolen anything. We'd borrowed things to find other things. That was hardly the same as stealing a countess's diamond necklace.

When I opened the door, holding my breath in terror of the bad news that waited in the hall, it was Amelia standing there with a giant grin to greet me.

"Bonjour! I'm here to play with Presley."

I exhaled in relief and stood back to let her in. "He's in the kitchen, making a mess of his water bowl."

She squealed and breezed past me. From the door across the hall, I could hear voices murmuring but couldn't make out the words they were saying.

Mac stealing a necklace from a guest? Unthinkable. What's more, unlikely. Last night he'd been here to give me the key to my room. When would he have had time to steal a necklace?

Although . . . when I'd called for him, the front desk had said he was unavailable. And I hadn't asked what he had been doing. Could he have been in that room, stealing that necklace, right when I needed to see him?

Implausible but not impossible. Darn. I hate when I use logic on myself. Even if I didn't believe he'd stolen it, I couldn't provide him a foolproof alibi either. That call to the front desk would be logged and the employee who took it questioned.

"Evelyn?" Amelia came up behind me, Presley in her arms. He was quite content to let her hold him, his little tail wagging so hard he vibrated in her grasp. "Is everything okay?"

"Yes." I shut the door. "Well. Not exactly. You know how I'm good at finding things?"

She nodded and sang out, "Tony, Tony!" in her adorable French accent, sending us both into a fit of giggles.

"Right," I said. "The countess has had a necklace go missing, and no one will let me look for it. It's driving me positively bonkers."

Presley licked her chin. She laughed and kissed his nose. "That's funny. You mean she can't remember her hiding place? I thought it was the best one I'd ever seen."

Once again, shock struck me motionless. "I beg your pardon? The countess has a hiding place?"

Amelia straightened Presley's blue blow. "I saw her from *my* hiding spot, which I thought was a particularly good one, because no one sees me, even when they walk past me. I'm not going to tell you what it is unless you pinkie swear not to say."

I held out my pinkie. "Deal."

She wrapped her pinkie around mine, and we kissed our thumbs simultaneously. I had to bend down quite a bit to achieve this, but it was worth it for the giant smile that bloomed over her face. "There are these potted plants at the end of the hall, and I can sit behind them and blend in. *Camouflage.* I see the countess, and she has a little ladder with her. She stands on it and looks around, and then she opened the grate."

"The grate? Oh, the vent!" The entire top floor has central air conditioning, including the hallway. Every few feet there are vents on the ceiling, painted to blend in.

"She put something in there, closed it up, and walked away. I tried to reach the grate because I thought it was such a good hiding spot, but it was too high. I think I'm probably too big to fit anyway. But I would like to try!"

I hauled Amelia, still holding Presley, into a hug and spun them around. She laughed and Presley barked. "You're a genius! Brilliant, brilliant Amelia! You've saved the whole day!"

When I set her back down, she shrugged and said, "It was nothing. Can we eat marshmallows again?"

"Of course we can! But I have to go do something first. Wait right here."

CHAPTER 21

My fingers grazed the bottom of the grate. I'm tall, but I wasn't quite tall enough. Pulling off my gloves, I looked around for the fastest solution. I could use Amelia as a stool, but I doubted her parents would appreciate that. My attention landed on the potted trees at the end of the hallway. Perfect!

I grabbed the terra-cotta edge of one and dragged it down the hall. Dirt sloshed over the sides like a too-full drink. Amelia groaned in displeasure from my doorway.

"My camouflage!"

"I'll put it back," I panted. "Promise. Pinkie promise!"

"You can't *say* pinkie promise. You have to *do* a pinkie promise!"

The planter directly under the air vent in question, I kicked off my heels and climbed up. It wobbled underneath me. I grabbed the vent and steadied us both, the greenery tickling my inner thighs. Popping open the grate took only a few seconds, and then I was blindly reaching in, dust bunnies running over my fingers.

Detective Hodgson chose that moment to walk out of the countess's room, Countess Dreadful herself and a small, bespectacled man who quite resembled an owl close behind.

"What do you think you're doing?" the detective asked.

"Helping," I replied.

The countess pointed at me. "She can't be in there! You can't be in there! Get her out of there." She smacked the detective's arm. He glared at her. "Get her down from there! She is not allowed."

Detective Hodgson arched a brow. "If you say so. Miss Murphy, please get down from there."

I touched velvet and grinned. "Yes, sir." Out of the air vent, I pulled a lovely rectangular box covered in navy-blue velvet. The small man squeaked and the countess frowned, but the detective smiled. He coughed to hide it.

I snapped the box open, revealing a gorgeous diamond necklace. Seven stones, each three carats. "Stunning," I said. "Is this what you were looking for, Countess?"

The small man approached me first. He smiled and pushed his glasses up his nose with both hands. "Hi. Hello. Hi. I'm James Barney. I work for Prestige Insurance. The countess called me in for a claim on this necklace. Might I see it?"

I handed it over.

Detective Hodgson helped me down in what I imagined to be his way of extending an olive branch. "Now," he said, when I was safely on the ground, "how did you know where that was?"

Smiling, I said, "I'm very good at finding things. Ask anyone."

"Countess," James Barney said, "I believe this belongs to you. And I also believe we won't need to file a claim."

She licked her teeth. "Yes. Thank you. The thief must have stashed it there before making a getaway. I'm sure they were planning to come back later."

Detective Hodgson nodded. "That's a good point."

"No, it is not," I said. "I have an eyewitness that saw *you* put the necklace there, Countess."

She gasped. "How dare you say such a thing! I demand to know my accuser at once."

"Me." Amelia stepped out from my doorway, Presley still in her arms. "I saw you."

"And who are you?" Detective Hodgson asked.

"The French diplomat's daughter," I said. "And my very good friend."

The countess glared. "Lies! Lies and slander. I will not stand for it! Not when they come from some hussy who entertains bellboys at all hours of the night."

"Hussy? Me?" It answered the *Who started the rumor?* question I'd been pondering, at least, though I didn't appreciate being called any names.

As of late, I'd been called far too many.

"That's a big claim coming from someone caught canoodling with an artist to get a good deal on a painting."

"Canoodling?" she repeated. "You silly girl, you know nothing! Mr. Bell was a dear friend. How *dare* you suggest anything untoward!" She snatched the box from James Barney's hand and stormed into her room, slamming the door behind her.

Amelia stuck her tongue out.

James Barney bowed his head. "My job here is done. Thank you so much for your assistance. And I do hope you catch the thief, Detective."

Hodgson gave the owl-like man a nod good-bye, and James Barney disappeared in the lift.

I fiddled with my pendant and turned to Hodgson. "You don't believe for a second in this thief theory, do you?"

"Hard not to," he said, "considering the record and opportunity Malcolm Cooper has."

"Mac had nothing to do with this. Amelia saw the countess stash the necklace!"

"That's what she says, yes." Hodgson stuck his hands in his coat pockets. "But she is also your little friend. And you are fond of Malcom Cooper. Maybe you gave him a warning, he told you where the necklace was, and you coached the diplomat's daughter into saying what you wanted her to say."

Amelia and I argued the point simultaneously. "I would never!" I said, while she exclaimed, "I saw what I saw!"

Detective Hodgson held up an empty palm. "That's enough. It's my job to follow the clues and find the culprit. Fortunately, the countess has her very expensive necklace back. Now if you ladies will excuse me, I need to go talk to Mr. Sharpe about what kind of people he has employed in your father's hotel."

"Mac will lose his job," I said.

He nodded. "Most likely."

"You mustn't tell Mr. Sharpe. Mac didn't steal it. I found it. We have an eyewitness who places the blame on the countess herself, probably trying to make a quick buck off insurance."

Detective Hodgson nodded again. "Could be," he said. "But I still need to tell Mr. Sharpe about the criminal record I uncovered. Just doing my duty, you see. If you hold me up any further, I will have you arrested."

"Arrested! Whatever for?"

"Obstruction, for one," he said. "Bet I could think of some others." With that, he tipped his hat and pressed the button for the lift.

Men! The lot of them. Ridiculous. And poor Mac, down in the lobby, hauling luggage. This would come as a shock. Add to that the embarrassment of getting fired. I hoped Mr. Sharpe wouldn't do it publicly.

If I hurried, I could get there first. I could call Daddy. I could throw a fit!

"Amelia," I said. "Do you feel like playing the elevator game with me?"

She bounced up on her toes. "I love the elevator game! Shall we bring Presley?"

"No, we need to hurry. Let's put him back in my room, and we'll get going. We have to beat the detective to the lobby."

The lift dinged, and Detective Hodgson stepped inside.

Amelia glared at him. "That won't be a problem." She kissed Presley between the ears and set him gently inside my apartment.

I shut and locked the door, then offered her my hand. She took it, and the two of us took off running to the steps.

CHAPTER 22

We raced down two flights of stairs.

"Go press the button on his elevator so it stops on the floor." I flung open the hallway door and ushered Amelia in. "But don't let him see you!"

She saluted me and ran to do her duty.

I kept going, barefoot, taking the steps two at a time, jumping six at once and hitting the landing running. Three more flights of stairs and I called the elevator again, running back to the hallway before it opened. That was twice he'd been delayed. I rounded the corner and saw two maids turning the key to call the service elevator.

I dashed in behind them and pressed the button for the lobby, breathlessly apologizing for commandeering their ride.

I'd make it to the office before the detective. And then I would throw the most massive fit of all fits and Mac would keep his job or Daddy would hear. And Daddy would not be pleased that Mr. Sharpe had caused me distress, of that I was sure.

I sprinted into the lobby, one hand holding my hat down on my head. Another luggage cart waited to take me out at the ankles, but I jumped over it like an Olympian. I'd never felt more athletic in my life.

I threw open the door to Mr. Sharpe's office. I'd beaten the detective! I'd won the elevator game!

His secretary arched an eyebrow. "Miss Murphy," she said, "how do you do?"

I sucked in a breath, and then another, and another. My heart pounded painfully in my chest. I couldn't get enough air. "Mr. . . ." I gasped. "Mr. . . ." Oh, dear heavens, I couldn't speak! "Wa"—massive inhale—"ter." I bent over and grasped my knees. "Water."

The secretary sighed, but she stood up and fetched me water from some mysterious place. It was cold and refreshing and soothed my scratchy throat, calmed my racing heart. Unfortunately, the door opened and Detective Hodgson walked inside before I finished.

No matter. I'd throw the fit in front of him. Let him see it, then. I'd thrown tantrums in front of more noteworthy people before.

He stared me up and down, his hands in his coat pockets, his hat low on his forehead. I felt the weight of his stare and the loss of it when he looked away, having found me panting and not worth any more of his time. "I need to speak to Mr. Sharpe please," he said to the secretary, "as soon as possible."

I'd never thrown a fit in front of someone as intimidating as the detective, though. No one who thought so little of me and had told me to my face. No one I'd wanted to impress like this before.

Darn. I couldn't throw a tantrum in front of him. I wanted his respect too badly. I'd have to do it once he left.

The phone rang on the secretary's desk before she could call for the manager. "Miss Murphy," she said, "there's a delivery out front for you."

Double darn! Henry's gift! That meant the press was here! I checked the pins holding my hat, straightened my veil, and with a wink at the detective, strolled out into the lobby, the marble flooring cold under my bare feet. I grimaced. I was going to have to go outside without shoes on. And my gloves! Had I left them in the hall? No matter. Act confident and smile and no one would be looking at my feet.

I went ahead and wiggled my wiggle dress down a bit, just in case.

Henry was waiting for me on the sidewalk. He grinned and held open his arms, but his eyes were dark and unsmiling.

"Darling," I said, and wrapped my arms around his neck. "I have a present for you!" A camera flashed when we embraced. I couldn't see where the photographer was, but I kissed Henry's cheek anyway. As if on cue, the brand-new Rolls-Royce Silver Cloud I'd bought for him rolled up. It was the ginchiest car, with a two-tone color scheme of soft blue over a shining silver. The big red bow on the hood made for a creamy photo prop.

Henry laughed, delighted.

"Do you like it, darling?"

"It's magnificent!"

After parking in front of us, the driver climbed out of the car and handed Henry the keys.

"Only the best for you, darling," I said.

There are always people coming and going out of the Pinnacle. And standing on the sidewalk, I had an excellent view. All the new arrivals, all the guests leaving, all the bellhops lugging luggage and doormen holding doors. So I saw with perfect clarity when Mac was escorted out of the hotel flanked by security on either side of him.

It was at that moment that Henry swept me up into his arms and planted a giant kiss square on my lips.

The camera flashed.

When the kiss ended, Mac was gone. Henry tipped the driver, as I was without both shoes and a purse, and placed his hand on the small of my back. "Let's head inside for a minute," he whispered in my ear. "You look like you've run a marathon."

"You're not wrong," I said. "I played the elevator game."

"The elevator game?" He nodded a greeting at the doormen, who ushered us inside. "Did you win?"

"No," I said. "I was too late."

The lobby was a bustle of noise around us. I didn't see Mr. Sharpe or Detective Hodgson. All I could see on the faces of every person who passed was the look Mac had given me when he was escorted out. Disappointment. Hurt. Embarrassment.

I wished he were here with me instead of Henry. What a horrible thing to think.

With his hand on my back, Henry led me to the boutique. "Let's get you some shoes. Size seven," he told Judy, who waited on us behind the counter. "Something in black. And charge it to Miss Murphy's room."

"Did you like the car, Henry?"

"It's perfect, darling."

Judy handed me a pair of black shoes with the Pinnacle emblem on the toes. "Best I can do," she said with an apology in her tone.

Ghastly things, but I supposed they were better than continuing to go barefoot.

"Thank you." I slipped them on and said to Henry, "You didn't even look inside."

He chuckled. "I don't drive, Evelyn. Actually, here." He handed me the keys. "You keep them. But the picture for the paper is priceless. He got that big kiss, and that'll run in the paper tomorrow, faster than any of those rumors could get around town. You're a genius, truly."

He didn't even want the car? And Mac . . . Mac was gone, and . . .

I blinked, desperately trying to keep the tears away. "I have to go, Henry. I'll, um, I'll see you later?"

He smiled, oblivious to my feelings. "Of course."

The tears wouldn't fall. Not in public. I wouldn't let them. I'd go up to my room and I'd call Daddy and I'd fix it. I'd fix all of it.

My new shoes squeaked when I walked. I ran my fingers over my cheeks and pressed down under my eyes, ordering myself not to cry.

Don't cry. Do not cry, Evelyn. This is not a big deal. A person is dead and the wrong man is in jail, for goodness' sake, and you're crying because your friend was fired.

"Miss Murphy?" a breathless male voice asked from behind me. "Excuse me, Miss Murphy?"

I sniffed and turned around.

Mr. Burrows stood behind me with a small box in his hand. "Malcom Cooper left this for you."

I took it, brows furrowed. Mac had left me something? What?

Mr. Burrows shoved his glasses up his nose. "Have a good day, Miss Murphy."

"You too." I waited until he was gone before opening the box. Inside were Mac's assortment of lockpicks. He'd remembered that I needed to break into Mr. Sharpe's office. He knew I needed him, even as he was escorted off the premises by security, losing his only job.

I covered my mouth with my hand.

Oh no.

I love him.

CHAPTER 23

With tears in my eyes and ugly squeaky shoes on my feet, I knocked on the ambassador's door. Amelia answered, grinning. Her grin fell when she saw the state I was in.

"Evelyn? Are you all right?"

"I'm fine. I was wondering . . . are you able to sneak out when your parents are asleep?"

She scoffed. "Of course."

"Good. I need your help. Late tonight. Will you come over to my place after midnight?"

"That depends on what you want me to help you with."

That brought a smile to my face. What a clever little girl. "I need you to be a lookout. I am going to break into a locked office and have a bit of a snoop."

Amelia squealed in delight. "Marvelous! I'd be delighted to be your lookout, Evelyn."

"Thank you ever so," I said. "See you tonight."

"See you tonight!"

Back in my suite, someone was humming. I gripped the doorknob, momentarily frightened, but it was only Florence, fluffing pillows.

"Good evening, Miss Murphy."

As my day maid, Florence only ever cleans during the day. I never expect to see her in the evening. "Hello, Florence. How are you?"

"Fine, thank you. I brought in your heels and gloves from the hall. And, I hope you don't mind me picking up a double shift? It's only—some of the other girls were talking, and I'd rather be the only one who pops in here for the time being."

The other girls had been talking? I unpinned my hat. It didn't take an active imagination to wonder about what. My face flushed and my eyes burned, but I blinked the pain away. Sweet Florence was protecting me the best way she knew how. She didn't deserve to deal with the emotional burden I was carrying.

"I see. Thank you ever so. It's been quite the day."

Florence nodded. "I've heard. I also heard—forgive me. It isn't my place."

I smiled at her, toed off my squeaky shoes. "Those are the best things to hear!"

She giggled, shook her head. "The girls were talking, and I happened to overhear. The countess's necklace wasn't stolen. She was trying to get insurance money."

I'd figured that much. "Do you know what she might need insurance money for? The count is rather wealthy."

"Haven't you heard, Miss Murphy? Between her gambling addiction and his bad investments, they're positively swimming in debt! At least, that's what the girls are saying."

Gambling addiction? Bad investments? Swimming in so much debt that she'd attempted insurance fraud? Was it bad enough that she'd also steal a painting or commit murder? And there was the possible affair to be noted, too. Perhaps that was the straw that had broken the proverbial camel's back.

"Miss Murphy? You all right?"

I realized my nose was wrinkled. I sniffed to smooth it out. "Yes, of course. That's fascinating, Florence. You always do hear the most interesting things."

She giggled again and then proceeded to fill me in on all the other gossip she'd overheard, which didn't have anything to do with me, while she turned down my apartment for bedtime. But I only half listened. My mind was racing.

It would be much, much better for me if the countess was a murderer and Henry was innocent. But that wasn't reason enough to suspect someone. Attempted insurance fraud might be, though.

★ ★ ★

Hoping that Presley would be too tired after his walk with Mr. Peters to react to Amelia's late-night arrival proved to be a waste of time. He perked up the moment she slipped into my penthouse. She cooed and threw herself down next to his bed.

"Mon chéri!" She rubbed her nose against his wet one. "How I've missed you!"

"You were here a few hours ago," I reminded her, slipping on a pair of leather gloves.

"Yes, but he is so cute. I can barely stand being away from him ever!"

I laughed because I understood. But Presley couldn't come with us on our visit to Mr. Sharpe's office. This wasn't like breaking into the Silver Room late at night with Mac at my side. Mr. Sharpe's office was off the lobby, and the lobby was always busy, no matter what time it was. Even if no one came into the office, they'd be walking near it, and if Presley barked once, we were done for. Didn't know how I'd explain away going through employee records, even to Daddy. Sleepwalking? But I was wearing all black, from the gloves on my hands to the boots on my feet.

Daddy would delight in my gung-ho, solve-it-yourself attitude if I phrased it the right way. But there was no telling what Mr. Sharpe might say to him to sway his opinion of me.

No, the only choice I had was to not get caught. There was no plan B. I had to know why Mr. Hall had been written up before, during his otherwise stellar career.

Stellar besides the art theft and the murder, of course.

I applied matte red lipstick in my hallway mirror. It's always important to look your best, even if you're hoping to not be seen. "Are you ready, Amelia?"

She dropped a kiss between Presley's ears. "I'll be back, my love. Wait for me."

Mr. Sharpe's office had a direct view to the lobby, which meant the lobby had a direct view to Mr. Sharpe's office. Amelia and I stood in the stairwell, peeking out from the door. I thought of being with Mac in the kitchen, behaving in much the same way. I missed him.

He'd been gone only a few hours, but I wasn't used to snooping without him.

"I'm going to need a distraction," I whispered to Amelia. "You up for it?"

"Of course I am! How long do you need?"

I pulled Mac's lock-picking kit out of my pocket. It felt heavier in my hand. "I'm not sure. A minute? At least."

Amelia nodded once. "One-minute distraction, coming right up." She skipped out of the stairwell, singing so loudly and off key in French that one by one every person in the lobby, guest and employee alike, turned to look at her. They watched as she skipped to the fountain, stared as she kicked off her shoes, and shrieked as she jumped in. Multiple employees went to the fountain in feeble attempts to get her out, but she splashed whoever came near and cackled.

I was not a natural lockpick. I'd watched Mac a handful of times, and I tried to copy him. Every few seconds I looked over my shoulder to make sure Amelia still had the crowd in the palm of her hand. It took the full minute to get the door open. My forehead was damp with nervous sweat by the time I finally made it inside.

I swapped Mac's lock-picking kit for a pen-sized flashlight. All of Mr. Sharpe's records were in metal filing cabinets behind his desk. Fortunately, he didn't bother locking the cabinets, but none of them were labeled on the outside. That meant there were twelve possible drawers for Mr. Hall's record to be located in.

I sighed and rolled up my sleeves. Hopefully, Amelia would have gotten out of trouble by now, and hopefully, she knew not to lead them to me here in the office. Shaking that thought away, I dug into the top cabinet on the left. Taxes. Not what I was looking for.

Three more drawers went much the same way until I finally found the employee records for *A–K*. Mac's file was in there.

I hesitated. I hadn't broken into this office to snoop on him. But seeing his name written in black ink on the top of a manila folder . . . this man that I love . . .

A thief from London.

I chewed the inside of my lip, tried to ignore the queasiness kicking around my gut. Looking at this file without his knowledge would be a breach of trust. Not looking would require a massive leap of faith.

I exhaled, nodded to myself.

Maybe Detective Hodgson was right about him, but that was a risk I was willing to take. I skipped over *C*, then *D*, and all the way to *H*.

Phil Hall, where are you? Haddock, Haim, Ham . . .

Where was Hall? It skipped right over him!

The doorknob moved.

I didn't have time to freeze.

As quietly and as quickly as possible, I closed the drawer and dove under Mr. Sharpe's desk, turning off my flashlight. This was it. I was going to get caught in the literal act of snooping. If only I had two less-than-ten-year-old girls helping me instead of one!

Someone entered the room.

From my hiding spot, I couldn't see who it was, but a beam of a flashlight illuminated the drawers I had rifled through. The mystery person moved almost silently across the dark office.

I got a good look at their black pants and sensible shoes but nothing else. The flashlight beam moved over the desk, and I held my breath, scared I'd been spotted. Above my head lit up like the Fourth of July, and I noticed a white square taped to the bottom of Mr. Sharpe's desk.

The mystery intruder located the drawer with the records faster than I did but came across the same trouble. Hall's folder was missing. The person left as silently as they had come. I counted to thirty in my head before peeling off the taped square. Hall's folder was missing no more.

CHAPTER 24

I read the folder by flashlight under Mr. Sharpe's desk, not daring to take it out of the room. The lobby was too crowded and too well lit to hide it in plain sight, my black sweater too tight to hide it underneath.

Plus there was the whole breaking-back-in-to-hide-it-again situation to think about.

With the flashlight in my mouth, I turned the pages. It was relatively thin, considering how many years Mr. Hall had been at the Pinnacle—first as a security guard, then working his way up to head of the whole department. The famed write-up had occurred recently. Six months ago, to be exact. The maid who had stolen cash out of the guest's safe had confessed, but only after an altercation with Hall.

Feminine cursive explained:

I shouldn't have done it. I'm so sorry. The money wasn't mine. I saw it, and I thought of my mother, and I acted on temptation. I shouldn't have done it and I understand that I must lose my job because of it. But Mr. Hall discovered that I had taken the money moments after the theft. He cornered me in the hallway and said he'd keep the secret, as long as I gave him half. I refused. Half would have been of little help to my mother. That's why he turned me in, because I wouldn't cave to his blackmail.

Mr. Sharpe had included the handwritten note, then typed underneath it:

She is convincing, but I am not convinced. Hall has been an exemplary employee for years. The word of a thief is not enough cause to end employment. Hall denies accusations.

Sharpe hadn't believed the maid was telling the truth, but what if she had been?

Worse than a blackmailer, Hall'd been arrested for theft and murder. Was Mr. Sharpe doubting his exemplary employee now? Was that why he had hidden the file? Because he regretted the paper trail that had felt so necessary earlier this year?

I fiddled with my pendant, bit my lip in thought. Between hiding a note like this and his alibi not matching Henry's, Mr. Sharpe was making himself a front-runner for my *Who killed Billie Bell?* bet with Mac.

I taped the folder back underneath the desk and crawled out, flashlight still in my mouth. My legs tingled from being cramped for so long in such a small space.

After standing up and touching my toes a few times, I sneaked back out of Mr. Sharpe's office. The lobby was sleepy. The number of new arrivals had significantly decreased, and the staff on the late shift were yawning and talking in hushed voices. Amelia was nowhere to be seen.

God bless that little French girl.

I checked my watch. A quarter after two. The few people milling about paid me no mind, as it wasn't entirely unusual for me to be wandering about the lobby this late. This is the city that never sleeps, after all.

The lift arrived in moments, and I rode it to the top floor, considering. There was only one person I could talk to about this, and he'd been fired. Did I call him now, so late at night? Or did I let him sleep and talk this out in the morning?

Knowing I wouldn't see his face tomorrow made the decision for me. After greeting Presley properly, as he so demanded, I called Mac.

"Evelyn," he said, "whadja find?"

I smiled into the receiver. "How did you know it was me?"

"I figured you'd call me after having your snoop," he said, "since I'm not there to sleep on your couch."

My smile drooped. "I'm sorry about that. I tried to get the detective to stop, but he doesn't care for my opinion. I'm going to talk to Daddy, though, and I'll get your job back, Mac. I promise."

He said, "Eh. That's life, Evelyn. I came to New York to start over, but my mistakes followed me. I had to pay the price sometime."

"Mac! Don't talk like that. You don't deserve to be fired. You're good at your job."

"It's just a job, Evelyn. I'll get another one. Now, tell me what you found." He yawned, loud and long. "I'm on pins and needles over here."

With a huff, I explained the folder hidden under Mr. Sharpe's desk and the paper trail I'd discovered.

"It's a good thing you went in when you did," Mac said. "If he's got half a brain, he'll shred the evidence."

"Mr. Sharpe is a company man. He won't shred evidence."

"But hiding it is A-OK?" Though I couldn't see him, in my mind's eye I pictured Mac shaking his head at me. "No, take my word for it. He's gonna destroy it. Shame you didn't nick it now while you had the chance."

"But why would I want it? Mac, I don't think Hall stole the painting, and I certainly don't think he killed Bell. Holding on to evidence that makes him look like a blackmailer is hardly in my best interest."

"The truth is the truth. One way or another, things are gonna be brought to the light."

It's very annoying when Mac is right and I am wrong. I don't like it, not even a little bit. "Fine," I said with a sigh, "I'll sneak back in before he gets to work in the morning and swipe it."

"Call me when you do," he said. "I can help you hide it if you're willing to meet me away from the hotel. I'm not allowed within one hundred feet."

"That's bonkers. You haven't stolen anything. I don't care what Countess Dreadful says! I'm going to talk to Daddy. I know you think you deserve this, but you don't. You haven't done anything wrong."

There was a smile in his voice when he said, "Well, except for all the locks I've picked with you."

"Right. But that was helping me out, Mac. Hardly a firable offense, though it does give me an idea. Tomorrow, would you go to the jail and speak with Hall? See what he has to say for himself about this whole blackmail business? Maybe he can illuminate something for us that we're missing here. I'll pay you double your usual fee."

"Double?" Mac swore in delight. "You've got yourself a deal."

★   ★   ★

I woke up early and dressed in a pastel floral sundress, put on my face, and got to work as soon as Mr. Peters took Presley for his morning walk.

The lift operator greeted me warmly. "You missed Mr. Presley," he said. "Such a good boy."

"Oh, I know," I said. "He's my favorite."

The operator pressed the button for the lobby. "Your favorite dog you've had?"

"No. My favorite of anything in the whole world."

"Ah, I see," he replied, not sounding like he understood at all. The elevator stopped in the lobby, and he waved good-bye.

With purpose, I strode to the manager's office. I needed the note under his desk before he arrived. It was a quarter till eight, giving me fifteen minutes to do the deed without being caught. Plenty of time.

Mr. Sharpe's door was locked. Curses.

Oh, that's right. I'd locked it myself on the way out last night so that Mr. Sharpe wouldn't notice anything was amiss. Foiled by my own careful planning.

I opened my purse and pulled out a compact and a lipstick. Anyone passing by would assume I was reapplying a red coat, but I was making sure no one was watching me from behind. Free and clear, I got out Mac's lock-picking kit. This morning it was much easier than last night, since I remembered what size pick had worked and how I'd maneuvered the lock into unlatching.

Everything was dark. I closed the door and made my way to Sharpe's inner office, finding it exactly as I'd left it.

Good. I'd beaten him in, and I'd get the evidence before he had a chance to get rid of it. Evidence that only piled more guilt onto the man I believed innocent, but Mac was right. The point was in finding out the truth, not in satisfying my own allegations.

The lights came on.

Oh no. My first instinct was to freeze. I was at Mr. Sharpe's desk! So close to what I wanted!

There was no point in hiding underneath it again. The lights were on and footsteps were coming closer, the workday having started earlier than planned. If Mr. Sharpe sat at his desk while I was under it, that would make for a pretty awkward discovery.

I did the only thing I could think of. I sat down on his chair and placed my feet on his desk.

"Miss Murphy!" Mr. Sharpe jumped in surprise when he turned on the lights in his inner office and saw me taking up his space. "I . . . what are you . . . it's early, and . . ." He cleared his throat. "Please don't put your dirty shoes on my things."

"These *shoes* are not dirty," I said. "They are *stilettos*, and they've never even been outside."

He frowned at me and set his briefcase down by my not-dirty stilettos. "All the same, I have much work to do, and you are rather in the way."

"Of course." Slowly, I set my feet on the ground. Even more slowly, I rose out of his chair. But I did not move from behind the desk.

He sighed and pinched the bridge of his nose. "Miss Murphy, to what do I owe the particular pleasure of this early-morning visit?"

"Well," I said, the affectation in my voice slightly higher than normal, "it's only that I don't know what to do with the car I bought Henry. He doesn't drive, you see. And I don't drive. Can you hire me a driver, Mr. Sharpe?"

"A driver," he repeated. "For you? But you don't ever leave the Pinnacle, Miss Murphy. For what reason would you ever require a driver?"

My mouth fell open. I covered my heart with my hand. It stopped beating for a second, making my lungs spasm, my throat clench. "I beg your pardon, Mr. Sharpe?"

"You are a recluse, Miss Murphy. Hiring a driver for you would be a waste of your father's resources, vast though they may be."

I held on to the back of his chair to keep standing on my thin heels. "A recluse? How dare you? Mr. Sharpe, you are an employee! How could you call me such a thing, in my father's hotel?"

He met my gaze, his dark eyes sharp, cutting. "You think me dafty, Miss Murphy? I know you. I know what you're doing in my office. You are nosy and spoiled. You think you have a right to go through my things, my documents, simply because your father is wealthy. Yes, your father is my boss. But *you* are not. You are nothing. You are a brat styled like Marilyn Monroe. And Miss Murphy, that does not a personality make."

I stumbled where I stood. No one had ever been so cruel to me before. Spoiled and nosy, a brat lacking personality? What was it with all these, these . . . these *men!* Calling me names to my face? A recluse?

Just because I didn't like to leave the hotel—no, not even that! I didn't *need* to leave the hotel. Everything I could want was here. And if something wasn't? I had it delivered. The benefit of being rich. I didn't have to wander the streets for entertainment! It was all brought to me.

Mr. Sharpe was jealous. Jealous of my father's wealth. Jealous of my . . . my . . .

I blinked rapidly, tears clouding my vision.

My what?

He was right.

I had absolutely nothing on my own for him to be jealous of.

I picked up my purse and left the office without another word. I couldn't risk him seeing me cry. He said my name, quietly and with regret, and I knew without hesitation he was only attempting the barest of apologies to keep me from tattling to Daddy. I didn't bother listening to the rest of it.

I bypassed the elevator and headed for the stairwell. I couldn't risk being seen crying, but the moment the heavy door closed, the tears fell. I'd known Mr. Sharpe almost all my life. For how much of it had he hated me?

With a sniff, I stuck my hand into my purse. There, next to the tissues, was the handwritten note of the fired maid and Mr. Sharpe's typed response.

A nosy, spoiled, personality-lacking brat I might be, but at least I had gotten what I'd come for.

CHAPTER 25

I secured the note in the zippered compartment in my purse, next to my favorite red lipstick and monogrammed compact. The tears wouldn't stop. Without personality? Me?

Yes, I wore whatever Marilyn Monroe was wearing. And I bought whatever makeup she wore. I used her favorite perfume, and I had my hair dyed her color. Sometimes I quoted her movies. And there was, of course, the pink dress from *Gentlemen Prefer Blondes* that I'd recreated for the now infamous art showing. But I had my own personality underneath all that hero worship.

I *did*.

Like he said, I'm nosy and spoiled. That's a personality, I'm pretty sure.

And now, with the evidence hidden safely in my clutch, I had my first clue. Maybe Mr. Sharpe had been mean to me because I was getting close. But why would he kill Bell? What motive could he possibly have for murder?

The motive for murder in detective novels is more often than not love. You love someone else's wife, you kill them. You need money to run away with your love, but your rich father says over his dead body, so you kill him. Love does funny things to a man, but as far as I knew, Mr. Sharpe wasn't in love with anyone. And hiding the note about Hall seemed to be about saving his own skin.

Perhaps the two of them were in on it together? Or maybe Sharpe had stolen the painting before the party, around the time Presley knocked him into the easel. Maybe he'd even been in the process of stealing it when my dog and I interrupted him. Hall found out and tried to blackmail Mr. Sharpe, but Mr. Sharpe killed the artist and made Hall look guilty.

Because Hall wasn't the murderer. There was no way. No one was stupid enough to kill a person with a knife engraved with their own initials. So, if he had teamed up with Mr. Sharpe for some unknown reason, Mr. Sharpe had been the one to plunge the knife in Bell's back. He'd planned on setting Hall up to take the fall. That was why he'd used the world's most obvious murder weapon. It explained why his alibi didn't match Henry's.

But why would Henry lie? If Sharpe was busy murdering Bell, he obviously wasn't retroactively adding a discount to Henry's stay.

I didn't want to believe Henry was capable of something so dastardly as murder, but I couldn't shake loose the image of that fight between him and Bell. He'd been so angry! So filled with rage. Something about Bell turned Henry into someone different than the person I knew and loved.

I also liked the countess for murder. With her money troubles, it wasn't hard to see how she, desperate for money, might end up killing a successful artist. She wanted something from him that he wouldn't give and in a fit of rage stabbed him in the back. That motive worked even if they were romantically involved. She could've seduced him to get access to his wallet, and when he chose his assistant over her, she snapped.

There was the assistant too. Tilly Bourke. But she'd mourned his death desperately, like a wife mourning a beloved husband. She was small, too delicate for the ugly work of murder. But he had cheated on her, and love and rage gave people all sorts of strength. Mr. Peters had backed up her alibi, though. She'd sent Bell to the room and hung back at the pool to pay off their tab. I'd seen her arrive, and by then Bell was already dead.

And what of that strange maid who had threatened me in the hallway? What role did she play in all this?

Someone was running down the stairs, huffing and puffing the whole way. I wiped my face dry on the back of my hand, but it was only Henry.

"Evelyn? Darling?" He panted as he stood in front of me, his forehead glistening with sweat. He wore gray sweatpants and a matching sweatshirt, a navy-blue towel thrown over his shoulder. He never missed an opportunity to look his best, even when exercising in the hotel stairwell. "Darling, what happened?"

"Mr. Sharpe and I got into a bit of an argument. Truthfully, it was less of an argument and more of a slaughter. He hates me."

"Don't be silly, my dear girl. Who could ever hate you?"

I sniffled. "It's true. He told me I was nosy and spoiled."

Henry wrapped an arm around my shoulders and held me against his side. "Those are two of my favorite things about you."

I shook my head. More tears came. "He called me a brat."

"You know what you want and how to get it. You should be proud of that."

"He said I was devoid of personality and hiding the fact by copying Marilyn Monroe."

Henry *tsk*ed and gently led me up the stairs. "Come now, don't be silly. He must be having a bad day. You and Mr. Sharpe go way back. He's known you since you were a child."

"Which is why this hurts so much." We made it to the second floor before I remembered the elevator exists. I pushed the door open and walked out into the hallway. "For how long has he hated me? My whole life?"

"Nonsense, no one could hate you. It's impossible." Henry pressed the button for the lift. "In an hour, he'll be knocking on your door to apologize. I guarantee."

"He'll apologize, all right. But only to keep me from calling Daddy and costing him his job. He won't mean it."

Henry wrapped his arm around me in another hug as the elevator doors opened.

"Miss Murphy. Mr. Fox." The liftboy greeted us. "Top floor?"

"Please," Henry said with his movie-star smile. He didn't let go of me the whole way up. I appreciated the comfort, but my mind wandered to the person I wanted holding me most.

How was Mac doing? Was he on his way to the jail? Would the police let him talk to Hall? Would Hall be willing to talk? Blackmail was a serious crime. Not as serious as murder, of course, but in for a penny, in for a pound, and all that.

When we reached the top floor, Henry guided me toward my room. "Let's get you comfortable. Some coffee, some music. I have an early call time at the theater this morning, but we could do dinner tonight? Would you like that?"

Presley trotted up to us when we stepped inside, his poofy tail wagging. His blue bow was askew on his forehead. Mr.

Peters did his best, but he was no Mac. I knelt down to fix the bow before scooping him up in my arms.

"I think we would like that," I said, rubbing my nose against Presley's little cold one. "Wouldn't we, baby? If only it were Friday. There's no wedding to crash on a Wednesday."

Henry chuckled. "We'll get a good window seat at the restaurant. What do you say? My treat."

"We'll be there with bells on."

"Good." He hesitated with his hand on the doorknob. "Say, Evelyn? What were you and Mr. Sharpe doing so early in the morning? Before the slaughter took place."

"Oh." My face warmed. "Well, you see . . ."

He exhaled so forcefully, my hair moved across my forehead.

"I think he has more information about Phil Hall than he is letting on, and I only wanted to find out about it. To help the police with their investigation, of course."

"The police don't need your help, darling. Mr. Sharpe is a good man. If he had important information, he would share it. You shouldn't be snooping around in his office."

I narrowed my eyes. "I thought you said you liked that I was nosy."

He grinned. "To a point, darling, to a point. But you aren't doing yourself any favors. The police have their man. Let them work it out. Bell was a horrible person anyway. I'm not sad he's dead. And you going around, poking your adorable nose into things? Look what it's done to your morning. It's brought you to tears. All of it could have been avoided if you'd stayed out of the whole thing."

At that, I could only nod. Henry wasn't right per se, but he wasn't wrong either.

"I'll see you tonight at dinner, darling. Rest up and get beautiful for me." He winked, flashed his perfect smile, and I giggled despite myself.

He opened the door and stepped out into the hallway.

"Henry," I said, still smiling. "Are we still best friends?"

"Of course. The very best." He winked again and closed the door.

The smile fell from my face. I held Presley against my cheek, let him lick my chin. "I don't know, Presley," I whispered. "Do best friends want you to change who you are?"

CHAPTER 26

I'd started contemplating what I wanted room service to bring Presley and I for lunch when the phone rang.

"Evelyn Murphy," I chirped into the receiver.

"Hey," Mac said. "I found something,"

"Ooo!" I sat down and crossed my legs. "You found something when I sent you to talk to Mr. Hall. What on earth was he hiding in his black-and-white jumpsuit?"

He chuckled. "No. He sent me on a goose chase. At least, I think he did. What I found doesn't make sense to me, but maybe it'll make sense to you. Can you come over?"

"Come over?" I fiddled with the pendant around my neck. "Like, to *Yonkers*?"

"Yes. To Yonkers. That is where I live."

The fiddling became pulling. I clutched the silver portrait of Saint Anthony tight in my fingers. "Why don't you come here? Better yet, why don't you tell me what you found over the phone? I can't handle the suspense, Mac."

"That's the thing. I don't know what it is I found. Well, I do know *what* it is, but I don't know how it helps him at all.

Besides, I can't go to the Pinnacle, remember? Mr. Sharpe made it crystal clear I wasn't welcome on the premises."

"But it's *my* hotel," I said. "If I want you to come over, what is Mr. Sharpe to do about it?"

"Ring the police, probably," Mac replied.

I rolled my eyes. "So what?"

"So, I left the station of my own free will, and I'd like to not go back there on someone else's whim."

Huffing, I acquiesced. "Fine. Tell me what you found."

"A book," he said. "Hall's high school yearbook. I think that's what he wanted me to get. He talked in riddles, Evelyn. I'll explain everything when you get here. You want the address?"

I copied his address down on a nearby pad of paper. Then I rolled the pen cap between my lips. "But how do I get there, Mac? Do I take a taxi? Do taxis go all the way to Yonkers?"

"If you got cash," Mac said, "they'll take you wherever you want to go. Or you could try the subway."

"The subway?" I about fell off my chair. "I should think not! Can you imagine? This dress on the subway!"

"I don't know what dress you're wearing. But no, you're right, I can't picture you in the subway. So give the driver my address, and I'll see you soon."

He hung up on me. He hung up on me!

I stared at the phone in shock, not ready for the conversation to be over. I felt as if I'd lost an argument.

I had to go to Yonkers? On my own? On a Wednesday?

My stomach growled. I hadn't even eaten yet!

I slammed the receiver down and hopped off the stool. Presley was a better clock than anything I wore around my wrist. He always knew when it was time to eat and was hot on my heels while I rifled through the pantry.

"Don't have time to order food today, Presley. Looks like peanut butter and jelly for me and a can for you."

Since he was a dog, as adorable and precious a dog as ever existed, he was grateful for food no matter what container it originated from. He gobbled up his canned goods while I made my sandwich, inwardly stewing.

Yonkers. All the way to Yonkers. And for a yearbook? What on earth could be in the yearbook that Hall thought would help him?

Did Hall think it would help him? Ugh, Mac. He hadn't given me enough to go on over the phone.

Yonkers. *Yonkers!* He had deliberately withheld information to get me to his apartment. I licked the butter knife clean of strawberry jelly. Part of me wanted to see his apartment. He'd been working at the Pinnacle for almost a year. We'd spent nearly every day together, but I had no idea how he lived, beyond the fact that he had only one phone and it was in his kitchen and he ate tinned veggies for dinner. Ick.

How much could fresh vegetables cost, anyway? Three dollars?

I dumped the dirty dishes in the sink and ate my sandwich standing up, still thinking. I was not looking forward to riding in a taxi. Maybe I could get one of the doormen to wave one down for me, and then all I'd have to do was tell him the address and pay him the money.

Better yet, I'd get one of the bellhops to drive my new car. Er, Henry's new car. He wasn't using it, and my name was on the title, so why not? At least then I'd be able to travel to Yonkers in the comfort of my own private vehicle.

I shivered at the thought of how many strangers sat in the back of a taxicab on any given day. Who knew what the state of their hygiene was, or the bottoms of their shoes, or if they left gum on the seat. What if I got gum on the bottom of my stilettos? I looked down at them while chewing. Since I was taking the Rolls, I wouldn't have to worry about changing for the ride, but what was Mac's apartment like? His personal hygiene was good, more or less, but what of his landlord or his neighbors? What was Yonkers even like?

Mr. Sharpe's voice rang out in my head, the word *recluse* resounding over and over again. And there, quietly underneath Mr. Sharpe, was Detective Hodgson warning me off Mac. Saying he was using me. Calling me stupid.

I'd show them both. I'd go to Yonkers, proving I wasn't a recluse.

I'd recover the yearbook Mac had and find the clue Hall had left for us, proving Mac wasn't using me and I wasn't stupid in one go.

I'd show both those men today, this very afternoon, and then they'd see.

I'm so much more than they think I am.

CHAPTER 27

I had to wait in line to talk to the concierge. A line! For the concierge! On a Wednesday in September, of all things. By the time I was waved to the podium by one of our tuxedo-wearing concierges, I had been standing for so long I felt light-headed and a bit woozy. Dehydrated, most likely.

I clutched Presley's purse closer to my body and smiled. "Hello. I need a driver, please."

He was narrow, the concierge. Narrow in the face and the shoulders and the hips. Even the grin he gave me was narrow. "A driver? You want me to call a car service, Miss . . . ?"

"Murphy." I said my last name slowly, so he wouldn't miss it. "Top floor." I added that in case he was new and didn't know the owner's last name. "And not a car service. I own a car. But I don't know how to drive it, so I need a driver. A bellboy will do fine. Please and thank you."

"A bellboy?" His narrow eyes glanced toward the phone on his podium. "I see. And to where do you require to be driven, Miss Murphy?"

"Yonkers." I pulled out Mac's address from underneath Presley's paws. "I need to go now. I'll also need the bellboy to hang around and wait for me to want to leave, and I am not sure when that will be."

Again, he gave me a narrow smile. "You want me to have a bellboy drive you to Yonkers for an unspecified amount of time? I am so sorry, Miss Murphy, but I can't do that. We've had an influx of guests, and it is all-hands-on-deck right now. I don't have a bellboy to spare, even for a short drive."

Looking around the lobby, it was clear to see he wasn't exaggerating.

I swallowed in a vain attempt to loosen the lump in my throat. What I needed was water. Or coffee. Or champagne. Preferably, chilled champagne and scrumptious caviar.

"Taxi it is." I clutched Mac's address tight in my hand. "Thank you for your help." What little there was he had given me, anyway.

He nodded at me and waved over the next in line.

My stomach felt sour, not in the mood for even the thought of caviar. I must've eaten my peanut butter and jelly too fast.

I weaved my way out of the lobby, my stilettos clacking against the exquisite marble flooring.

Should I change now that I would have to take a taxi? I checked my watch. It was already one thirty, and anyway, my outfit was adorable. I wanted to see Mac's face when he saw me in the short sundress and towering stiletto heels. I'd curled my hair ever so gently and pinned it up, exposing my neck. My lipstick, instead of the usual Marilyn red, was a soft peach.

Maybe he still wanted things to be a casual bit of fun, but I didn't, and it was a wonder what the right outfit could do to a man's sense of commitment.

The lobby was so packed with people that they sucked up all the available air, leaving behind something thin and polluted.

It was a relief when the doors opened and I inhaled the fresh air. Normally, that was all it took to settle my nervous stomach. But the whiff of late summer and the exhaust of passing cars did nothing to help me.

In my life, I'd never hailed a single taxi. They drove past the Pinnacle now, slow and yellow, stopping for whoever held up a hand, or for guests checking in.

I walked down the stairs and onto the sidewalk. Bellboys hurried about with golden carts, hauling luggage out of trunks and answering questions for guests yet to check in. Valets with keys in their hands hopped into cars and hurried to park them in the Pinnacle's garage. Glamorous young women and their older male companions chirped along, talking about taking in a show or where they were going to grab dinner.

With a deep breath of the city's thick summer air, I raised my hand and called out, "Taxi!"

What do you know? One stopped right in front of me, the passenger window rolled down.

"Hello," I said. "Can you take me to Yonkers? I have money."

The driver made a phlegm-filled noise in response that caused me to physically recoil.

"Yeah, lady, I can take you to Yonkers. You got an address?"

Grimacing, I handed him the slip of paper through the open window, feeling a bit like I was giving him my last lifeline. I didn't have Mac's address memorized. What if he lost it and then I had to use a public phone to call him?

"You gonna get in or what?" He continued to sit in his seat, making absolutely no effort to open my door for me.

I frowned but opened up the back door and slid inside. Presley set his two front paws on the edge of the purse when I put it down on the seat next to me, his tail wagging and his ears upright. He hadn't been in a car since he was my little puppy bear. I scratched his head.

The car rolled forward. My hand shook over his fur. Presley rubbed his cold nose on my palm, and I resumed his rightful pats as we pulled into slow-moving traffic.

Turning my head, I could still see the Pinnacle, but every second it got smaller and smaller until I could no longer see the bellboys and the valets, the glamorous women and their rich companions, the doormen and the guests. Even the Pinnacle's own gleaming white walls and Chateauesque emerald-green towered roof slipped away.

My stomach flipped. Curse that sandwich! I'd never eat peanut butter and jelly again for as long as I lived.

Bile hit the back of my throat. I swallowed, my neck tight, my mouth dry. I didn't want to throw up, not in the back of this taxi!

"Hey, lady," the driver said, "you gonna spew?"

I wanted to respond, to demand he call me by my name or insist that I had never done and would never do something so grotesque as spewing, but my breathing was too erratic to make room for speech.

My heart pounded in my chest, squeezed in on itself, exploded inside of me, only to do it all again.

Over and over, my heart constricted itself into oblivion.

"I can't breathe," I gasped out. "I'm having a heart attack! Take me back to the hotel!"

I don't remember much of the ride back, except the driver spent the time swearing up a storm.

Tingles traveled up and down my arms, burning as they went. My hands and feet went numb. Presley stared up at me with his tongue hanging out of his mouth, and I couldn't even bop it.

The moment the taxi stopped outside the Pinnacle, I forced the door open and stumbled out. My legs didn't work. I was on all fours on the sidewalk, my limbs shaking beneath me.

What a day to wear a short sundress.

The driver ran out of the taxi and waved his arms above his head, yelling for help. Not that his help wasn't appreciated, of course, but his dramatics were unnecessary, as every set of eyes on the block were turned toward the hotel heiress dying on the steps of her inheritance.

This was it. I was dying. And Mac would never get to see me in my adorable outfit.

CHAPTER 28

"Hey! Hey! This broad needs a doctor!" The taxi driver stood over me, waving his arms like he was trying to land a plane.

I couldn't catch my breath enough to properly explain how little I liked being referred to as "this broad."

"Come on, I can't have another fare die on me! They'll take my license!"

A middle-aged man wearing an expensive suit, but an abominably ugly brown and white checkered tie, came jogging down the stairs. He had a bag in his hand that was not quite a briefcase, but it was made from real leather all the same. He knelt down next to me and placed two fingers on my neck.

"Your heart rate is elevated," he said.

"Are you . . . a . . . doctor?"

He nodded once and popped open his bag, pulling out a stethoscope. "Are you experiencing any pain?"

"Pain?" Presley furiously licked my elbow. "What kind of pain?"

Listening to my lungs, he gave me a glare over his crescent-shaped bifocals. "Any kind of pain. Burning, tightening, stabbing?"

My mind's eye conjured up the image of Billie Bell, a knife sticking out of his back. And then the last time I'd seen my mother. I grimaced. "Don't say stabbing. No, I'm not in pain. Not really. I can't catch my breath. My hands are tingling."

He moved his stethoscope from my ribs to my heart, a deep frown on his face.

"Oh God, it's a heart attack, isn't it? I'm dying, I'm dying, I know it, I'm dying, I'm—"

"Please," he interrupted, loud and rude. "I am trying to evaluate you, and your incessant blathering isn't helping. Now, what is your name?"

Another man yelling at me? This one a doctor? On the steps of my own hotel! The absolute nerve. "Miss Evelyn Elizabeth Grace Murphy," I replied, my anger letting my lungs expand somewhat normally. "My father owns the hotel you're staying in."

"It's a very nice hotel," he said. "Congratulations to your father. Now." He draped the stethoscope around his neck and held my wrist in his hand. "I want you to breathe as I breathe. Can you do that for me, Miss Murphy? In through your nose"—he demonstrated this as if I were a small, dumb child—"hold it in, and out through your mouth." He exhaled. "And breathe in."

I breathed in through my nose.

"Hold," he said.

I held my breath.

"Out."

I exhaled through my nose. We did this together seven or eight times. He checked my pulse around my wrist. "It's better," he said. "How do you feel?"

It took me a second to register his question, but when I did, I gave myself a quick evaluation. Stunningly, I felt better. Not great. Still a bit dizzy and like I might break down in tears at any moment, but my hands no longer tingled and I wasn't short of breath.

"Better, thank you. Should we call an ambulance to be safe?"

"That's your decision," he said, "but in my professional estimation, you've suffered an attack of anxiety. Have you ever seen an analyst?"

Sniffing lightly, I settled Presley in my lap, in no rush to leave my seat on the sidewalk, even though I did not care for where this conversation was going. "I fail to see how that is any of your business."

"I see." He set his stethoscope back in his bag. "That is a yes, then. I'm going to assume you received a diagnosis you didn't agree with."

Presley put his paws on my chest and licked my chin. Poor baby was worried about his mommy. I cooed and scratched his ears and thoroughly ignored the doctor.

"I suggest you get back in touch with your analyst." The doctor groaned when he stood. "Without having your history in front of me, I couldn't say what triggered your anxiety, nor give you proper advice as to how to treat it. Have a good day, Miss Murphy."

"I didn't catch your name, Doctor?"

"It's Smith," he said, and climbed into the back of the taxi that had almost killed me. "Be seeing you."

The cabby who'd called me a broad was still waiting to be paid and so was available to lend me a hand and pull me onto my stiletto heels. I shook but stayed upright, Presley tucked safely in my arms.

Mr. Burrows quickly descended the stairs to hold my elbow. Had someone gone inside and informed the front desk I was in trouble?

It was the first time I'd looked around since arriving back to the safety of the Pinnacle. All the well-dressed women and their rich, older male counterparts, the elderly ladies in sweaters with big gold brooches, the staff in green and thick-brimmed hats—every single one of them was looking at me. Their motions hadn't stopped. Everyone continued on doing what they needed to do—this was New York, after all—but they were all very much aware of the owner's daughter splayed out on the dirty sidewalk.

My cheeks burned, but I paid the cabby well.

I swayed on my too-tall shoes and decided that leaning on the staff member offering assistance was better than falling down in front of everyone gawking like I had performed some trick. "I'm going to the front desk," I said. "I need to leave a message for Mr. Fox, and I'd like the bill for Dr. Smith's room charged to me for the duration of his stay."

"I can do that for you, ma'am," Mr. Burrows said, walking me up the stairs. "What would you like the message for Mr. Fox to say?"

"I'm afraid I need to cancel dinner. I'm not feeling well."

CHAPTER 29

Mr. Sharpe almost knocked me over in his haste to replace Mr. Burrows at my side. "Miss Murphy! Dear me, Miss Murphy! What happened? Are you ill? Did you fall? Do you need to go to hospital?"

I held up the flat of my palm to stop his barrage of questions. Tears pressed against the backs of my eyes, and I couldn't tell if it was because of the anxiety attack I had suffered or seeing Mr. Sharpe's face again after the hurtful words he'd hurled at me earlier.

"I'll be fine. I need to lie down for a minute. Maybe take a bath to wash off the sidewalk from my skin. Your concern is most appreciated, Mr. Sharpe."

To his benefit, his face reddened and his back stiffened at the remark.

Good. I hoped he was embarrassed about how he had spoken to me earlier. He should be. Frankly, he should be fired for it. Daddy wouldn't take kindly to one of his employees calling me any sort of name.

"Please, Miss Murphy, let me accompany you to your room. Have you not anyone you want me to call for you? A doctor? Your father?"

"As I said, I'll be fine." Nevertheless, he insisted on riding the elevator to the top floor with me. As the operator closed the door, an idea appeared in my—admittedly hazy—mind. "I'm surprised you want me to speak to Daddy, Mr. Sharpe."

Sure enough, he stiffened again beside me.

"I haven't had a chance to call him all morning," I said. "We have ever so much to catch up on."

"Certainly. I know your father cares for you."

I didn't like his tone of voice, slick with fake humility.

Glancing at him from the corner of my eye, I said, "He does hate to have me inconvenienced or upset in any way. It's easier for him if I am kept content."

The elevator stopped, and Mr. Sharpe walked me to my door. "It seems as though collapsing on the public sidewalk is a bit more than being inconvenienced, Miss Murphy."

"But you see, I had such an awful, awful morning. It contributed to my fainting spell. Daddy would absolutely rage if he heard it."

"Rage," Mr. Sharpe repeated, a shine on his upper lip. I unlocked the door and set Presley down but didn't immediately follow him inside.

"Rage." I glanced up at the air vents in the ceiling and fluttered my eyelashes, the carefully held back tears let loose. "Daddy, everyone is so mean to me. My best friend in the whole world was cast away from me. I'm so lonely, and so hurt, and so scared. Oh Daddy, won't you push up your visit? Can't you come here for a bit and help me with all this mess?"

Mr. Sharpe held up both hands in surrender. "I get your point." He reached into his jacket pocket and pulled out a monogrammed hankie. "Dry your tears. You want Mr. Cooper allowed on the premises again."

I dried my face, frowned at the amount of makeup that came off on the white cotton. "Very much so, yes."

"Then he will be allowed on the premises, but only under your direct supervision. He will not be given his job back, and he is not to wander unsupervised. If you want him, he is entirely your responsibility."

"That's a deal, Mr. Sharpe." I held out my hand. "You won't regret it."

He shook my hand with a loud sigh. "Have a good day, Miss Murphy. Or, at least, a better day." He took his hanky, and I waited until he was back in the elevator before stepping into my apartment and locking the door.

There. The easy part was over. Mac could come to me and I wouldn't have to go all the way to Yonkers.

Now for the hard part. I would have to call my analyst. That darned woman. How dare she end up being right about me! Shell shock and agoraphobia, she had said. Written down in red ink like a scarlet letter. I'd fired her on the spot and hadn't spoken to her in a year.

I had someone I loved now. Someone who lived all the way in Yonkers. I'd never get the opportunity to snoop around his personal belongings if I couldn't leave the Pinnacle's grounds.

I settled down on my couch, and with Presley on my lap, I made two phone calls. The first to Mac.

"I'm sorry, I won't be able to make it to Yonkers. I had a bit of a . . . medical situation. But I've cleared it with Mr. Sharpe that you're allowed on the premises as long as you stay by me. Will you come over, Mac? Please?"

"Medical thing? Evelyn, are you all right?"

"I'll be fine," I said, and I almost started to believe it. "But I'd like to see you. And your clue."

"I'll be right there, Evelyn. Don't worry."

Don't worry. If only it was that easy.

"See you soon, Mac." But I hoped he heard the truth. I was in love with him. And I *was* worried about it.

CHAPTER 30

The second call was to my analyst. It took me a while to make it, a quarter of an hour spent staring my reflection down in my bathroom mirror, and when I did call, it was her secretary I reached.

She asked me to hold.

"Miss Murphy," Dr. Sanders said, after a few short moments, "so happy you've decided to move on with our sessions."

"Oh, no, that's not why I'm calling. I don't need sessions, only advice."

"Advice?" I heard her sigh. "Miss Murphy, I'm in between clients right now. I don't have time for—"

"Quick advice," I promised. "Do you remember the last time we spoke?"

The long cord of the kitchen phone allowed me room to roam. Presley watched me, his little head moving back and forth like a spectator at a tennis match, while I carved out a path in front of the refrigerator.

She *hmm*ed. "The last time I saw you was to discuss your diagnoses. Agoraphobia and shell shock. You did not agree with my assessments."

"I still don't," I said. "I'm not crazy. I'm eccentric. Lots of wealthy people are! Seems completely unnecessary to label that as something more than it is."

"Was it the words I used to describe your conditions that so offended you, or was it my reasoning behind it?"

I scoffed. "Both, I should say."

"I see. Miss Murphy, when was the last time you left the Pinnacle?"

Standing still before the sink, I replied, "Today."

"Ah." I could hear her scribble something down over the receiver. "Let me rephrase. When was the last time you success-fully left the hotel?"

Hmm. When was the last time I'd left the hotel? *Successfully,* as she so rudely put it. I cleared my throat as I thought. "Well," I said, and cleared my throat once more. I must be coming down with something. "It's hard to remember an exact date."

"Guess," she said, "as close as you can. Maybe if you can remember what you were doing, it would narrow the date down."

I started pacing again. "I suppose it was for Henry's latest premiere. In the summer."

"The summer of what year?" Dr. Sanders asked, in a tone of voice that suggested she already knew the answer. "This year? Or last?"

I swallowed down my immediate, snarky reply. After a deep, steadying breath, I answered, "Last summer."

His movie had come out in July 1957. Had I really not left the hotel in fourteen months? My head started to pound. I pressed my fingertips against my temples and closed my eyes. The studio had thrown a huge party for the first showing. It had been packed with people, as close together as sardines in a can.

When we arrived, the press were lined up to take his picture. They shouted his name, and as he held me to his side and smiled for the cameras, I couldn't escape. I'd had to stand there and bear it with a grin or risk collapsing on the red carpet for all the world to see.

In the fourteen months since, I'd been locked inside this building. The first time I had dared try to leave it, I'd had a full-blown attack of anxiety on the sidewalk like some sort of freak.

"Goodness gracious." I sat down on my kitchen floor. "I can't believe it."

"What can't you believe, Miss Murphy?"

I opened my eyes, my vision blurry with tears. Presley sat in my lap. "You're right, Dr. Sanders."

Her voice was softer when she asked, "What was I right about, Miss Murphy?"

"As it turns out, I might be the teensiest, weensiest bit agoraphobic."

She wrote something down, and her pen squeaked across the page. "What happened today when you tried to leave the hotel?"

"I didn't try." I gathered Presley up against my chest. "I left the hotel and hailed a taxi. But then I felt like I was dying, like I was having a heart attack. I had to come back to the hotel and be checked by a doctor. I'm fine; he said it was an attack of anxiety. But I do not want to feel like that. Ever again."

"I can help you, Miss Murphy," Dr. Sanders said. "Why don't we schedule an appointment?"

Scheduling an appointment meant visiting her office. Visiting her office meant leaving the hotel. The outside world was so big, and there were so many people, and what if I had to ride the subway one day? What would I wear?

But Mac lived outside the hotel, and soon he'd work outside the hotel too. What if the only way I could see him would be to leave the Pinnacle? What if he left me, the way everyone always had, because I couldn't?

Henry, he was to debut on Broadway soon. Would I miss his big play?

What if, one day, Mac and I got married and I had a baby. Would I give birth in my suite? Would my child be forced to spend every day indoors, never going outside? Never seeing the beach or the zoo? An amusement park? Paris at night?

My mother had made sure my childhood was glorious. I'd traveled all around the world before my fifth birthday. I'd had tea parties with real princesses, ridden on the backs of elephants, witnessed the wonders of the pyramids all before I could even bathe myself. Manhattan was our home base, and Mom loved the Pinnacle most of all. I think that's why Daddy bought the hotel in the first place. But she made sure I was a child of the world as much as I was a New Yorker.

What kind of a mother would I be if I couldn't leave the Pinnacle's grounds? What kind of life could I lead stuck inside this one building for the rest of it?

But what if I tried and failed? What if I kept almost dying on sidewalks every time I tried to step outside? How would I even make it to her office?

I had a murder to solve, and I'd never be able to think clearly if another attack of anxiety was always waiting for me right around the corner.

"I promise I will think about it," I said. "Is there anything I can do now, though?"

Her pen squeaked again. "There is a breathing technique I can help you with before I have to meet my next client. First, can you tell me where in your body you feel your fear?"

What a strange question. I didn't answer.

There was a smile in her voice when she said, "Close your eyes. And focus inward. What do you feel inside of you?"

I *was* paying her for her advice—her secretary had informed me of that before she sent the call over. I might as well take it, no matter how weird.

I closed my eyes and focused inward. What did I feel?

"My chest," I said, thinking hard and doing my best to put words to the feeling. An almost impossible task for me since I was a small child. "It's tingly. Uncomfortable. I don't like it."

"Good," Dr. Sanders said. "That's good. What you do next is sit with it for a while. Sit with it, know that what you're feeling is your fear, but know that you are safe. Sit with it until you are used to the feeling."

"And then what? Because I don't think I'll ever be used to this feeling."

"Then you do a little exercise, where you picture yourself as a small child. You picture this small-child version of you talking to you now and telling you about their fear. You tell that small-child version exactly what I've told you. You're safe. Everything is okay. You are not alone."

I cried. Hysterical and ugly.

This is what you get for listening to analysts. The absolute audacity of this woman who I was paying for her expertise.

"That's good, Evelyn," she said. "You're doing great."

CHAPTER 31

There was a knock on the door.

"Evelyn?" Mac asked.

"In here," I said from my spot on the kitchen floor. I snatched a nearby dish towel and wiped my face. "Thank you, Dr. Sanders."

"You're welcome, Miss Murphy. Think about what I said?"

I nodded even though she couldn't see. "I promise."

Mac spotted me, and his expression glowed with relief. My heart felt as though it were filled with bees. What a silly thing to feel. Nervous and scared and happy, all at once, at just seeing the way he looked at me.

"Evelyn." He collapsed at my side and wrapped his arms around my shoulders, gathering me up in a hug. "I'm so glad you're okay. You are okay, aren't you?" He pulled back far enough to look me in the eyes, his hands warm on my bare skin.

I couldn't maintain eye contact for long, the gray of his eyes too much for me. I only wanted to kiss him. I didn't want him to know the dark parts of my life. What if it scared him? What if he never kissed me again because of it?

"I'm doing better, thank you," I said. "I was on the phone with my doctor."

"A doctor?" He looked me over, still not letting go. "Are you okay? Do we need to go to hospital?"

My heart felt split in two pieces. Did I tell Mac what was really going on? Or did I keep hiding it from him?

If he didn't want to kiss me once he found out about my past, then maybe he didn't deserve to kiss me at all.

I took hold of his hand and squeezed tight. Presley licked our joined fingers.

"Mac," I said, "about a year ago, Dr. Sanders diagnosed me with agoraphobia. I didn't believe it at the time. But she's right. I'm the teensiest, weensiest bit agoraphobic."

"Agoraphobic?" Mac blinked twice. "You're scared of spiders? What does that have to do with anything that happened today?"

"I'm not afraid of spiders. No, that's not true. I am. They are terrifying. But that's not my problem. My problem is that I haven't left the hotel since last summer. Fourteen months I've stayed inside this building, and today, when I tried to go to Yonkers to see you, I had an anxiety attack. I thought I was dying. I sat on the *sidewalk*, Mac, in my pretty dress!"

The tears came back. With my free hand, I wiped my nose clean. I was a slobbering mess. "I thought I was dying, and it was all because I left the hotel. I'm sorry. I'm so sorry."

Mac held my chin between two fingers. "Evelyn," he whispered, "what are you sorry for?" His calloused thumb wiped away my tears. "This isn't your fault. You didn't do anything wrong."

I closed my eyes because I couldn't take the sincerity, the kindness in his gaze, without feeling the urge to tell him everything.

I love you, I love you, isn't that terrible?

He kissed my forehead, let his lips linger. "It's okay, Evelyn." His mouth moved over my skin. "I'm not going anywhere."

If anything, that only made me cry more. I wrapped my arms around him and held on for all I was worth, soaking his shirt in my tears.

Presley wiggled his way out with a sneeze and jumped to the floor, trotting off to his bed.

Sniffing, I asked, "You don't think I'm crazy?"

He chuckled. "I didn't say that. Not after all the locks you've made me pick and the late nights we've spent snooping around. But this, this fear? That's not *crazy*, Evelyn. That's life."

"It isn't only agoraphobia." I sat up and stared at my knees. It was easier to say what I needed to say if I didn't have to look at him while doing it. "I was also diagnosed with shell shock."

"Shell shock? Like a soldier?"

I nodded. "You probably know that my mother died when I was little." My fingers found the pendant around my neck. The last present she'd ever given me. "But what you don't know, what I don't like to talk about, what no one who worked here at the time is allowed to talk about, is that my mother . . . she was murdered. And I . . . I've always been so good at finding things, you know." The tears stuck in my throat, clogging my voice. "And I found her. I found her, and she was, she was . . ."

I collapsed against him. I hadn't shared details of that night in years. My mother, dead in an alleyway, outside the toy shop I'd begged her to take me to a week before Christmas. Her body all alone in the cold, like she was trash. And I, at six years old, had found her before the security guards did.

"Her murderer has never been brought to justice. For a while, I thought I'd find him. That I'd track him down and bring him to the police. But then I'd leave the hotel and wonder . . . was he watching me? Was he out there, waiting to kill me too? And then I stopped leaving the hotel altogether."

Mac swore and rubbed my back. "I didn't know. That's— damn, that's horrible. No wonder you're whatever that word is that doesn't mean afraid of spiders. And no wonder you want to find out who killed Billie Bell."

I sniffed. "She died outside the hotel. Since then, the Pinnacle is safe and everywhere else is a gamble. But now that the Pinnacle isn't safe . . . what do I do?"

"We solve it, that's what we do." He kissed my cheek. "Speaking of which, I brought that clue. You wanna see it?"

"Of course."

He left the kitchen to grab it. I blew my nose in the dish towel.

"Here." Mac came back into the kitchen and handed me the yearbook. He didn't sit down next to me, instead opting to lean against the counter. I bit my tongue to keep from begging for more hugs.

It was a standard high school yearbook. I flipped from front to back, back to front, with no idea what I was looking for. I shook my head and stared up at the nearest lightbulb to keep from crying again.

"I don't know what I'm doing, Mac. I can't even read this right now."

He scratched his temple. "You know what I think?"

I shook my head.

"I think you gotta get back up on the horse. Come with me to take Presley on his walk. You'll conquer the Park and clear your head."

My mouth fell open. "You can't be serious."

"Seriously serious. I'll be there. So will the dog. We'll keep you safe. Plus we're close to home. I won't let anything bad happen to you, Evelyn. We can do this together."

There was a crazy sense in what he was saying. I was scared of having another attack of anxiety. Maybe if I could do the thing I was scared of and not have another one, I wouldn't be so scared. If I wasn't so scared, I'd be able to focus on the task at hand. Theoretically, of course.

Still. I wasn't a fan of the idea.

I pouted my lips. "I have to go outside again? Twice in one day?" I pulled on the hem of my dress miserably. "And in the same outfit? Now, that's *crazy*. What if someone sees?"

He checked his watch. "Go change. Presley can wait a bit more."

I pouted harder.

"Come on, Evelyn. It won't be so bad. We're in this together."

"Are you sure you want to do this with me?" I couldn't look him in the eyes. He was too handsome, too kind. My casual friend. "I understand if this is all too much."

But Mac knelt down at my side and took my hand in his. "Wherever you need me, that's where I'll go."

CHAPTER 32

After changing into beige slacks, a button-down pink blouse, and adorable pink flats, I put Presley in his purse and followed Mac to the lift.

"I don't want to have another attack of anxiety," I said. "One was quite enough."

"We'll leave before it gets that bad." Mac told the liftboy to take us to the lobby. "There's this pretzel cart Presley loves. They give him cheese every time."

"You give my dog Park cheese?" Shock replaced fear. "Malcolm Cooper, I should have you arrested!"

Mac held up a hand in surrender. "*I* don't give it to him. The guy behind the cart gives it to him. Not my fault Presley loves it. Besides, when I'm walking him, he's the boss."

"He's the boss even when you're not walking him." I rubbed my nose against his perfect little wet one. "Isn't that right, baby? You're the best boy, and you deserve better than Park cheese."

"That Park cheese is delicious," Mac said. "I'm gonna get you some. You'll see. I'll make a proper New Yorker out of you yet."

"You're from London! I was born here, Malcolm."

He shook his head and flashed a playful grin. "Sad that I'm more of a New Yorker than you, ain't it?"

We arrived at the lobby floor. Mac stepped out first, but I hesitated to follow. All these people, did they know what had happened to me earlier? Had they witnessed my panic, seen me lying on the sidewalk? Had they hear the rumors from Mr. Burrows or Mr. Sharpe? Would they say anything now? If I could go the rest of my life without detailing what happened on that sidewalk, it'd be too soon.

"Evelyn," Mac asked, "you ready?"

"No. But let's do it anyway."

"That's my girl."

I chose to ignore how his words made my stomach twist and stepped out into the lobby. Mac kept his pace in front of me. For a second, I wondered why he wasn't at my side holding my hand, but then I saw people turning their heads and glancing our way before going back to whatever they were doing. He was right. I was still Henry's girlfriend, and Mac was still the man I had gotten caught with in the mail room with my hair stuck in his zipper. We needed to at least pretend we were respecting Henry's wishes.

I held my breath when we stepped into the daylight. The sun was setting, the air was cooling, and the scent of exhaust was still fresh in the air.

Presley wiggled so hard in his purse I had no choice but to set him on the ground and hold his leash instead. "You want Mommy to take you on a walk, baby?"

He knew the way. Presley trotted down the steps like he owned the place—which wasn't too far from the truth—and I followed his lead, Mac taking up the rear. We crossed the spot on the sidewalk where I'd had my attack of anxiety and kept right on strolling until the pavement changed colors and trees surrounded us. Central Park was like a different world here in the city. I took a deep breath.

Still smelled like exhaust. But what can you do?

Mac touched my elbow. "What do you think?"

"I think," I said, "I'd like to try a pretzel with Park cheese."

He kissed my cheek. "I'll go get it. Um. Actually." He made a show of patting his empty pockets. I rolled my eyes but fished several dollar bills out of my wallet.

"Keep the change," I said.

"Always do!"

He jogged off. I shook my head at Presley. "So hard to get good help these days."

He jumped up on my legs, his little paws patting my knees. I unhooked his leash, and he merrily pounced on low-flying dragonflies while I took a seat on a nearby bench. The Pinnacle stood tall above the trees of Central Park. Mac was only a few paces away, waiting in line at a pretzel cart.

What was I feeling? I closed my eyes and focused inward. That tingly sensation in my chest was still there, along with a knot in my stomach. I was nervous. That feeling was *nervous*. But I was all right. Mac and Presley were here with me. The Pinnacle was within running distance.

I pictured little six-year-old me, being tucked into bed by a stranger. Her new nanny. Her mom was never coming back. Little six-year-old me was nervous her new nanny wouldn't be nice. She was nervous they wouldn't get along. She was nervous she'd never feel loved again.

But I told her that everything was going to be okay. Her new nanny was wonderful. And not only would Nanny love her, the little girl would grow to love Nanny back.

She was safe. Everything was okay. She was not alone.

"Hey." Mac's voice pulled me out of my exercise. He sat down next to me with a pretzel in one hand and a cup of street cheese in the other.

Presley noticed his arrival and gave up his hunt for low-hanging flies, tail wagging so hard his whole body shook waiting for his prize.

Mac set the cup on the grass and held my hand. "Evelyn, it's okay. We're here."

"I know." I smiled and dried my face. "I think that's why I'm crying. Because you're here."

Hurt darkened his gray eyes. "You want me to leave?"

"No." I held his hand tight. "Not at all."

I wanted to tell him then, but I couldn't get my tongue to form the words. *I love you, Mac. Sorry about that. It's gonna be tough on you because I do not have myself put together. Not even a little bit. Not even at all.*

I rested my head on Mac's shoulder and stole the pretzel. "Thank you for this," I said. "It is delicious."

"Hey, you paid for it." He kissed my hair. "You gonna give me a bite?"

I held it up, and he ate out of my hand.

"Better with cheese," he assured me after swallowing. "You wanna try?"

I laughed. Presley was lying on the grass, trying to clean his face with his little paws, his whiskers and nose orange.

"I'll try next time."

"So there will be a next time?"

I nodded against his shoulder. "Yes,"

There had to be. I wanted to snoop through his apartment, and I certainly couldn't do that from my hotel room suite.

"Let's finish our pretzel," I said. "I'm ready to look at that yearbook now."

Chapter 33

"Hey," Mac said when we crossed the street. He took Presley's leash from me and jerked his head to the side. "Let's go in through the kitchen."

I shrugged. Why not? It was easy to keep up with his brisk pace in my pink flats, and I praised myself for my shoe choice. I wasn't sure I'd ever wear those stilettos again without thinking about one of the worst days of my life. Getting yelled at by Mr. Sharpe in them, the attack of anxiety that had me lying down on the literal ground. Not that those incidents were the shoes' fault, of course, but negative associations didn't always make the most logical sense.

Mac tapped his knuckles against the kitchen door three times, and it swung open. Chef Marco stood there smiling, his bushy eyebrows so high up on his forehead they almost touched his glorious hat.

"Good, you made it!" Chef Marco said, which was a curious thing to say to someone you were not expecting. "It's ready."

"Thanks." Mac held the door open for me. "Appreciate it."

I looked around at the kitchen, the dozens of cooks chopping and getting ready for the dinner rush, fulfilling room service orders and preparing dessert. "Appreciate what? What's going on?"

"Mr. Cooper asked me to make you your favorite soup." Chef Marco led us to a tray on a nearby silver serving table. It held a large covered bowl of homemade potato soup, with shredded cheese and chopped-up bacon as optional sides, plus two empty bowls and two spoons and two cloth napkins. "Do you want a drink? Some champagne? Vodka?"

"We're all set," Mac said, and slid Presley's leash down to his wrist before picking up the tray. "Thanks a lot, Marco."

"Anything for Miss Murphy," said Chef Marco.

I felt it again, in my chest, that weird tingly feeling. But this time it didn't feel like fear; it felt like happiness. How was it possible that two such different feelings could elicit such a similar reaction inside my body? I'd have to talk to Dr. Sanders about that. Feelings were weird. I didn't care for them.

Mac and Presley and I made our way to the service elevator, and when the doors closed, I turned to him. "Mac? You ordered me my favorite soup?"

He didn't look at me, kept his attention on the climbing numbers above the door. "Only 'cause I thought you were sick."

I'd never wanted to kiss anyone more than I did at that moment. Too bad the tray was in the way. "That is the sweetest thing. Thank you ever so."

His cheeks reddened, but he still didn't look at me. "Don't mention it."

The door opened, and we walked the opposite way down the hall to my room. It was strange to come from this direction, as I didn't usually use the service elevator in my day-to-day life. Everything about this day had been strange, right down to the tingling in my heart. As I unlocked my door and released Presley from his leash, the tingling increased until I could feel it in my throat, behind my lips. I was going to kiss Mac like he'd never been kissed before, and he didn't even know what was coming to him.

He had absolutely no idea I was so deeply in love with him. I had half a mind to move him into a room in the Pinnacle tonight. Or figure out a way to get Mac to marry me. He wasn't Catholic, which would mean a hefty donation to a priest willing to bend the rules.

He didn't need a job. I'd take care of him for the rest of his life, the way he always took care of me.

Mac set the tray down on the entry side table. "Anyway, they charged it to your room, and I made sure there was enough for me. So really, I should be thanking y—"

I kissed him. I didn't close the door, I didn't check where Presley was, I didn't even make sure we were all alone. I grabbed his face and kissed him. Hard at first, and then softer, his hands on my waist, his tongue in my mouth.

Someone gasped.

My mind was too fuzzy from the kiss to properly register what had happened, much less disentangle myself from Mac. But after a few blinks, I saw a strange, beautiful girl in the doorway.

Mac made a strangled noise low in his throat before he finally exclaimed, "Poppy!"

Poppy? I looked at her, this girl staring at me in my doorway, back to Mac, my fingers clutching his shirt, and back to the girl. Heart-shaped face, dark-brown hair, gray eyes. I knew her. Where did I know her?

Oh! "Ghost maid!"

"Ghost maid?" Mac dropped his hands from my waist. "What are you talking about?"

"I know you. You're the strange maid who threatened me in the hallway."

"I didn't threaten you," she replied. "I warned you. There's a difference. And now, here you are, up to it again. Messing with Mac."

Mac repeated, "Messing with?" and I glared at him. Was he capable only of parroting half a sentence?

Finally letting go of Mac, I stared this strange maid down. Her gray eyes were piercing and familiar. "You told me not to investigate Bell's murder."

"No, I didn't! I told you to leave Mac alone!"

"What?" Mac and I said at the same time.

Mac said, "Poppy, you didn't."

I said, "Why on earth would you warn me to leave Mac alone? Oh no, are you his girlfriend? Mac, you absolute scoundrel! How *could* you?"

"No, no, no!" Mac held up his hands. "This is my little sister. This is Poppy. Poppy, Evelyn isn't messing with me. She's my friend. We're only friends, isn't that right, Evelyn? We have some casual fun every once in a while, but it's nothing. Really."

It's nothing. Really.

The tingling in my neck fell all the way to the bottom of my stomach. I thought I might vomit right there on my pink shoes. Moments ago I'd been thinking of moving him in, making him a kept husband, of brown-haired, gray-eyed children—and then to hear him say, so nonchalantly, *It's nothing. Really.*

"Ah," Poppy whispered. "I see." She *tsk*ed her brother. "Idiot."

"What did I do?"

Poppy set her cold hand on my arm. How could she be so cold to the touch and her brother so warm? "I'm sorry, Miss Murphy. I thought you were toying with him. I didn't realize what was going on." Once more she *tsk*ed at Mac and said, "Idiot."

Mac made that strangled noise in his throat again, followed by a hollow bark of a laugh. "Gee, thanks, little sister. Thanks a lot."

How obvious was my love for Mac that this girl I barely knew could see it on my face? Did that mean he knew it too and took advantage of it to get free kisses and big tips? Had he been using me all this time, like Detective Hodgson said?

Poppy squeezed my arm. "Would you like some tea, Miss Murphy?"

I nodded.

"Make us some tea, you bloody idiot."

Mac whistled out of his nose, a sound I'd never heard before, and stomped off to the kitchen, mumbling curse words and rude names under his breath.

Poppy picked up my tray of dinner, the very same one that had almost made me make a fool of myself in front of a man who didn't love me back, and carried it to my dining room table. "Looks delicious."

"Yeah? You want some? You can have Mac's bowl."

She grinned. "I think we just became friends, Miss Murphy."

"In that case, you must call me Evelyn. I insist."

She set the tray down, and I served the soup.

After a few quiet moments of watching the steam rise from our bowls, Mac came out with tea service for three and an overexaggerated frown on his face. "My sister and my best friend. Ruining my dinner plans. Yet again."

He could starve for all I cared.

I sighed at my own lie. I didn't even believe myself. "We'll split it three ways," I said. "There are bowls above the sink."

He smiled at me, in the way that made my stomach hurt worse, and got his bowl while Poppy poured herself some tea.

"I am sorry about my idiot brother. He'll figure it out. Eventually."

"Figure what out?" Mac asked, making himself comfortable at my side.

I couldn't look at his face, instead keeping my full attention on his bowl as I filled it up. Chef Marco had made sure we had enough to feed an army, and splitting it three ways was no problem.

"How stupid you are," Poppy said in a perky voice. "Of course."

Mac grumbled. I slid him his bowl and he thanked me, but I didn't reply. I felt his eyes on me the entire time I added cheese and bacon to my bowl.

My heart ached as if he had reached inside my chest and wrapped a fist around it. Heat pressed against the backs of my eyes and ran down my throat, scratching me from the inside out. The intensity of his gaze made my cheek itch. He stared at me like he was trying to solve an impossible math problem.

I didn't like it at all, so I said, "Hey, Mac? Where's that yearbook?"

It was Hall's junior yearbook. I found him under *H*. He had a thick mustache even at seventeen. But there was nothing in the pages of his classmates' smiling black-and-white faces that gave any sort of clue. Or even a hint of a clue.

"What are we looking for?" I asked Mac. "What did he say?"

Mac shrugged, took a big bite of mostly bacon and cheese. "Don't know," he said, mouth full. "He started talking about his high school days and how things have a way of all coming back around. He talked about high school a lot. Maybe he was bored. He coulda been messing with me."

I flipped to the back of the book, where every student's name was listed along with page numbers corresponding to their photos. Not counting Hall's class picture, his face appeared on two pages. Flipping to the front of the yearbook, I found the collage pages for extracurricular groups.

"What about high school?" I asked. "A certain class or friend in particular?"

"No. That's all he kept saying. That things have a way of coming back around, like in high school. It didn't make sense to me, but I figured he thought the cops were listening in on us."

I searched for Hall's mustached face in the pictures of teens participating in debate or in the chess club, his two extracurriculars. There were a lot of other teenagers around him. Some smiling in posed pictures, others busy in candids. My eyes slid from face to face, studying each one.

Was he trying to say the real killer had been in high school with him? Was he trying to say he was being framed by someone he had gone to high school with? And if either of those was true, why not tell the police?

There was something about the debate club collages, though I couldn't put my finger on what. Hall had participated in debate with four other boys and three other girls. They wore matching coats and knee-high socks. I didn't recognize any of them besides Hall, but something nagged at the base of my brain.

There was something there.

It was like looking at those pictures side by side where you have to spot seven differences in an otherwise identical image. I was missing whatever it was Hall wanted me to find.

But I was close.

I snapped the book closed out of frustration. "What if this isn't even about the murder?"

Poppy started piling up the dirty bowls. "What do you mean?"

"I'm looking for a connection to the killer, but what if he's trying to get us to look for a connection to the robbery?" I held my face in my hands, tugged at my increasingly messy curls. I needed a bath, pronto. "I think I need to break back into the original crime scene and snoop around. Maybe if I can solve the robbery, the murder will start to make sense. Maybe this was never about the murder at all. Maybe this has always been about the painting."

"Murder seems more important than a robbery to me, Evelyn," said Poppy.

I shrugged. "Depends on the motives."

"Either way," Mac broke in, still staring at me like he saw right through me, "it's getting late. We'll think about it after getting some sleep, especially after the day you've had."

He was right, because of course he was. Mac's being-right-most-of-the-time thing was becoming most annoying.

"It is getting late. You both should stay here for the night instead of going all the way back to Yonkers."

Mac scooped Presley off the ground and settled him in his lap. "What do you say, boy? You gonna share the couch with me?"

Poppy cleared the table with practiced ease, and if I hadn't been so exhausted, I'd have felt guilty about being a terrible hostess. "Thank you, Evelyn, but I actually have a date tonight."

Mac choked on his own spit. "What! This late? With who?"

She grinned over her shoulder. "Burrows."

"Burrows!" Mac and I exclaimed simultaneously.

Mac said, "That square?"

And I said, "*Glasses*?"

Poppy ran the water in the sink and rolled up her sleeves. "The square with the glasses is sweet to me. I like him. I was gonna tell you not to wait up, Mac, but now I don't have to."

He gagged in response.

I couldn't help but smile at him. He was a good big brother. I'd always wanted siblings growing up. It was hard to be a kid all alone in a big city, no matter how diligent and kind Nanny was. But if I'd had to choose between having a big brother or a little sister, I would have wanted someone like Amelia. Someone to help me in my adventures and not fret about who I was spending my time with.

Mac smiled at me, winked, and my face flushed. I stared down at the yearbook for want of something to do. Now I was going to spend the night alone with the man I loved who didn't love me back. And darn it all, I wanted to be alone with him as much as I never wanted to see him again.

Poppy finished washing up and told us both good-bye.

"You'll be by in the morning? Help us look around the Silver Room?" I asked.

"First thing!" She ruffled Mac's hair and scratched Presley's ears on her way out. Presley wagged his tail, and I was sold. He liked her as much as I did. Looked like I really had made a new friend. A female one, at that! What progress.

"I'm gonna have a smoke." Mac jerked his thumb in the direction of my balcony. "You want some air?"

The double glass doors showed the Pinnacle's view of the Park, of the city's skyline lit up at night and the inky black sky. My heart squeezed in my chest, but I didn't feel like I was dying, so I forced myself to smile at him. "Sounds nice."

Something thunked against the carpet when he left. I scooped up his lighter and followed after him.

CHAPTER 34

The night was beautiful. So were Mac's hands. What right did he have to have such large, pretty hands? He patted his pockets, frowning. His tan fingers around a cigarette, his eyes on the skyline.

I handed him the lighter without saying anything.

He smiled at me, and my stomach squeezed behind my belly button.

"Thanks." He lit up a smoke, and I stared at the way his fingers held it.

I tucked my feet underneath me on the oversized patio chair. Presley balanced on my knees and wagged his tail. His tongue lolled at the city spread out before him. Cars honked, dogs barked, children cried, and Presley was having a blast taking it all in.

I couldn't enjoy the same view, as I was too distracted by the man smoking in front of me.

For Pete's sake. I needed to get a hold of myself. He was a *man*. So was half the population of earth! I could have my pick of them—if I ever left the hotel, anyway.

Or even if I didn't! The Pinnacle was a destination all in itself. It wasn't unusual for dukes to stroll in on vacation. I'd have to keep Burrows in my pocket so he could give me a heads-up on when such visitors might be arriving and enjoy me in one of my many cute bikinis.

"Look, Evelyn," Mac said, blowing out a big puff of smoke. He didn't say anything.

I stared at him, eyebrows raised, wondering what it was he wanted me to look at.

He shook his head, took another hit off his cigarette. "I mean," he said, "this isn't easy for me. But after what happened with Poppy calling me an idiot . . ."

Oh. Oh no. He was breaking up with me. Could you break up with a friend that you kiss from time to time?

He'd figured it out, as Poppy had said he would, and now he was cutting the cord. I could no longer be casual, and he wasn't up for anything more. He was going to leave.

Everyone leaves.

I gathered Presley up close to my chest and hurried my nose in his fur. What was I going to do without Mac? Things were so strained with Henry. I was about to be friendless. Would Poppy still want to talk to me after this?

I'd be all alone all over again.

"Mac," I said, holding Presley tight. "It's okay. Don't worry about it. *Please.*"

He looked at me with that same intense stare, the one that looked right through me. "I gotta say it, Evelyn. If I don't do it now, I don't know if I ever will."

I shook my head. "You don't have to say anything. I understand. I really do."

He chuckled humorlessly. "You do? What do you understand, Evelyn?"

I bit my trembling lip. Was he about to tear me down too? Would this day never end?

"Do you understand how hard it is for a guy like me to even talk to a girl like you? You're this beautiful princess. And I haul luggage for a living.

"I saw you my first day at work and dropped this giant box right on my toes. Sharpe warned me after that. He said you were off-limits, that you were—that you *are* so special. After that, I took every opportunity I could to be close to you. To see if you'd notice me. I didn't think you'd ever want me, you know? But I thought I could, damn. I thought I could serve you. Be a bloody servant.

"I'd walk your dog and pick up your trash and take in your dry cleaning. Just for you to look me in the eyes. The tips helped, sure. It's just me and Poppy here, and I gotta take care of her, you know? But the money was nothing more than a bonus. You were what I wanted. I didn't expect you to kiss me. I didn't expect you to like kissing me. I kept saying it was casual, it was fun, because if I let myself believe it was anything more than that and then you changed your mind, I'd be crushed. Devastated. Do you understand that, Evelyn?"

He took a final drag off his cigarette and tossed it off the railing. "It's never been casual for me."

Boys like Mac often know exactly what to say to a girl to get what they want from them. I knew, because I'd fallen for it before. I'd make that mistake and listened to boys who only wanted one thing from me. There was a chance he was doing that now. That he was using me like Detective Hodgson had said. That he didn't mean it at all. That he only wanted to spend the night in my bed instead of on my couch.

But I decided to believe him. Because I wanted him to spend the night in my bed instead of on my couch too.

★　★　★

Later. After. Curled up with him under the covers, safe and happy, his warm, beautiful hands holding me, I decided it didn't matter what other people thought. What Detective Hodgson thought, or Mr. Sharpe, or anyone else in the entire world. Even Daddy!

I loved him. And that's what mattered.

I tucked my head under his chin, pressed my face against his neck. He had more hair than I'd expected, down his chest and his abdomen, over his forearms and legs. I liked it. I liked everything about Mac. I liked the muscles in his arms and thighs, the softness of his belly, the broad width of his shoulders.

"I suppose I'll have to break the news to Henry and the press," I said. "That is, as long as that's what you want?"

He kissed my hair. "Whatever you want. That's what I want."

"What I want is to break into the Silver Room with your sister in the morning."

He chuckled, a rumble in his throat. "Then that's what we'll do."

CHAPTER 35

I could've slept for days. Turns out facing your biggest fears and confessing your feelings in one day is a bit hard on the body. But Poppy let herself in with a maid's key and pulled open every curtain in my suite.

"Good morning!" she singsonged. "Fear not, lovebirds. I see nothing! I hear nothing! And I will say nothing. Well, except in my weekly letter to Gran. But she'll never believe it." She stood in the doorway with her hands on her hips and a smile on her face. "Who's ready for some breaking and entering?"

Mac groaned.

All the light made my head ache. I buried my face in Presley's soft fur. How late had we stayed up last night? My body protested every movement, complained that I'd fallen asleep only a minute ago and what I needed was more. As soon as possible.

"Up, up! Hurry, the both of you. May I remind you, I'm here because you *asked*. I'd much rather still be with my beau! Speaking of." She smiled bigger. "Burrows is buying us time with Mr. Sharpe. Which means we don't have long."

"You are a terrible influence on your little sister," I said.

Mac rolled out of bed. He underestimated the amount of mattress left and fell. From the ground, he cried, "I'm fine. Don't worry."

"We weren't," said Poppy. She clapped her hands. "Let's go!"

* * *

Presley wouldn't settle until Poppy picked him up and carried him. Mac huffed out a "Traitor," and I grinned.

"Now you know how I feel."

We sneaked out of the kitchen with a wave to Chef Marco and walked along the back of the hotel, past the busy tennis courts and through the crowds of guests and employees alike going about their mornings.

The back door into the Silver Room was at the far corner of the hotel. Mac dropped to his knees, and Poppy and I stood in front of him, chatting casually while keeping a lookout. Anyone who passed by saw two young women and a dog watching a rather uninteresting game of tennis and gossiping about the attractive instructor.

"Brad's not that good-looking for a bloke," Mac said when the lock gave. "What's more, he always smells like cheese."

The Silver Room was different than the night of the robbery, the tables and chairs set up for whatever tonight's schedule called for. A charity benefit, it looked like. That would make things difficult but not impossible.

"So," I said, ignoring the room as it was now and picturing it as it had been that night. "His artwork covered the walls. Gaudy, bougie things. Right here"—I stood where the easel had been—"was his grand unveiling. Mr. Hall stood before it." I put Mac where Hall had stood. "Henry and I, the count and countess, we were over here." I guided Presley and Poppy half-way across the room. "That's where we were when the fight broke out."

"I still think Henry was in on it," Mac called out, and his voice echoed in the vast room. "Why else would someone that boring start a fight so public?"

Mac had a point, as annoying as it was. "Henry didn't do it," I said. "I know it."

"How do you know it?"

"I just know it. Now be quiet, I'm thinking."

There had been people everywhere. Up the stairs, milling about the floor. Had whoever stole the masterpiece been able to sleight-of-hand it out of the frame and out a window without a roomful of people noticing?

"It's possible but highly unlikely," I said. "I think it was stolen before the party. Mr. Hall wasn't guarding it when I came in to check the flowers, but the room was busy with staff members and Mr. Sharpe."

"Mr. Sharpe?" Poppy asked. "What was he doing?"

"I don't know what he was doing, but I do know that he knocked right into the easel in question when Presley got underfoot."

She scratched my dog under his chin. "Did you interrupt the manager stealing the painting, good boy?"

He wagged his tail.

"Come on," Mac said. "No way. Mr. Sharpe's too square to rob his own hotel. It was Henry. He's always seemed a dodgy fellow."

I bit my lip. "Henry did tell me he popped into the Silver Room before getting ready to pick me up. He said there were people milling about."

Mac clapped his hands and yelled out, "Aha!"

I glared at him. "What *aha*?"

"Maybe there weren't people milling about. Maybe he snuck in here and stole the painting."

"*Fine*, maybe he did." I rolled my eyes. "But why would he do that?"

"Because he hated Bell, right? Hated him so much he got in a fight with him in the middle of his show. He gets word of the big reveal and he sneaks in here early to sabotage it. Nicks the painting so Bell's big moment is ruined and scarpers off before anyone's the wiser."

Poppy tilted her head to the side. "But who killed Mr. Bell?"

Mac scratched his ear. "I don't know. Henry, I guess. Yeah, definitely Henry. See, Bell figured it was Henry and confronts him about it. Maybe threatens to go to the police, and Henry can't have a theft on his record. That'd ruin his career. So he kills him and frames up Hall."

The worst part about Mac's argument was its plausibility.

"Forget Henry for a moment. Do you remember when Detective Hodgson questioned us that night? He said the only people he couldn't account for during the reveal were us, Henry and Mr. Sharpe, and the Count and Countess Dreadful. Henry and Mr. Sharpe were getting drinks at one of the bars. But what were the Dreadfuls doing?"

"Didn't you say that the countess was having an affair with Bell? And that the assistant found out about it?" Mac asked.

Poppy hopped on her tiptoes. "An affair? How exciting!"

I knuckled my forehead. "There's still too many suspects in play. Let's go talk to Miss Bourke. She'll be the easiest to deal with, and hopefully we can cross her off the list quickly."

CHAPTER 36

Tilly Bourke did not come to the door after several rounds of knocking. Mac looked left and right before he dropped to his knees again and worked on the lock. Poppy shook her head.

"I do have the keys," she said. "I clean on this floor."

The door swung open. Mac grinned up at me, then at his sister.

She rolled her eyes.

I breezed past the siblings and surveyed the room. Tilly was absent, probably off grabbing a bite to eat and a cup of coffee like a sensible person. The stacks of paintings were littered about her room. Some covered, some not.

Poppy shut the door, Presley still in her arms. "Now what?"

Mac rubbed his hands together. "Now we snoop."

I nodded. "Might as well. Would be a waste to break in like that and not even have a small look about. Don't you think, Poppy?"

She seemed doubtful but keen, and the three of us started going through Miss Bourke's drawers and closet.

"What are we looking for?" Poppy asked.

"You'll know when you find it," I said, wrist-deep in neatly rolled socks. "Something unusual stashed in a curious place."

Poppy started leafing through the paintings. "These are beautiful," she said. "Almost kaleidoscopic."

"Are you a connoisseur of art, Poppy?"

She smiled at me. "I've fancied myself an artist. But bills come first."

"That's right," said Mac, opening up Tilly's suitcase. "And don't you forget it."

That struck me as particularly sad. Bills came before art? Poor Poppy had to clean for a living and couldn't pursue her passion. Mac had told me my tips supported the both of them, but I hadn't exactly been thinking of practical things when he'd said it.

I moved to the stack of landscapes by the front door. How many were there? I made a quick count of every painting I could see. Thirty-two. Thirty-two canvases. Was that how many had been here when I had spoken with Tilly? Many had been covered in tarps, and I hadn't counted. Now, though, with all of them fully exposed, I could see they'd been sorted. Landscapes with bridges; landscapes with flowers; half-naked women sunbathing in fields in that overdone Parisian way, except with splashes of jaundiced yellow.

Where was the landscape the countess had loved so much? With all the pinks?

Poppy made a thoughtful noise in her throat, quiet enough to be meaningful. I covered the canvases back up with a tarp and found her nearby with Presley in one hand and a sketch in the other.

"It's beautiful," she said, and showed it to me. A pencil sketch of a wood bridge over a rolling river. "I didn't know Mr. Bell was left-handed."

My nose wrinkled. "What do you mean?"

"The cross-hatching in the sketch. See?" Mac came over, and Poppy showed it to him too. "It goes from upper left to lower right. Handedness is harder to tell in paint, but in a sketch like this, it's impossible to hide. You know, Leonardo Da Vinci was left-handed."

"Left-handed," I repeated, staring at the sketch. It was infinitely prettier than the garish things Bill had painted, probably because it was in black and white.

"Did I do it?" Poppy asked. "Did I find a clue?"

Mac clapped his sister on the shoulder. "Sure did."

"Left-handed," I said again, now pacing the room back and forth. "That means something. But what?"

"It means we've been in here for long enough," Mac said. "Better split before she comes back."

Once again, Mac was right.

"Put everything back the way we found it." I took the sketch from Poppy. "Except for this. I have a feeling this might come in handy later." I folded up the sketch and stuck it in my clutch, in the same pocket as Mr. Sharpe's note.

Mr. Sharpe. Hmm.

"Is it rare?" I asked. "Forgive me if that is a stupid question. I confess I spend most of my time in the hotel."

"Is what rare?" Poppy asked.

"Left-handedness. You see, the only left-handed person I know is Mr. Sharpe."

Mac fluttered a tarp over a stack of canvases, hiding the nearly naked women. "It's not rare. Uncommon, more like."

I nodded, chewed the inside of my cheek. Three clues in and still not a single idea where to go.

★   ★   ★

Carefully, the four of us made our way to the stairwell at the end of the hall. I didn't want to risk running into Miss Bourke in the elevator and then having to lie to her face.

Several guests came out of their rooms as we walked by, but none of them was connected to Tilly Bourke. I simply smiled and kept on. Mac held my hand. I don't know when he reached for me, maybe before the guests, maybe after, but I laced our fingers together and squeezed. I didn't care who saw anymore. In fact, I wanted to announce it to the entire hotel, if not the entire world. I was in love! Wasn't that beautiful?

Daddy wouldn't be too keen, but he'd grow to accept it, like he'd grown to accept the bunny I had adopted as a child. And then the second bunny. And then all the little baby bunnies those two bunnies made because Nanny had thought they were two girl bunnies, but alas, they were not. Daddy wanted me to be happy more than he wanted anything else. Mac made me happy.

Henry jogged down the stairs in his gray-and-blue exercise outfit, a sweatband on his forehead, white sneakers on his feet.

"Evelyn!" He greeted me from the top of the stairs.

I waved back with a smile. Mac loosened his hold on my hand, but I tightened my grip. No time like the present, after all.

"You sure?" Mac whispered.

I nodded, squeezed his fingers again. "I've never been more sure about anything."

Henry came to a stop in front of his, his brow furrowed. He looked from Mac to Poppy to me and back again. "Evelyn? What's going on?"

"Henry. I think it's time we had a bit of a chat. Are you free?"

"For you? Of course, darling." He was putting on a show for Poppy's sake. "I heard you were sick. You canceled our dinner plans last night. I was most disappointed."

"That's what I need to talk to you about. Will you two excuse us, please? You can take Presley back to my room. Thank you ever so."

Mac kissed my cheek before he left. Henry glared at him but kept his mouth shut. We waited until the Cooper siblings and Presley cleared the stairwell before we started our long-overdue conversation.

Henry was not pleased.

CHAPTER 37

"What is the meaning of this?" Henry looked hurt, and it shook me a little. There was no one left to put on a show for. He was being honest. He took me by the arm and led me into the corner of the stairwell, standing so he could see if anyone was going up or down. "Evelyn," he whispered, "I thought we had an understanding."

"I know, and I'm sorry," I said, keeping my voice down. "But I haven't made it public with Mac, not yet. I intend to. Soon."

He clenched his jaw so tight the crunch of his teeth echoed in the empty stairwell.

"I'm in love with him. Desperately. And I don't want to hide it, Henry. You understand, don't you?"

Henry closed his eyes, and with his jaw still clenched, his hands fists at his sides, I thought of his altercation with Bell in the middle of the party. But Henry swallowed hard, his Adam's apple bobbing. When he looked at me, his perfect blue eyes were shining with unshed tears.

"Of course I understand. Of course I want you to find love, Evelyn. To love and be loved in return. That's everything I could ever hope for. For you, I mean. I'll talk to my people this afternoon, and we'll leak a story to the press about an amicable split. How does that sound?"

My Henry. Always such a gentleman. "That sounds marvelous. Thank you ever so."

He dabbed at his face with the matching towel flung over his shoulder. "I suppose I should find new accommodations."

"What! Whatever for?"

"It will look a little funny, won't it? My continuing to stay at the hotel of my heiress ex-girlfriend?"

"I think that should only lend credence to our amicable split story." I reached out and grabbed his elbow. "You mustn't leave, Henry. I'll miss you too much."

That was the truth. There was only a small part of me that wanted him to stay because I thought him guilty. There was the faintest, remotest chance that he might indeed have had something to do with Bell's death or the stolen painting—both preposterous accusations—but just in case, I wanted him close by.

Just in case.

He narrowed his perfect eyes at me. "I see," he said. "This has nothing to do with Bell's death?"

I licked my lips. "No, of course not."

"Or the stolen painting?"

I batted my lashes. "Why ever would you think that? You're my best friend, Henry. I want you near me. I wouldn't get to see you if you stayed at a different hotel. Besides, the Pinnacle is the finest hotel in all of New York."

He sighed. "That is true. Plus, I can't beat the discount."

Squealing in delight, I hopped up on my toes and kissed his cheek. "That settles it. Thank you, Henry. I do love you, you know."

"I know." He held my chin between two fingers. "I love you too. If only we could've made it work, eh, darling?"

I smiled as he kissed my forehead. "I do have to wonder, though, darling."

"Hmm?"

"Are you ever going to tell me why you hated Mr. Bell so?"

Mac came running down the stairwell, his hair a mess, his chest heaving. "Evelyn!" he called, breaking Henry and I apart rather abruptly. Goodness, couldn't he have waited a few minutes while I broke up with my pretend boyfriend and possibly got to interview him about the gruesome murder of an artist? He tried to talk, but his breathing was too heavy, and he coughed on his words.

Henry asked, "Did you run all the way down here from the top floor? Got to pace yourself, old sport."

Mac wiped his mouth with the back of his hand and then finally said, "Come quick! You won't believe this!"

★ ★ ★

The *this* I was not going to believe turned out to be my room.

Ransacked.

Every drawer open. All the contents of every counter toppled, splayed out on the ground. Everything I owned a whirlwind in my pink haven.

Poppy wrapped her free arm around me, the other clutching a wiggling, barking Presley. "Evelyn! I'm so sorry! This is terrible!"

I grabbed for Presley. Only his soft fur could comfort me. I stared, unblinking, at the mess my life was.

What had happened? Who had done this?

"*Who did this?*" I whirled on my heels. "Call the police," I ordered Henry, who had followed me and Mac up. I'd opted to take the elevator instead of the stairs, giving Mac a chance to catch his breath. "Call the police and tell them there's been a robbery!"

"A robbery?" Henry asked, craning his neck to look into my apartment. "What's been stolen? They'll ask."

"I don't know what's been stolen. I haven't had a chance to do inventory yet, but I want the police here now. Ask for Detective Hodgson specifically. Here." I thrusted Presley into Mac's unsuspecting chest, ignored the *oomph* sound they both made at the contact. "I know who did this. That *dreadful* woman!"

I'd never been angrier in my life than when I pounded on the countess's door. How dare she! How dare she enter my own space and bring it to chaos! What right did she have to go through my things?

I thought then—between my fourth and fifth knock—of going through Tilly Bourke's room not thirty minutes earlier. But that was searching for clues, not creating destruction for destruction's sake.

The countess flung the door open, her mascara askew, a robe draped akimbo over her bare skin. She started screaming at me in Italian, so I started screaming in Russian.

I don't speak Russian, but Nanny had a Russian grandmother who'd taught her all the naughty words.

I shoved my shoulder into the door to pry it open. She resisted, but I was more ferocious. The count lay on the bed, a pillow over his lap, smoking. Peeking out in the corner of the room was the kaleidoscopic landscape that had been missing from Tilly's collection.

"I knew it!" I shouted. The crowd of my friends had gathered around us. It wasn't every day you saw an enraged hotel heiress get into a slap fight with a mostly naked countess, so I didn't blame them. "I knew it! Well, I didn't know it, but I had a feeling! She stole a painting!"

"You nosy little brat!" The countess blocked me from entering the room with her entire body.

The count waved at me from the bed. I waved back, momentarily distracted by his smiling face and cheerful disposition. A squiffy Thursday morning. Good for him.

"How dare you come in my room and accuse me of thievery!"

"How dare you come into my room and destroy it!"

"I have no idea what you're talking about!"

I grabbed her by the elbow and tugged. She dug in her heels, but I was not to be denied. She was only two doors down from me, across the hallway. Our fighting had brought out other guests, including the diplomat from France and Amelia, who was all too happy to cheer me on.

Her mother shushed her.

Amelia gave me a thumbs-up instead.

"Here! Look at this! Why would you do this? What did I do to you to deserve this?"

The countess clutched her robe against her chest, stared openmouthed into my apartment. Then she laughed. Threw her head back and lost herself to hysterics.

I had the sudden, sinking revelation that she hadn't set my apartment to disarray.

As the countess continued cackling, my nose wrinkled. Who else, then? Mac and Poppy were with me, so they were off the suspect list. I had taken Mr. Sharpe's note. Maybe he was looking for it? What about the owner of those sensible shoes who had come into Mr. Sharpe's office to snoop the same night I had?

No matter who it was, I wasn't about to apologize to Countess Dreadful.

"Oh, fine, then!" I said. "The police are on their way. I'm sure they'll want to know all about the painting in your room."

I strolled past her with my chin held head high and slammed the door behind me.

CHAPTER 38

About three seconds later, Mac opened the door and walked in with Presley in his arms. "You, er, left me out there. With all of them."

I collapsed on my couch, so angry I could cry. In fact, I did cry. I flung my arms over my face to hide my tears from Mac. I couldn't believe how much of a fool of myself I had made in the hallway. In front of Mac and Poppy, Amelia, and Henry. Soon Mr. Sharpe would be knocking on my door to tell me off for yelling at a guest, and now I wouldn't have anything to hold over him. We were back on equal footing, as far as Daddy was concerned.

And where was Florence? My apartment was a *mess*!

"Hey, Evelyn?" Mac touched my crossed ankles with his large, warm hands. "You all right?"

"I'm fine," I sniffed. "Angry and confused, but fine." And I would continue to be confused unless I could figure out what had been stolen, if anything. That would narrow down the suspect list.

I wiped my face and hopped off the couch so fast Mac stumbled on his feet.

"We need to go through the mess and see what's been taken. Quickly, Mac! The police will be here any minute!"

⋆ ⋆ ⋆

Even my underclothes had been gone through. Dumped unceremoniously on the floor, cotton and lace mixed together like an animal had rooted through them.

I had a hard time picturing Mr. Sharpe rifling through my bras, panties, girdles, and hose, but I had lived in New York all my life and spent my free time reading newspapers and detective stories. People could behave one way in public and a totally different way in private. They could even change their personality based on who they were talking to. I'd certainly done it enough. Sometimes playing the ingenue was the only way to get someone's attention.

My diamonds were all accounted for, thank goodness. Pearls, gems, gold, silver. None of my jewelry had been taken. In the closet, every dress and jacket I owned had been unhung and tossed about willy-nilly. Chanel and Balmain and Dior, treated like little more than off-the-rack pieces. And my shoes and handbags! For heaven's sake! Every shoe overturned, every handbag gone through.

But nothing had been taken.

"I'm not noticing anything missing in the kitchen," Mac called out, "but they did smash a plate."

As the plates were the property of the hotel, I could forgive that. But balling up my Balenciaga gloves and leaving them by the trash can? Unforgivable.

"It's going to take hours to clean all this up!" The angry tears restarted. This was my *sanctuary*. My one safe place in the big, scary world. And someone had come in and touched every part of it, destroyed every space, stolen nothing but my peace. After the robbery in the Silver Room and the dead body on a guest floor, I'd at least had the sanctity of my suite. Now my entire home had been violated.

I held the pendant of Saint Anthony and closed my eyes. Tried to remember my mother. Tried to remember her smile, the sound of her voice, the way her eyes lit up when she laughed. She was so beautiful. But the image faded, and instead I saw her in that alleyway, the knife in her chest, the blood in her mouth.

There was a knock on the door. I opened my eyes as Mac poked his head into my bedroom, still clutching Presley lest there be something in the mess that might hurt his paws. "Hey, Evelyn? The police are here."

★ ★ ★

A single police officer took pictures of my apartment while Detective Hodgson sat with me in my kitchen. I supposed he was more comfortable around broken plates and open utensils drawers than the pile of underwear on my bedroom floor.

"Miss Murphy," he said, "good to see you again, though I am sorry for the circumstances."

I managed a polite smile. Detective Hodgson was one person who did not respond well to an ingenue. That was unusual for a man, but he seemed not to have the best interpersonal skills. He and Daddy would be pals if their paths ever crossed, I was certain.

"Better something like this than another murder," I said. "Or a theft."

He tapped his pen against his notebook. "Was anything stolen, Miss Murphy?"

"A painting."

He sighed. "I'm aware of the stolen painting from Mr. Bell's art show—"

"No," I interrupted. "Recently. One of his paintings was stolen from his assistant's room. It's in the countess's room now. She's the thief. You should go see for yourself!"

Detective Hodgson furrowed his brow. "And how do you know it was missing from the assistant's room?"

"Because I was in there, and I looked for it, and it wasn't there! You've got to believe me. The countess is up to something."

"When were you in Miss Bourke's room?"

I crossed my legs on the stool, smoothed out my blouse. "This morning." I did not like where this conversation was going.

"And was Miss Bourke in the room with you?"

I drummed my fingers on my knees and stared at the wall behind the detective. Was that a grease stain? I'd have to speak to Florence about it.

"Miss Murphy?"

My gaze snapped to the detective's unhappy face. "Hmm?"

He pinched the bridge of his nose between his thumb and index finger. "Did you admit to me that you broke into Miss Bourke's room?"

"That's such a terrible way of looking at it. I was trying to help, you see."

"Help with what?"

This conversation was veering uncomfortably off track. "Detective Hodgson, while I appreciate your concern about the

Pinnacle's guest rooms, I did nothing illegal or out of bounds. I have access to every inch of this hotel whenever I determine it necessary."

A bald-faced lie. I wasn't allowed to snoop through guest rooms. Of course, that had never stopped me before, but I'd also never let my anger cloud my judgment and loosen my tongue enough to admit it to a *cop* before either.

"What *is* important is the fact that the countess stole a dead man's painting. And my apartment was ransacked, as I'm sure you've noticed."

He tapped his pen against his notepad again. "Yes, that's why we're here. Was anything stolen from your apartment, Miss Murphy?"

"I haven't had a chance to catalog everything yet. But, after a first look around . . . no. Nothing."

"Who has a key to your room?"

"The maid staff," I said. "Mr. Peters, the bartender at the pool. He had been walking Presley for me while Mac, um, took some time off. I need to get that back from him today, actually. There's probably a copy of it somewhere for the use of the general hotel staff. I get packages delivered, and sometimes I want them waiting for me in my room if I'm busy at an appointment when they arrive."

"I see," he said, "so almost anyone who has come into the hotel and has enough forethought could have broken in."

"That's if they used a key," I added. "They could also have picked the lock."

He opened his mouth, closed it again. With a shake of his head, he said, "I was about to ask how a young lady in your station knows about lock picking, but that's a silly question, and I don't like to ask those. Miss Murphy, I will do my best to see who broke into your room and made a mess."

"We need the motive first. What were they looking for and why, and then we'll have our culprit."

He sighed again as he stood up. "Yes, Miss Murphy, I do understand what police work is. Have a good day."

I didn't get up. I sat there, staring at the grease stain, my nose wrinkled. If nothing was stolen, the intruder must have been after the note from Mr. Sharpe's office currently in my clutch. Which meant that there were only two suspects: Mr. Sharpe and whoever had been wearing those sensible shoes while I was hiding under the desk.

CHAPTER 39

Since I didn't know the identity of the second person, I decided to talk to Mr. Sharpe as soon as possible. This proved not very difficult, as he was in the hallway with the myriad top-floor guests upset by either my outburst, my destroyed room, the police presence, or all of the above.

While I didn't want to deal with my fellow guests, I knew better than to stroll out there after my previous behavior, all haughty and unapologetic. I tucked my chin to my chest and looked at the group under my eyelashes.

"Good morning, all," I said, and the hubbub fell away. "I am terribly sorry about my behavior. I shouldn't have gotten physical with the countess like that. I was upset about the state of my room, you see, and my emotions overrode my common sense."

Amelia patted my arm. "It's okay, Evelyn. Everyone gets upset when their stuff is messed with. Anyway, I think the countess did have something to do with it."

Her mother whispered admonishments in French, but Amelia and I shared a smile.

"Might I steal Mr. Sharpe for a moment? I'd like to show him the damage done and see if he will lend me a few extra maids today to help clean it up."

There was a general murmur of agreement, though I got the sense I wasn't completely forgiven yet. I'd have to make it up to my neighbors later. Perhaps a party thrown in their honor? Good food and good alcohol went a long way toward soothing ruffled feathers.

Parties would have to wait. For now, I had a mystery to solve.

"Mr. Sharpe?"

"Of course, Miss Murphy. Of course." His accent was thicker today than normal, a habit of his under times of stress. I found it rather charming, putting my inner feelings for him at complete odds. On the one hand, he'd possibly ransacked my apartment to steal back the note I had sto—*borrowed* from him.

On the other hand, he respected his position and feared for his job so much that he was nervous about all the police activity in the last week.

I wondered if it had cost us guests. Daddy wouldn't be happy about that.

"As you can see"—I threw open the door and found Mac feeding Presley and himself pieces of cheddar cheese I'd been keeping in the fridge—"it's an absolute disaster."

Mac looked at both of us, left cheek full to bursting, and then around the room.

I bit back a smile and guided Mr. Sharpe in. Mr. Sharpe stared harder at Mac than he did at the destruction around us.

"I wanted you to see it, because it will take more than me and Florence and Mr. Cooper here to get it back to rights."

"Of course, Miss Murphy. Whatever you need, Miss Murphy. And Mr. Cooper. You sure look comfortable in Miss Murphy's private room. What a surprise to see *you* here and not Mr. Fox."

Mac swallowed and shrugged one shoulder.

"He's taking care of Presley for me again!" I said, lest Daddy find out Mac spent the night in my bedroom. "And I also wanted to speak to you because . . ." I locked my door, a loud click as it slid into place. "I have a sneaking suspicion you are the one behind this."

He stared at me, aghast. "Me? What? Why would you think such a thing?"

"Well, for one, when you first saw my room, you were not surprised by the damage," I said. "Which means it wasn't the first time you had seen it."

He swallowed hard, his Adam's apple bobbing. "Miss Murphy, I swear to you, I did not do this."

"But it isn't the first time you've seen it," Mac said.

Mr. Sharpe glared at him. "No," he said. He sighed and looked at me. "When Burrows wouldn't leave me alone, I figured . . . well, I know how loyal Miss Cooper is to her brother, and how loyal Mr. Cooper is to you, and that Miss Cooper and Mr. Burrows are seeing one another. It didn't take much to put two and two together that he was distracting me for your sake. I knocked on the door, no one answered, but it wasn't locked either. When I came in, it looked like this." He moved his arms around in a general gesture.

"And so what did you do?" I asked.

"I know you took that note, Evelyn. I only wanted it back. It isn't what it looks like."

"You didn't answer the question." Mac came up to Mr. Sharpe's other side, Presley munching on a block of cheese in his arms. "What did you do after you saw her apartment like this?"

Mr. Sharpe didn't answer, but he didn't have to. I saw it in the look of disappointment that crossed his face. Not in the situation, but in himself.

"I don't have your note," I lied. "I'm sorry that you wasted your time looking for it."

He stared at me, eye to eye, and his disappointment flashed from himself to me. He knew I was lying, but there was nothing he could do about it.

Him being disappointed in me made my insides squirm, my toes curl in my shoes. I bit my tongue to keep from blurting out the truth. I needed to do the right thing, even if it meant making enemies along the way.

But why couldn't everyone *like* me?

"I'll pull some staff together," he said. "We'll get you back to rights in no time. Perhaps Mr. Fox will be able to help you?"

I didn't know why he was throwing Henry in my face like that, except that he was mad at me and trying to poke an injury. "Perhaps," I replied, not wanting to divulge the fact that Henry and I had broken up. "We are the best of friends, you know."

"Have a good day, Miss Murphy. Mr. Cooper." He unlocked the door and left us alone in the mess we hadn't made.

I put my hands on my hips and tapped my foot on the ground, nose wrinkling. Something was close. Something was right there, right on the tip of my brain, but I couldn't quite think it out.

"Evelyn?" asked Mac. "You on to something?"

"Not quite," I said. "But I know what I need to do next. And I need your help."

"Anything."

The sincerity in his voice pulled me out of my thinking slump. I kissed him quick on the cheek, rubbed Presley between the ears. "I am convinced now more than ever of Hall's innocence. But if I'm going to get any usable help from him, I'm the one who needs to talk to him. Face-to-face. Which means I have to leave the hotel and visit the police station. Mac, I know this is a lot to ask, but will you drive my Rolls-Royce?"

I was sure the top-floor guests still gathered outside could hear Mac's resounding whoop.

CHAPTER 40

"I don't think we should bring the dog to the police station," Mac said. "Coppers are not, er, dog friendly."

I looked at him like he was nuts. "What, are you nuts? And leave Presley in this mess?" I found his purse amid the chaos of my apartment and set him inside, leash ready to go. I slipped in Hall's yearbook too, underneath Presley's furry belly. "He'll be fine! A perfect little gentleman. No one will even know he's with us!"

The clutch with my precious clues I kept under my arm, pressed against my side. I wasn't about to let Sharpe's note out of my sight. Not now, after what had happened to my beautiful suite.

Mac sighed, resigned, and opened the door for me. "I'll leave it unlocked, shall I?"

"Hopefully the maids will have gotten to it before we get back. The idea of having to sort through all this?" I shuddered. "It's positively worse than leaving the property!"

The elevator stopped multiple times on the way down to pick up more and more people. I smiled at them all, my hand in

Mac's. It was a struggle the whole way down. Not so much that I had to be polite to the guests, but that there were so many of them in such a small space. An omen of what was waiting for me once I left the safety and familiarity of the Pinnacle's lobby. Strangers, closing in on me. Watching me. Sizing me up and passing judgment, and who knew if they were even judging the right things? Like my clothes or my hair or my makeup? What if they were judging my personality? What if they found me lacking? What if one of them was a killer and was planning on offing me? And given the fact that Billie Bell had been murdered in this hotel, there was a chance, however small, that one of the strangers in the elevator was, in fact, a murderer.

Mac squeezed my fingers when we arrived at the lobby floor. "Halfway there."

That was hardly the truth, but I appreciated his encouragement, so I kissed his cheek. "Let's ask Burrows to fetch the car for us," I said. "You'll give him the key?"

"Sure, sure. I still get to drive it, though, right?" His grin was as wide as it was ridiculous. "I've never been inside a Rolls before, much less driven one."

"Well, they aren't built for the drivers, lover. They're built for the ones being driven. But I'm happy you're excited."

His cheeks went red, I wasn't sure from what, but his smile stayed the same. "Hey, Burrows!" he shouted over the line of people waiting to get to the front desk. "Need a favor for the princess!"

Burrows dropped whatever he was holding, picked it up, hit the back of his head on the desk, dropped it again. The other people behind the counter rolled their eyes, and a few guests chuckled. Burrows held up a finger telling Mac to wait, and so we did.

I hugged myself and looked around the lobby. I'd be leaving it soon, but I'd be back. That same day! In and out. See Hall face-to-face, ask a few questions, and come home. Easy peasy. I could do that. I would do that! With Presley and Mac at my side, I could do anything.

Someone touched me.

I jumped straight up in the air—and so did my heart—and landed with a thud and the attention of everyone nearby.

"Easy, easy," Mac said, grabbing on to me, while Presley poked his head out of his purse and yipped.

"I'm so sorry!" squeaked a high-pitched voice, "I only wanted to say hi. Golly, Miss Murphy, are you all right?"

I covered my heart with my hand. It had, fortunately, found its way back inside my chest. "Miss Bourke." I licked my lips and forced them into a smile. "How good to see you! I was thinking about you this morning."

While rummaging through her room, but I didn't need to tell her that.

She pushed her glasses up her nose with the back of her hand. "I heard about the break-in, Miss Murphy. How awful! Was very much stolen?"

I leaned in to whisper conspiratorially, "Absolutely nothing. That's the thing. Someone went in there, made an absolute mess of everything, and then left." I snapped my fingers. "Lickety-split."

Burrows jogged up to us, breathing heavily. "Good day, Miss Murphy," he said.

"Good to see you back on the property, Cooper."

"Yep." Mac wiped his hands across his imaginary lapels. "Old Sharpe had to cave when it came to where and where not I was allowed to trespass."

"I know. I read the memo."

Now that was news to me. "There was a memo?"

Burrows nodded. "Yes, I believe in it that old Sharpe referred to Mr. Cooper as your, um, *new pet*."

Tilly lost herself to an obviously fake cough while I fell into giggles. Mac dropped his imaginary lapels, shoulders slumped.

Burrows wiped his palms with a white kerchief. "How may I help you?"

Tilly Bourke scratched Presley's ears. "I better get going. But it was nice to see you. Shall we have tea together soon?"

"I'd love that," I said, meaning it. It would give me a chance to question her again. "Have a good day, Miss Bourke."

She walked outside, and Mac dug the keys out his pocket, making a show of it all. Holding them in his fingers, jangling them about, like a hypnotist about to put someone under. "Be a dear, my good fellow, and bring the Rolls around, will you?" He set them carefully in Burrows's hand. "And don't be rough with it. That car isn't like my sister."

I'd never seen a man as pale as Burrows pink up quite so quickly or so beautifully. He shuffled away to fetch the car from the garage and bring it out front.

Mac grinned at me. "Gonna be a great day, Evelyn. I can feel it. I've got a very keen sense about these things, you know."

"My room was broken into this morning, Malcolm."

He waved a hand as if to wipe my words out of the air. "You didn't lose anything, and other people are cleaning it up."

"All my Chanels touched the ground. The *ground*! What if I can't salvage them?"

"You can't wash them off?"

I felt dizzy on my feet. "With water? And soap? I have so much to teach you, lover."

He went red again. Rubbed the back of his neck, cleared his throat. "Why are you calling me that?"

"It's what you are, isn't it?" I bounced up on my tiptoes to rub my nose against his. "*Lover*. Or do you prefer *pet*?"

He surprised me with a kiss. Right there in the middle of the lobby. Arm around my waist, bending me backward.

A kiss for the papers without even a photographer present.

My brain was in a fog when he let me go, but I registered the sparkle in his gray eyes, the confidence of his smile.

"Guess we're public knowledge now," he said.

The fog had yet to clear. I could only nod. At that moment, fortunately for my sense of pride, Burrows came back with the keys in hand. "Here you go! Have a good day!"

"Great day," Mac corrected. "We are having a *great* day!"

The Rolls-Royce Silver Cloud shone in the afternoon sun as it idled at the sidewalk. I held Mac's arm as we walked down the steps and waited as he opened the door for me.

"Just so you know," he said, after I was safely inside and he was sliding in behind the steering wheel, "your country has this all backward."

The seats were a plump red leather, the mahogany dashboard highly polished. The gauges, handles, and wheel were black with silver accents. I nodded my approval. Daddy's assistant had done an excellent job. I'd told her ginchy, and she had delivered ginchy.

I settled Presley's purse in my lap and straightened his blue bow. "Has what all backward?"

He gestured at the steering wheel. "I learned to drive on the other side. Should be fine, though. It's all . . . transferrable information."

I held on to Presley's purse. Mac did not exactly strike confidence.

"If you say so," I said.

"I do. I say so." He grinned at me, though it didn't reach his eyes. "Great day, Evelyn. It's a great day. Remember that."

Humming noncommittally, I grasped the door handle for a sense of security, however false it might be. Mac pulled out into the steady flow of traffic. So far, so good.

Mac said, "Hall hasn't been before a judge yet, so they're still holding him at the station."

"Do you know how to get there from here? Is it much different than going there from Yonkers?"

"No, no, it's fine. I know where I'm going." He was glancing down at the speedometer, back up at the street, back down again. His shifty eyes were making me nervous. "I know where we are. It's, uh, it's fine." But not as nervous as his voice was making me.

I held on to Presley's purse and the door handle even tighter. Presley licked my chin. "Mac? Mac, what's wrong?"

"Nothing," he said. His foot stomped on the brake. "Nothing is wrong. Nothing is—nothing is happening. Nothing is happening!"

"Mac?"

The cars in front of us were bright rows of red lights. But we were not slowing down. If anything, we were getting faster.

"Mac! Mac, brakes!"

"I'm hitting the brakes! I'm—"

We crashed.

CHAPTER 41

I woke up in a hospital bed. In a *double* room. There was an older lady in the bed next to me, our thin orange curtains pulled back so we could stare at each other. Or at least, so she could stare at me while I slept. And stare she continued to do, her eyes wide and unblinking.

Had she died? Was I in a room with a corpse?

She sneezed.

I almost fell out of the bed, I startled so hard.

"Nurse!" I yelled, and then immediately winced. Yelling made my head hurt. Or rather, my head hurt and yelling made it worse. "Nurse!"

A middle-aged woman in nurse's whites came in and smiled at me, too big to be real. "Yes?"

"What is happening? Why have I been put in a double room? Where is Mac? Where is my dog?"

The nurse kept smiling. "You were in a car accident. The police are investigating. I don't know of anyone named Mac or any dog. You were brought on an ambulance quite alone, but the paramedics said your name was Murphy."

"Evelyn Elizabeth Grace Murphy," I said. "My father owns the Pinnacle Hotel. Mac is my boyfriend, and he was driving the car. My dog was with me. He was on my lap." My lips trembled, my eyes burned. "He was on my lap. He's perfect. My little baby. Where is he?"

Her smile faltered. "I am sorry, Miss Murphy. I don't know. Is there anyone you want me to call? Anyone who should be with you right now?"

Mac should be with me. Presley should be with me. They were, they had been . . . and now . . . ? Now what?

"Detective Hodgson," I said. "Please call Detective Hodgson."

"Miss Murphy, I am sure the police are doing all they can. What you need is to rest. Why don't I talk to the doctor about getting you some more medication, hmm? How's your head?"

"It hurts like the dickens, but I don't need sleep right now. I need to speak to Detective Hodgson immediately, and if you won't call him for me, then I need to get to the police station."

Oh dear, the hospital and the police station in one day. What would Dr. Sanders say about that?

"Not possible, Miss Murphy. You were in a car accident. The doctors are worried about a concussion or whiplash. You'll be kept overnight."

I guffawed. I was not spending the night outside the Pinnacle. Absolutely, positively, no way, no how.

"I need a phone and I need it now. I must speak to Detective Hodgson at once."

"Yeah, yeah," said a familiar voice as the detective himself strolled into the room. He took off his black fedora, nodded at the nurse and my not-dead roommate. "If you'll excuse us for a minute. I need to have a private conversation with your patient."

The nurse shrugged and closed the curtain around my bed. So much for privacy.

"Where is Mac?" I demanded. "Where is Presley?"

"Elvis?" Detective Hodgson squinted his dark eyes. "Fort Hood, last I heard on the radio."

"No, my dog. Where's my dog? Is he okay?" Tears blurred my vision, choked my throat. "Please, is he okay? Oh God, my baby. My baby!"

"Miss Murphy, please." His tone was short, but his expression was pleading. I had the sudden realization that though the detective was not a man who could be manipulated by a pretty face, he couldn't stand to be around a woman crying.

Tears. The ultimate weapon.

Detective Hodgson pulled his notepad out of his coat pocket and flipped to the middle. "Your dog was taken to a nearby veterinarian. The reports of the officers on the scene were that he seemed uninjured but refused to leave your side, and presented a danger to the policewoman attending to your injuries."

My little bear cub, protecting his mama.

"And Mac?"

"Mac was brought to this hospital, but I haven't checked on him yet. You were my top priority."

That gave me pause. I was his top priority? That was a new experience for me. "He wasn't . . . he wasn't dead, though, right?"

Detective Hodgson checked his notepad. "The officer I spoke to said he'd been conscious but groggy. Bleeding from the forehead but nothing life-threatening."

I wiped my face dry with the itchy hospital blanket. "He was bleeding?"

"And talking," the detective reminded me. "I'm sure he's fine."

"I need to see him."

He held up a finger. "In a second. Don't you want to know why I'm here?"

"Because you're starting to care about me?"

He scoffed. "The brake lines on your Rolls-Royce were cut. Snipped, more like. Enough to cause an accident after you'd driven about half a mile."

"You mean that someone tried to kill me?"

"You or Mr. Cooper, yes."

"But probably me," I said, "because he's a bellhop."

The detective set his hat on the foot of my bed. "He *was* a bellhop. For a time. After leading a life of crime."

It was my turn to scoff. Ridiculous. Detective Hodgson was wrong. No one from Mac's previous life of petty theft would even know to snip the lines of my Rolls-Royce. What were the odds he'd ever drive me out of the hotel if I wasn't actively attempting to solve a crime? No, I must be close, and someone was spooked. They'd tried to kill me before I could uncover the truth.

"I need to speak with Phil Hall."

Hodgson shook his head.

"Miss Murphy. I have been nothing but patient with you."

Well, that was fundamentally not true. My face must've displayed my disbelief, because he gave me a sheepish look.

"As patient as I can be with some busybody interfering with police work," he said. "But Phil Hall had nothing to do with this attempt on your life. He's been behind bars this whole time."

"Exactly. So if he was responsible for the murder or the theft, why were my brakes tampered with? If you had the right man, I wouldn't have been in a car accident today. Somebody tried to kill me because I'm close. And I'll be closer if I can talk to Mr. Hall."

"Or, as I said, they were trying to kill Mr. Cooper and you were simply collateral damage."

I shook my head, bit my lip. Stubborn man! Like reasoning with a wall. I tossed off my blankets, revealing my bare legs. Someone had undressed me—I hoped female hospital staff—and put me in the ugliest beige-and-blue hospital gown ever created.

"What are you doing?" Detective Hodgson asked. "You're under observation. You can't—"

I scooted to the edge of the bed and set my feet on the floor. "I am going to find Mac. Yell for the nurses if you want, Detective. But this will give you the opportunity to investigate the mystery attackers of Mac's past who happened to have a lucky guess that the Rolls was mine—that I, a known homebody, would need Mac to drive it today, of all days. Very lucky, these mystery attackers."

He snatched up his hat, grumbling something too rude to repeat under his breath, before finally holding out his arm. "Fine. But don't fall down and bust your head open. I don't need to be yelled at by two nurses today."

I stood with his help. My legs shook, but he was stable, and I leaned heavily against him. I thought of Daddy and how he had handled me after Mom died. Like glass, scared I would break. Handing me off to the first person he could because I was too fragile.

I shook my head, pushed those thoughts away. "A nurse yelled at you?"

"At the front desk." He pulled back the curtains, and the metal hangers scraped against the rod. My roommate continued to stare, unblinking. "She was not impressed by my badge and told me so."

I patted his arm. "And yet you persevered and made it to my bedside. I knew you were starting to like me, Detective."

CHAPTER 42

The linoleum floor was cold on my feet, and my backside felt a surprising breeze. With one arm clutched around the detective's, I kept the back of my gown closed with my free hand.

"Disgusting," I said, "look at me!"

The detective obliged.

"No, please don't! No one should ever look at me in this monstrosity again."

He rolled his eyes and looked away.

The nurse sneaking a muffin at the nurses' station pointed down the hall toward Mac's room, and we both thanked her.

"I can't believe Mac is going to see me in this." It took a surprising amount of effort to stay covered up. "Maybe I should change first."

Detective Hodgson pushed the door open and said, "Too late."

The first thing I noticed was that Mac had a private room. I didn't have time to be incensed, because the second thing I noticed was Mac, lying on his back, a bandage on his forehead. Unconscious.

I ran to his side, headache and modesty forgotten.

"Mac?" I held his hand in mine. "Mac, can you hear me?"

Detective Hodgson cleared his throat. "I'll, uh, I'll go find the doctor." He shut the door behind him, but I barely noticed he'd left at all.

Mac. My poor Mac. His eyes fluttered behind his closed eyes, violent purple under both like he'd lost a fight. I place my hand on the side of his face. "Mac?" I whispered. "Please, Mac. I need you to wake up. Okay? Can you wake up?"

I traced his bruises with a trembling thumb. The bandage over his forehead was fresh, hiding the damage from me. Detective Hodgson would've been told if it was life-threatening. Wouldn't he? And he'd said Mac was talking after the crash. Groggy, he'd said. Groggy but talking.

He was fine. "You're gonna be fine." Tears blurred my vision until he was nothing more than a water stain before me. "You are fine." My knees buckled, legs trembled. I collapsed on the floor beside his bed, my head swimming. I couldn't see. I couldn't breathe. Every jagged inhale tore my throat.

Someone had tried to kill me, and Mac had gotten hurt. Someone had hurt Mac because I was being a spoiled busybody and sticking my nose in places it didn't belong. Mac was bleeding on a hospital bed, and it was all my fault.

"Miss Murphy?" a male voice asked. It sounded like Daddy, but that was impossible. Daddy was never around when I needed him most. "Miss Murphy?"

Detective Hodgson walked around Mac's bed. He took off his hat and stared down at me, his mouth wide open.

I was kneeling on the linoleum floor, shaking like Presley during a thunderstorm.

"Do you need a . . . is this an . . . are you hurt?"

I shook my head, teeth chattering. "Attack of," I gasped, "anxiety. Need a . . . minute."

He dragged a chair over from under the window and helped me sit.

"Put your head between your knees," he said, "and breathe."

For lack of a better idea, I did what he said. With my head between my knees, I closed my eyes and took a deep breath. What was it that Dr. Sanders had said? What am I feeling, and where do I feel it?

Behind my eyes. A buzzing so loud I could feel it in my ears, pulsating with every breath. In my stomach, a knot so tight it threatened to burst out of me at any moment. I was terrified. I was guilty. I'd been selfish, and the one person in the world I loved more than Presley had gotten hurt because of it.

I pictured myself as a young child. Hiding off the boiler room, like Amelia. What would I say to Amelia in this situation?

It isn't your fault there are bad people in this world. You did what you thought was right. You did the right thing during a scary time, and that's the bravest thing anyone could do. You are brave. You are strong. And Mac is fine.

I wiped my face dry on the sleeve of my paper gown and sat up. Detective Hodgson stared down at me. "Feeling better?"

I nodded and took Mac's hand. Warm. He was always warm when I held him. And he was warm now too. Because he was fine. I held his hand between both of mine. His fingers were exquisite. Long and tan. I could picture them holding his cigarettes. Could remember what they felt like touching me. That was only a night ago. We'd had one night, and now someone was trying to kill us.

But who?

I was brave, and I would keep going. I would find who did this. I would find whoever had hurt Mac, and I would make sure justice was served.

Who'd known I was taking the car today? The only one we'd told was Burrows. Burrows, a killer? I didn't know him well. He seemed nervous all the time. And those sweaty palms of his! Signs of a guilty conscience? He had started dating Poppy at a convenient time.

What was his motive? I supposed it could be money related. He couldn't be a millionaire working behind the mail desk.

So, he'd stolen the painting, and Bell had found out, and when confronted, Burrows got the best of the eccentric artist. Or! Or . . .

That day he'd walked me up to Tilly's room. I'd assumed their awkwardness around each other was due to their lack of social grace, but maybe it had resulted from their knowing each other beforehand and having to act like strangers in front of me?

I tapped my finger against the back of Mac's hand. I knew what he would say, if he were awake. He'd say it was Henry.

Henry did know about the car. I'd bought it for him, after all. He could've cut the brake lines at any time after being gifted the car. Was that why he'd refused to drive it? Because he'd sabotaged it?

Why else would any sane person turn down a free Rolls-Royce?

Oh dear God. Had it been Henry all along?

Detective Hodgson moved another chair on the opposite side of the bed and sat down with a groan. "The doctor is busy," he said, "but I've been promised he'll stop here as soon as he can. Maybe you can tell him about . . ." He waved his arm at me, encompassing my episode without saying the words.

"Thank you." I didn't look at him, though. I kept staring at Mac's hand. Wondered how it would look with a gold band on the ring finger. Wondered if we'd ever get that chance now that someone was trying to kill us.

Maybe it was Henry. Maybe it was Burrows. I didn't care who it was. I loved Mac, and I was going to keep him safe. If that meant solving the case and throwing my best friend in jail, then that's what it meant.

"Miss Murphy?" Hodgson asked. "You sure you're okay?"

"My head hurts. But otherwise I'm fine."

He pulled out his notepad and pen from his jacket pocket. "Mind if I ask you a few questions, then?"

I smiled. "Ask away."

"Is there anyone you've recently had any issues with? Someone you've had a disagreement with, or gotten into a fight?"

"No," I said. "No, no one." I sniffed. "Well."

"Well?"

"Mr. Sharpe and I haven't been seeing eye to eye lately. I, um, suspected he was the one who tore up my room, actually. He says he didn't, though. And then there was that altercation with the countess."

His pen scratched over the paper.

"Because you claimed she stole a painting?"

I shrugged a shoulder instead of answering. "I did recently break up with Henry Fox, but he took it very well, and was understanding of my new relationship with Mac."

He wrote that down too.

Henry had been understanding. We'd hugged! We'd shared a special moment. But he was an incredibly gifted actor. Was it possible he was acting like he was happy for me?

"Is there anyone else you can think of, Miss Murphy?"

Was that everyone, then? Everyone who might have it out for me? Burrows, Henry, Mr. Sharpe, and Countess Dreadful. "I did run into Tilly Bourke before the car accident," I said. "But she seemed blissfully unaware of me snooping through her room, so I doubt she cut the brake lines as an act of revenge. Besides, how would she even have known about the car?"

Mac said, "You did put it in the paper."

I jumped out of my seat and grabbed his face with both hands. "Oh, Mac," I said, kissing his face all over, "you scared me! Are you okay?"

He squished up his nose as I kissed every inch of skin I could reach, a sloppy grin overtaking his lips. "I feel hungover, but yeah, I'm okay. How are you?"

"I'm fine. A bit of a headache." I pulled away to look in his kind gray eyes, my hands still on his cheeks. The bandage covered the whole right side of his forehead, dipping down into his eyebrow. "Oh, lover, does it hurt? Will it scar? Scars are all the rage, you know. You'll look ever so ginchy with a scar!"

Mac touched his bandage. "They gave me something for the pain. It doesn't hurt right now. But where's Presley? God, Evelyn, is he—"

"He's all right." I smiled to reassure him. "Detective Hodgson says they took him to a vet as a precaution. More to keep the officers safe from the vicious bear cub who was protecting his mama."

Mac tucked a strand of my hair behind my ear, left his hand pressed against me. "Thank the Lord we're all okay. Or do I thank your Tony for that one?"

The fact that he remembered the saint I kept closest to my heart when he wasn't Catholic turned my insides to goo.

I kissed him.

"Anthony is the patron saint of lost things and missing people, so no, I wouldn't thank him for saving us from the crash. Someone cut our brake lines, didn't they, Detective?"

Poor Detective Hodgson. We'd been so lovey-dovey in front of him, alone in this hospital room. He was staring at the clock on the wall like it was a modern wonder of the universe. "Uh." He coughed, shook his head. Finally, he looked at us. "Yeah. Yeah, someone had it out for you. One of you, anyway. Or both."

In an overly loud whisper, I said to Mac, "The good detective theorizes that one of your old criminal buddies from London tracked you down here, to my brand-new car, and had a lucky guess that you might drive my car one day."

Detective Hodgson sighed so hard it sounded like he had emptied himself of all air. "That's only one idea, Miss Murphy. It is plausible, no matter how sarcastic you are when you present it."

Mac took my hands off his face and held them in each of his. "But the only person who knew we were taking the car was—"

"Burrows," I finished. "Yeah."

He whistled. "Wow. Poppy is gonna be furious."

"At us or at him?"

"Both, I'd wager."

"Burrows?" Detective Hodgson asked.

Right. Should probably inform the man investigating the crash about the most likely suspect. "He works behind the mail desk at the hotel," I said. "We had him bring the car around for us. As far as we know, he's the only one who knew we were taking the car today."

Detective Hodgson rubbed his palms over his slacks before standing up. "And what did you mean, Mr. Cooper, when you said Miss Murphy put it in the paper?"

"The Rolls was a gift for Henry," I answered, before Mac could. "Called a photographer to take a picture of it and everything."

"I see." He pulled his notebook out and scribbled something down. "So it's entirely possible whoever cut the brake lines wasn't after you two at all, but instead Henry Fox. Why were you driving Mr. Fox's car, Miss Murphy?"

Someone had tried to kill Henry? I couldn't believe it, but Hodgson made sense. Certainly it made more sense than some random person from Mac's past getting lucky. It was a public gift, and nobody knew Henry had refused it but me.

My eyes were puffy, and blinking seemed to only make them dryer. I closed them for a minute to gather my thoughts. Either Henry was the target or I was. And if I was, it was because I was close to solving the murder. Which meant the murderer themselves had the drop on me and knew I was taking Henry's car.

What else did they know about me?

"He didn't want it," I said, opening my dry eyes. "He told me he doesn't drive."

The detective tucked his notebook away. "I'll go speak to this Burrows and your Mr. Fox. See if I can get this sorted. You guys take it easy. If you're lucky, the doctors will release you in the morning."

I stared at Mac. He stared at me. And then in perfect unison, we threw our heads back and laughed.

"Oh, no, no. No." I wiped the tears off my face. "No, we will not be spending a night here at this hospital. No."

"With all due respect, it ain't up to you, Miss Murphy. If the doctors want to keep you under observation, you need to comply."

"Detective." I smiled at him. "This is America and I'm wealthy. I don't have to do anything I don't want to do."

"There's no use fighting with her, Detective," Mac said. "She's stubborn, this one."

What he said was true, but nevertheless, I gently slapped his arm out of principle.

"And you, Mr. Cooper? You're going to get up and leave?"

He shrugged. "Yeah, why not? I feel hungover, nothing I haven't dealt with before. Besides, we got a murder to solve. If it is Burrows, my sister is in trouble. You expect me to lie here on my ass when my sister is in danger?"

Detective Hodgson sucked his teeth. "I guess not."

"Please," I said to the detective, "we still need your help."

"My help?" He huffed. "All I've been doing is helping you, Miss Murphy."

I could think of at least three reasons why that wasn't true but kept going as if he hadn't spoken. "We need you to take us to Mr. Hall. Please. If it wasn't him that killed Bell, that means the killer is still out there, and they are trying to hurt us."

Detective Hodgson stared down at me. I wasn't exactly sure what he was looking for, but I stared right back at him. If I could handle a man like Daddy, I could handle a man like Hodgson.

"Please, sir. He'll talk to me. He trusts me. Let me try. Please. The worst thing that happens is you get more evidence in your case against him. I'll tell you everything he says. Please, Detective."

He swore. "I'm going to regret this, aren't I? Fine. We'll meet in the lobby. Don't make me regret this, you hear me?"

I nodded. Oof, too hard. I put a hand to my head and forced a smile. "Promise. Do you want to do a pinkie promise? Those are kept no matter what, you know."

He glared at me and left the room.

CHAPTER 43

I dressed in my high-waisted denim jeans and white button-down blouse. Was the blouse a touch on the see-through side in the harsh overhead hospital lighting? Yes, but only a touch, and my lingerie was modest. As far as lingerie goes, anyway. The blouse had been wrinkled in the crash but not stained, and anyway, *anything* was better than the paper hospital gown, even wrinkly see-through clothing.

I attempted to fix my platinum-blonde curls in the mirror above the sink in my and my roommate's private bathroom. The mirror itself was warped, giving my bare face a bit of a funhouse mirror effect of my forehead being too large and my chin too small. I missed my makeup. The rough fabric of the hospital pillowcase had made my hair frizz, and my roots were coming in dark. But there was nothing to do about that now.

I had to go to the police station and conduct an interview. I could do this. I would do this! Mac and Presley—and even Detective Hodgson—would be there with me.

Besides, it was only Mr. Hall. A man, like any other man. And I knew how to handle men.

I nodded at my reflection and strolled out into my shared hospital room. My roommate still stared at me. I waited to see if she would blink, or sneeze, or show any sign of life, but she continued to stare.

Setting my hands on my hips, I asked, "Well?"

She licked her lips. "Harlot."

"Really?" I looked down at my outfit. I'd thought it more professional than harlot-y. I grinned. It was an even better ensemble than I'd thought! "Wonderful, thank you ever so! I do hope you get well soon."

She sniffed and kept staring.

I left the hospital room with a happy wave and followed the signs to the lobby.

My head still hurt, and no one had given me more medicine, but I could get something back at the Pinnacle. I needed to use this perfect ensemble to get information out of a murder suspect before Detective Hodgson changed his mind. There was something about almost dying that gave you a bit of a free pass. People were willing to extend a helping hand where they wouldn't have otherwise. I'd need to write that down when I got home for future reference.

There was a chance I had suffered a concussion and wasn't thinking quite clearly, but it was a chance I was willing to take. Mac and Detective Hodgson were waiting for me in the lobby. Mac was dressed in the same outfit as earlier, only now he was sporting bloodstains over the right shoulder that would never come out. Shame. He looked so good in blue.

"My car is parked out back," the detective said. "They moved Hall this morning to a small station that mostly handles transfers."

"You know the way?" I asked.

"Of course."

"And do you know the way to the vet? Because we need to make a quick stop and get Presley first."

He sighed. "Of course."

★   ★   ★

The small station didn't entertain a lot of visitors, so there wasn't a place for me to sit and talk with Mr. Hall. Instead, we were walked to his holding cell and allowed to speak with him as he stood behind bars. He looked fine. Unshaven but well-fed, wearing a frumpy black-and-white jumpsuit. With a little tailoring, he'd look like a hundred bucks.

I peeked inside the purse to check on Presley. He was asleep, and anyway, it wouldn't be professional for my little puppy to pop out in the middle of all these hardened criminals.

Hardened criminals was a bit dramatic. Most of them seemed to be drunk people sleeping off a hard night, or ladies of the evening who wouldn't be working for a few more evenings. Still. Better safe than sorry.

"Hello, Mr. Hall, how are you?" I smiled. "It's good to see you again."

He smiled back. "Good to see you too, Miss Murphy. Mr. Cooper." He glanced at the detective, then stared at my shoes.

Ah, he wasn't going to talk in front of Hodgson. I raised my eyebrows at the man in question, who glared back for a long while before eventually admitting his defeat. "I'll be back in five minutes."

"Wonderful! Thank you ever so." I slid Presley's purse off my shoulder, dug out the yearbook. With a bright smile, I handed the purse to him. "Will you hold this for me, please?"

His lips twisted, his jaw twitched, but he took the purse and walked off nonetheless. I grinned. He was starting to come around to liking me, I could feel it.

Mac reached through the bars to pat Hall on the shoulder. "Good to see you again, man. I found that book you sent me looking for. I don't understand it, but I found it."

Mr. Hall kept looking at my shoes. "And you, Miss Murphy? Did you look at it?"

"I did." I watched him, studied his posture. He didn't seem nervous. Afraid? Had I been wrong about him? Was he a killer? No, of course not. He wasn't a killer. But he was guilty of something. "I must admit, I didn't understand the purpose of your yearbook either."

"You didn't notice anyone who . . ." Hall shifted on his feet, raised his eyes to meet mine. They were darkened by shame. "Someone who looked familiar? Besides me, I mean."

"Well . . ." There had been something, hadn't there? My nose wrinkled as I forced myself to remember. There had been something about his debate club picture. I propped the book on my forearm and flipped the pages until I found it. Hall's thick mustache. Matching coats and knee-high socks. Three girls and four boys. "Oh," I said. "Oh, I see it now. That's Bell—he was in your debate club!"

He was skinnier, shorter, and without any glorious facial hair, but that grin, that snarky grin was the same. I should have recognized it the moment I saw it. I decided to cut myself some slack, since I had experienced an attack of anxiety, spoken to my therapist for the first time in months, and confessed my feelings to Mac all on that same day.

"You know him from high school?" Mac shook his head. "Phil, mate, you aren't doing yourself any favors."

"I didn't kill him!" Mr. Hall wasn't lying. He grabbed the bars and pushed his face close to Mac's. "I swear it! I didn't kill him, and I didn't steal that painting."

The first piece of the puzzle clicked in place. "No, you didn't. But you recognized him and knew he was a boy from Brooklyn and not whoever he was pretending to be. You recognized him and blackmailed him. Didn't you, Mr. Hall? You threatened to reveal his true identity unless he paid you. Just like you black-mailed the maid who stole from a guest."

He started to protest, so I handed Mac the book and pulled out the note from my clutch.

It took Hall a moment to realize what it was. He hunched low and stared at the ground. "She didn't need all that money. We coulda split it. She coulda helped her mom, and I coulda helped mine. What was the harm in that? But she was so upset. Said if she didn't get all of it, she didn't want none of it. So she ratted me out to Sharpe."

"But Mr. Sharpe took your side." I slipped the note back inside my clutch. "You got to keep your job but didn't get the money. So when Bell came, and you figured out who he was—"

"He's rich!" Hall looked me in the eye. "He coulda given me the money from one painting, and I woulda kept my mouth shut forever."

Mac recoiled in disgust. "Until you needed some money again. Then you would've been back, knocking on his door. I'm gutted, mate. I thought you were better than this. Blackmail? I'd rather you were a thief. There's an art to that, at least."

I remembered Amelia telling me about the argument she had overheard between Bell and his assistant. *How could you?* Tilly kept saying. Tilly had explained it as an argument over a beautiful woman, but maybe it was about money instead. "Did Bell agree to pay you?" I asked.

Hall nodded but didn't say anything else.

A police officer in blue interrupted us. "Hello," he said, "Detective Hodgson says your time is up. I'm supposed to take you to him."

I wrapped my hand around the bars separating me from Mr. Hall. "Thank you for being honest with me. I appreciate it. And I will do everything I can to clear your name of murder." I smiled at him, and he smiled back at me, hesitant and unsure. "It goes without saying, of course, that you are fired and no longer welcome on the Pinnacle premises. Have a great day!"

CHAPTER 44

Detective Hodgson leaned on the sergeant's station, his hat crooked on his head. He looked tired, as if he'd been the one in a recent car accident. He waved his hand at the purse on the floor. "Your dog."

Presley was sleeping like the good little boy he was, so I picked up his purse and tucked it under my arm and let him sleep on.

"Thank you ever so, Detective. Speaking with Mr. Hall was enlightening."

"Did you get what you wanted, then?"

"Yes, and you'll be glad to know he is definitely not your killer. And not a thief either! Merely a common blackmailer."

Hodgson pinched the bridge of his nose with his thumb and forefinger, his eyes squeezed shut tight. "Why would that make me happy, Miss Murphy? I arrested him because the evidence is stacked against him. Of course he told you he wasn't the killer."

I shrugged a shoulder. "I suppose we'll have to agree to disagree. For now. Here, take this evidence." Mac gave him the yearbook. "You should find particular interest in the debate club picture."

"I should, should I?" He opened his eyes long enough to glare at me, then closed them again and released a long, drawn-out sigh. "You were right about one thing, as much as it hurts me to admit it."

"You don't say?"

"The countess was up to something. That painting? She was attempting to sell it. On the black market. We picked up her fence."

"A fence?" I looked at Mac for clarification. "Why are they picking up fences? Why would the countess even have a fence in the hotel, wh—"

Mac shook his head once. "A fence is somebody who sells illegal things."

My mouth fell open in understanding. "She stole the painting and was attempting to sell it?"

"No," said the detective. "She says she bought the painting fair and square, and we were able to confirm that with Bell's assistant. But the fence was trying to sell it on the black market as the painting that was stolen from the art show."

Nose wrinkling, I set a hand on my hip. That felt . . . *familiar*, somehow. "It wasn't the stolen painting, though. She forced me to admire it on the wall at the party. Now why would she say it was stolen when she was selling it?"

"Figured she could get more money," Mac said with a sniff. "Probably. I don't know much about these criminal types myself, but a painting stolen in such a big, splashy way? That's bound to draw attention from your more nefarious collectors."

The idea of nefarious art collectors was a silly one. I giggled, dug my knuckles into my forehead. I needed to lie down. "Thank you again, Detective. But I think it's time for me to go home and rest. All this thinking is giving me a headache." That and the car accident, probably. "Will you give me a call if you figure out who cut my brake line, please?"

"Of course, Miss Murphy."

"Because it wasn't Mr. Hall," I said. "And he didn't kill the artist or steal the painting either."

He glared at me. "As you've said. Have a good night, Miss Murphy."

Mac reached for my hand and tugged me toward the station door, but I smiled brightly at the detective. "We're going to be friends," I told him. "I can feel it. In my heart."

He turned his glare to Mac, who tugged harder.

"Come on, Evelyn," he whispered, "before you get us both arrested."

I wiggled my fingers good-bye at Detective Hodgson and allowed Mac to lead me outside the station. "He's warming up to me, lover. I wouldn't be surprised if he actually starts wanting my advice."

He waved over a taxi. "You sure you want to go back to the hotel? And not the hospital? Get checked for a head injury?"

Mac opened the taxi door, and I slid inside. "I assure you, I'm fine. Better than ever! Well, besides this pounding headache, but that's to be expected. I need a good night's rest and some heavy pain medication and I'll be set."

"And where are you going to get pain medication from if not the hospital? Pinnacle, please," Mac said to the driver. He put his arm around my shoulders and kissed my temple. "You got a stash I don't know about under your bed?"

"Not quite. I have something even better."

CHAPTER 45

Dr. Smith did not seem to appreciate being my "something better," as he grumbled quite rudely at me over the phone before agreeing to see me. The sun had set, yes, but it was still early. What did he mean, *asleep*? Before eight? Nonsense. He must've been lying to get out of seeing me, but since I was paying for his stay, which I took no joy in reminding him about, he had no choice but to see me.

I tucked my legs underneath me on my pink chaise longue, my head pounding and my mind whirling. I was so close, I knew it, if only I could stop hurting long enough to focus.

"Hey, you hungry?" Mac asked. He was sitting on the couch, his head in his hands.

I smiled at him. "You going to cook for me, Mr. Cooper?"

"No, I was going to order for you. I can't cook to save my life."

"Tinned veggies," I said, remembering our phone call from earlier in the week. "How on earth do you survive?"

"Don't knock tinned veg, now." He stretched out his long legs and tapped his toes against my knees. "Healthy and long-lasting."

The chaise was so soft and the room was warm. I could almost forget the pounding in my head. The maids had done an excellent job straightening up while we were gone, though I hadn't checked any drawers or the closet to see if they'd managed to get everything organized or if they'd done a quick clean instead. It didn't matter. As long as it was put away, I could think.

Or I *would* think, once my headache went away.

There was a knock on the door, followed by a soft female voice saying, "Knock, knock." Poppy poked her head in the apartment and smiled when she saw us. "Good evening, Miss Murphy."

"You don't have to knock and say *Knock, knock*," I said. "Redundant."

Poppy shut the door behind her and carried in a small bag. "She okay?"

"Bit delirious," Mac said. "Hit her head in the car accident."

"And you?"

"Bit delirious," said Mac. "Hit my head in the car accident."

"Do you two need to go to hospital?"

"No, we two do not," I replied. "We're fine. Besides, Dr. Smith will be up in a minute to verify that we are fine."

Poppy set her bag down on the floor. "Brought you a change of clothes," she said. "Figured you might want a shower and didn't expect you to come home."

Mac pushed his foot against my thigh. "I'll have to clear it with the boss first."

"I'm not your boss," I said. "I'm your girlfriend."

"There's a difference now?"

Poppy giggled, shook her head. "I was planning on going out tonight. Are you two sure you're okay? Because, quite honestly, you look terrible."

"Going out with who?" Mac asked. "Please don't tell me it's Burrows."

"Of course it's Burrows. He asked me to go steady last night."

Presley came out of my bedroom and headed straight for Poppy. I narrowed my eyes at him. He was supposed to be my dog, but here he was, flirting with every pretty girl he came across.

She scooped him up and scratched under his chin.

"Poppy, there's something we need to tell you," I said.

She froze, open mouth parting into a wide smile. "You're getting married! Oh, I *knew* it!"

Mac choked on his spit. He sat up straight and clutched his throat.

I laughed, and it made my headache pound. "Golly, Poppy," I said with a grimace. "It's been a single day. But we need to talk to you about the accident."

There was another knock on the door.

"That'll be the doctor," I said.

"Why don't I take this little guy out for his walk, and we can talk after?" Poppy offered.

I nodded, winced in immediate regret. "Thank you."

She welcomed Dr. Smith into the apartment before taking Presley out for his walk.

Dr. Smith did look rather sleep rumpled, though it was possible his face was naturally grumpy. "Miss Murphy," he said in a deep, unhappy voice, his leather bag in his hand. "You rang?"

"Yes, hello, good to see you again. Are you enjoying your room?"

He set his bag down on the end table by the couch, started rifling through it. "Yes. What seems to be the problem?"

"We were in a car accident earlier today. I was hoping you would give us something to relieve the headache."

"Car accident? You need to go to the hospital, Miss Murphy, so they can run tests to see if you aren't concussed."

"I was at the hospital. They put me in a room with another person. Can you believe that?"

He stared down at me like he did, in fact, believe that.

"Anyway, I'm not going back, so can you give me something? Please and thank you."

Dr. Smith grumbled and pulled a small flashlight out of his bag. Without talking to me, he waved a light in both my eyes. Then he checked me over with his stethoscope.

"Your turn," he said to Mac, and did the same exam.

When he was done, he gave me a full bottle of aspirin. "I don't have anything stronger than this. Take two and call me in the morning. If you don't die in the night, that is."

Aspirin? I had aspirin in my bathroom. I frowned but thanked him.

"Wait, wait," Mac said. "*Are* we about to die?"

Dr. Smith rolled his eyes. "She's fine. You're fine. Have a good night. I'm going back to bed."

He left without another word.

"His bedside manner leaves a bit to be desired," I said, "but at least he confirmed I don't need to go back to that ghastly hospital. Water, Mac?"

"Oh, right." He disappeared into the kitchen and came back with a glass of water. "Here, give me some." I gave him two of the aspirin, and we shared the water. "What a day."

"Was it as great as you thought it was going to be?"

He grinned, shook his head. "I can be wrong every once in a while. But don't tell anybody."

Poppy and Presley came back in the room, this time without knocking or saying *Knock, knock.* She hung up his leash in the entryway before sitting with us. "What did the doctor say?"

Presley hopped off her lap. He curled up on his white, creamy bed and started cleaning his face.

"That we're fine and we're definitely not going to die," Mac said. He did not sound convincing.

Poppy raised her eyebrows in obvious alarm.

"But anyway. Listen, Poppy." He rubbed his palm over his face. "Look, the brake lines were cut. They were cut just enough so that the car would run for a few minutes before causing an accident. And the only person who knew we were taking the car today was Burrows."

Poppy's pretty face was stuck in an expression of shock and disbelief. "No," she said, "not possible. He's so sweet! He wouldn't hurt a fly. Evelyn, you don't think he could do something like that, do you?"

Truth be told, I wanted it to be Burrows more than I wanted it to be Henry. At least then I could put someone in jail who deserved to be there and wasn't one of my dearest friends. But beyond that selfish desire, I didn't know.

I said, "Poppy, it's late and we're both hurt. Maybe you could spend the night and look after Presley for me? I'll tip you well. We can talk to Burrows tomorrow. All of us, together."

Her lips quivered, but she nodded. "Let me ring him and cancel. You do look frightful. But I think you're both wrong about him. I really do."

"I hope you're right," Mac said.

I didn't agree with him. I hoped with everything in me she was wrong.

CHAPTER 46

The shrill ringing of the phone woke us up. Ugh. What time was it? The ticking clock face displayed five past six. I missed the receiver on the first two swipes, my hand bumping into *Hickory Dickory Death*—six chapters left.

"Blargh," Mac said, rolling over. And then, more helpfully, "Forsmithwhatchafor?"

My fingers finally landed on the receiver. I grabbed hold and moved it to the general vicinity of my face. "Hello?"

"Evelyn." It was Henry on the other line. "Evelyn, can we talk?"

I raked my fingers through my hair. Or attempted to. They got snagged on knots in the middle of my head. "Talk?" I repeated, my brain still waking up. "What? Oh. Sure. Of course. What do you want to talk about?" I was waking up now. "What's wrong? Henry, are you okay?"

"I'm fine." His voice was quiet, a bit slurred. It did not sound fine. "I need to talk to you. Can you come to my room?"

"Um." The blankets pooled in my lap when I sat up. "Your room?"

"Three oh nine," he said. "Please, Evelyn. It's important."

"Okay, okay. Of course. I'll come over. Let me get dressed. Mac and Poppy are sleeping—"

"Come alone," he said. "Please."

Alone? With Henry? A week ago I wouldn't have even batted an eye at the thought, but now? After everything that had happened?

Henry was my friend. And yes, maybe Mac was right and Henry was both an international movie star and art thief turned murderer. But he was my friend first, and I was positive he'd never hurt me.

"I'll be right there."

"See you soon."

He hung up. I stared at the phone in my hand, still trying to make sense of what was going on. "Henry wants me to go to his room," I said. "Alone."

But Mac had fallen back asleep, mouth open and snoring softly, his soft under eyes still a bit puffy and purple. The bandage on his forehead was dingy. I'd have to get some new ones for him.

I got dressed in a pink, cashmere sweater and a white skirt, slipped on beige sandals. A bit of mascara and a smudge of peach lipstick and I was on my way. Poppy slept on the couch, Presley curled up on her stomach.

I thought about waking her up and telling her where I was going. After all, she hadn't been in a car accident. But we'd made her cancel her date, and I felt too guilty to shake her awake this early in the morning. So I scribbled a note on the pad by the kitchen phone and locked the door behind me.

My stomach rumbled on the elevator ride down to the third floor. I'd forgotten to eat the night before. At least my head felt much better! After breakfast I'd be able to think. I was so very close.

The liftboy opened the elevator doors. I clutched the pendant around my neck and stepped out into the hallway. I hoped Henry hadn't called me down to confess to either the theft or the murder. I hoped very much that Mac was wrong for once.

If Henry was about to confess, would I lie for him and let Mr. Hall take the fall? Poor man. Dastardly blackmailer, but not deserving of a murder charge.

What was I going to do? *Oh, Tony, Tony, Tony . . . the murderer is lost and must be found.*

Henry opened the door after one knock. "Good morning, darling," he greeted me, all the usual cheer missing from his voice, even the proper pronunciation of *darling*. He slid a cup of coffee in my hand. "Thought you might need this."

I sipped it gratefully. A little cream and a lot of sugar, the way I like it.

"Have you had breakfast?" I asked him. "I'm starving. Is there any food in your fridge?"

He shook his head. "I could call for room service?"

I dismissed it with a wave of my hand. It would take too long, and I didn't want to be stuck in Henry's room after a big murder confession waiting for a bagel to be delivered.

"Come on, then," he said. "Let's sit."

His room was much smaller than my suite. We sat at a square wooden table in the living room, pushed underneath a large mirror. A tense silence followed as we drank our coffees. Was he going to confess? Should I let him? I wanted to shut him up, to beg him to stop, but I needed to know. It was a desperate, longing need deep down inside of me. In my very soul. I needed to know who had stolen the painting and how, and I needed to know who had stabbed Bell in the back. I needed to know it like I needed the coffee in my mug or Mac by my side or Presley in my lap. I'd found that body. And I would find the killer if it was the last thing I ever did.

"You and Malcolm Cooper, eh?" he asked. "Still going strong?"

"I do believe it's only been a day since I told you. So yes, still going strong."

Henry seemed to be having trouble with his hands. He held his mug in both palms, set it down, and tapped his fingers against the table. Leaned back in his chair and put his hands behind his head. Shifted again, clutched his hands into fists on top of the table, before pulling them into his lap and tapping his knees. Then he laid them flat on either side of his coffee mug.

"For goodness' sake, Henry!" I exclaimed, when I couldn't take any more. "What on earth has got you fidgeting so?"

"You asked if I was ever going to tell you about my relation-ship with Billie Bell."

I nodded once, kept my mouth shut. I didn't want to say something that would spook him into not telling me what I craved to know.

"The truth is," he said, "he caught me and . . . a *friend* in a compromising situation."

"A friend," I repeated, thinking back to that argument in the Silver Room. What had Bell said? It was so hard to get good help these days? "Your friend wasn't a fellow actor?"

"No, a waiter. We'd been . . . spending some time together. It was nice. We got along swimmingly." Henry took a slow sip of his coffee, a deep sadness darkening his bright eyes. "I took my friend to a party at one of those little lounges, you know, that are very European about things. I thought it a safe space. Bell was there.

"There was plenty of alcohol involved. I'll say that in Bell's defense. My friend and I slipped into a back room for a quick rendezvous, and Bell snuck in after us. He managed to snap a photo. And then he taunted me with it."

He stared down at his hands, flexed into fists on the table. I reached out and took hold of one. He smiled at me, but it rang false.

"I destroyed the camera and threatened him within an inch of his life." He sighed. "It was a nice camera too. A sleek little Royer Savoy. I pulled out the film, but I was so angry I didn't stop there. I stomped on that camera until it was in pieces and my friend was yelling at me, and Billie . . . that idiot was laughing. Nothing upset him. Not anything I did or said, and I believe I said quite a bit. That was the end of that. Or so I thought. Drunken shenanigans. No evidence to back it up. Nothing to worry about."

I squeezed his wrist. "But then he reminded you of it, and you snapped. In public. Not a good look, Henry."

"Not my finest moment," Henry agreed. "We knew each other, Evelyn. We ran in the same circle. Him being a drunk jerk, that I could forgive. But him threatening me while stone-cold sober? That was terrifying. Absolutely terrifying. He could've ruined me. My career. My *whole* life. I shouldn't have snapped, and I am embarrassed by my behavior. But he threatened me, and I saw red."

"I understand why you did what you did. And I'm so terribly sorry that you have to hide who you are. It's not fair, Henry."

He moved his hand to grasp mine and didn't reply.

"I have to ask, though, Henry. I am sorry for asking this. But . . ." I took a deep breath and steeled myself. "Were you involved in the theft of the painting and the subsequent death of Billie Bell?"

There was no sign of hesitation when he replied, "Of course not! I wanted to break his teeth, not kill him. His paintings are ghastly! Where would I display such an eyesore?"

Me and Henry have always had the same taste in things.

"Thank you for being honest. I *knew* you didn't kill him, but I had to ask. You understand, don't you?" That wasn't totally the truth. I'd hoped he hadn't murdered Bell, I'd prayed he hadn't murdered Bell, I'd felt within my heart he hadn't murdered Bell, but I had never been sure. Not until this conversation.

If Henry knew I was lying to be polite, he didn't show it. He smiled at me and kissed my knuckles. "I should've told you sooner. I was embarrassed. I was embarrassed by my behavior, and my friend insisted we stop seeing each other after what happened with Bell. I suppose I was a bit heartbroken."

"Are you still?" I asked. "Heartbroken, I mean?"

He smiled again. "No. I have been feeling more and more myself as of late."

"Wonderful. I'm happy to hear it, Henry."

"You'll still come to my play, won't you? You can bring that boy of yours."

A Broadway play? As in, a large, public event outside the walls of the Pinnacle? The last time I had gone to one of those with Henry, it had been so traumatic I'd stayed inside the hotel for fourteen months after.

Henry looked at me, his eyes big and hopeful, and darn it all! I'd have to call Dr. Sanders and make the appointment she wanted.

"Yes," I said. "Yes, you can count me and Mac in for opening night."

The smile he gave me made up for all our recent tension over the last few days.

He sniffed. "Let me take you back to your room? You need to eat, and I haven't yet had a proper conversation with this new beau of yours."

"You want to talk to Mac?" I chuckled. "Whatever about?"

"To threaten him, of course, as all good best friends should. You're a catch, Evelyn. No! Forgive me. You're *the* catch! Don't ever let him forget it. I sure won't."

Tears pressed against the backs of my eyes. I smiled bright to keep them away. What with my shell shock and the teensy-weensy bit of agoraphobia I suffered from, I didn't feel much like a catch. Mac could do better if he wanted. Someone who could leave her home without needing a hand to hold and a dog in her purse. "You're too sweet to me, Henry."

"I mean every word." He kissed my knuckles again. "Come on. Let's get you back up to your room."

CHAPTER 47

We caught Poppy at the door, dressed for work. "Good morning, Evelyn. Mr. Fox."

"Have you been introduced?" I asked Henry.

He shook his head. "We met briefly during the hubbub yesterday, but I'm afraid I didn't catch your name."

"This is Poppy," I said. "Mac's little sister."

Henry offered her his hand, flashed his movie-star smile. "Nice to officially meet you, Poppy."

She giggled and blushed. He had that effect on everyone.

Mac came to the doorway, wearing blue striped pajama bottoms and a white undershirt. He rested his elbow on the doorframe and raised an eyebrow. "Mornin'."

Almost everyone.

I rolled my eyes. Was Mac really blocking off access to my apartment like he owned the place? Men. So territorial!

"I've got to clock in or I'll get written up," Poppy said. "See you later, Evelyn. Nice to meet you, Mr. Fox!"

She darted toward the service elevator, and we watched her go.

"Ordered you an egg white omelet," Mac told me. "Tried to put it up high enough that Presley won't get it, but he's being awfully quiet."

I shrugged, even though my heart sang in my chest. He'd ordered me breakfast without ever being asked, knew what I liked to eat without being reminded. "Won't be the first meal I've shared with him."

Mac nodded his chin at Henry. "What did you two get up to this early in the morning? Hmm?"

"We had coffee," I said. "It was nice to catch up."

Henry kissed my temple. Then he held out his hand to Mac.

Mac stared at it for several long moments before he finally relaxed his territorial posture and shook Henry's hand.

"You're a good man, Mr. Cooper. And you've got the greatest girl in the whole world right here."

Mac smiled. Legitimately, warmly, and my singing heart took flight. Could the two most important men in my life—after Daddy and Presley, of course—actually become friends?

"Don't I know it." Mac wrapped his arm around my shoulders when Henry dropped their handshake.

"I'll let you get back to your morning," Henry said. "Thank you for coffee. And thank you for listening."

"I'm always here for you, Henry." Literally. Always at the Pinnacle.

Mac and I walked into the apartment, shutting the door behind us. I toed off my sandals and left them near the entrance. Sure enough, Presley had hopped his little way onto the table. I shook my head at him and set him down on the ground. "You can finish what we don't eat."

"So, coffee, huh?" Mac asked, tucking into breakfast. "You guys talk about anything interesting? His play, the car accident, the murder?"

"Oh, his play!" I'd forgotten to ask him the date of his opening night! If I was going to schedule an appointment with Dr. Sanders, I had to know what we were working toward.

"Henry!" I ran out of the suite. "Wait, Henry!" Out in the hall, a small group of top-floor guests were waiting for the elevator. "Excuse me," I greeted my neighbors, "have you seen Henry Fox?"

There was an excited whisper among the guests as they recognized his name, but they shook their heads and told me they hadn't seen him. Strange. He'd walked out only a few seconds before I had. Where could he have gone? The service elevator? You needed a key for that.

The stairs, then.

Yes, he must've. I'd seen him run up and down those stairs for his cardio many times since he'd checked in last week. Though every time he'd been wearing a fashionable athletic outfit, not jeans and a T-shirt as he had been for breakfast. No matter. Maybe he wanted to walk in peace, away from adoring fans.

The guests loaded into the elevator and disappeared as I stood out in the hallway, thinking to myself, and when they were gone, a little voice startled me from my thoughts.

"I know where he went," she said with a thick French accent, "but I will not tell you, because you ruined my last hiding spot."

"Oh, Amelia!" I covered my heart with my hand. "Where are you?" I scanned my surroundings and found her under one of the decorative tables. "That's not such a great hiding spot."

She nodded. "I know. But as I said, you destroyed the plant I was hiding behind before. To stand on. His name was Jeffrey, and you killed him."

I chewed my cheek to keep from laughing. "I am ever so sorry, Miss Amelia. I did need it to find the necklace the countess had hidden, remember? Can I make it up to you? With marshmallows and chocolate? And snuggles from Presley?"

Amelia turned her nose up at me, sniffed. "I suppose that will suffice. I'm still not sure I should tell you. What if you ruin his hiding spot too?"

Henry, hiding? "He didn't take the stairs?" And he hadn't taken the elevator. Where would he, a grown man, hide in a hallway?

Oh, dear God! How stupid could I be? I smacked myself in the forehead. How could I not have seen it before now?

"Amelia, please forgive me! Come by later and I'll make up Jeffrey's death to you, okay?"

I ran back into my apartment. Mac sat at the table, sharing his omelet with Presley. "Bit cold," he said, his mouth full of eggs. "And the dog ate most of it."

"Enough of that now!" I grabbed my sandals. "I figured it out!"

"Figured what out?"

I slipped the shoes on my feet. "Why the table was moved, of course!"

Mac stood up and grabbed hold of Presley, though he said, "Table? What table?" as he followed me out the door.

★　★　★

"This table!"

Yes, I had waited to speak again until we were at the spot where I had discovered the dead body of Billie Bell. But it was worth it for the look of recognition that crossed Mac's face.

Or that would crossed it, if he'd understood what I was talking about.

"I spoke to Florence after Bell's death," I explained. "The one thing she said was weird about this hallway—besides the corpse with the knife in its back—was that *this* table was off-center."

The table in question had been moved back, the police tape gone, new guests allowed in these rooms. The only noticeable difference now was the patch of carpet that had replaced the bloodstained piece the maids could never get clean.

I held out my arms. Brows furrowed, Mac gave me Presley. "Now," I said, "move that table for me, lover."

He groaned the entire time. Unnecessarily loudly, if you ask me, making the noise only for attention. Granted, the veins in his neck did bulge as he pushed the heavy table, the two vases of fresh flowers wobbling precariously as it slid across the carpet. Perhaps he needed to run the stairs with Henry a few times.

Mac wiped imaginary sweat off his forehead with the back of his hand and then used that hand to gesture at the table he'd moved.

"Excellent, thank you." I gave him Presley back.

The floral wallpaper was perfect. It took close examination to find the seam, but find it I did. And with one good push, the hidden door opened up.

Mac swore.

He obviously didn't know about the Pinnacle's history. Owned by the Mafia and used during Prohibition to store and run alcohol. I'd spent my childhood hiding in a secret room off the boiler, never once thinking there would be other hidden rooms or secret passages connecting them.

Stupid girl. If there was one hidden room in a Mafia-built hotel, why wouldn't there be more?

How Henry knew about the secret hallways was a mystery in itself, and not one I could think about currently. Because the first thing I saw inside the passageway was a bloody handprint.

Mac swore again, more viciously this time.

"Flashlight," I said, hand out.

"Flashlight?" Mac repeated. "Evie, I'm in my *pajamas*."

"Lighter, then. And don't call me Evie."

"Why not?" He slipped his Zippo lighter into my hand. "You keep calling me lover."

I clicked the lighter on and held it up to the handprint. "You're welcome," I replied, no longer listening to him. It was a left-hand print.

Or, rather, a partial of one. A pinkie, index finger, and the left side of the hand were so thick on the wall, it was as if it had been painted there. The rest of the hand was fainter, harder to see, and harder to tell the size of. There was a line in the center of the pinkie. A scar? A ring? Something had caused the print to split in half. They had killed Bell, slipped into this passageway, and found their way out without ever being caught. Possibly coming back around to the crime scene to establish their alibi.

What were the odds that both Billie Bell and his murderer were left-handed?

Stupid. Stupid Evelyn. I shook my head in an attempt to get my nose to smooth out, but it was stuck in its wrinkled state. "Mac," I said. "Call Detective Hodgson. And then call everyone else. It's time to have a party."

CHAPTER 48

My outfit needed to be dramatic. It wasn't every day a girl got to reveal a murder plot to her friends and colleagues, after all. I went with a backless black ball gown. Dior, of course.

Backless for the drama of it all. Black because the party was in honor of a murderer.

Mac handled ordering the food from the kitchen. A delectable spread of shrimp cocktail and pigs in a blanket, maybe a good cheesy fondue with pears and potatoes for dipping, would be an excellent thing for my guests to munch on while I laid out the truth. And some chilled champagne to celebrate after Detective Hodgson made an arrest.

If he made an arrest.

He would. He would see things my way. I'd make sure of it. In this dress, who wouldn't take me seriously?

I put on a pair of white wedges that tied in a delicate bow around my ankles, slipped on white gloves, and made sure my bubblegum-pink lipstick wasn't on my teeth. The tiniest bit of my natural color was starting to come in at the root, brunette eroding the blonde. I hadn't seen myself as a brunette in years. Mac had never seen me with my natural color.

Maybe it was time for a change.

I strode out of my bedroom. Mac was sitting with Presley on the couch, Elvis's record spinning on the player. His bandage was fresh, and he wore a pair of blue jeans and a plain white T-shirt.

I gave a twirl so my boys could fully appreciate the outfit I'd chosen. Mac dropped the glass of water he was holding, spilling it all over the carpet.

"That good, huh?" I grinned. "Good to know."

"I don't understand what's happening," Mac said, seemingly with difficulty, "but I'm happy to be a part of it."

Someone knocked. Since I was standing, and Mac still sat on the couch with his eyes wide and his mouth hanging open, I answered it.

Detective Hodgson raised both eyebrows at me in lieu of a proper greeting.

No matter. He wasn't the type of man who was impressed by looks. I'd have to win him over with my intellect. Luckily, I'd read every Chesterton story ever published. I had a handle on this. Soon the detective and I would be good friends.

"I've done as you asked," he said, walking into my suite. "Checked out the hidden hallway myself."

"No one saw you, right? Don't want to risk the real thief and killer fleeing when we're so close to the finish."

Detective Hodgson looked me up and down in that searching yet unimpressed way of his. "Do you mean to say that you solved an art theft and a murder case all on your own, Miss Murphy?"

I smiled at him, batted my eyelashes. "Oh, is it very difficult?"

There was another knock on the door. Mr. Sharpe had arrived.

"Miss Murphy," he said, his Scottish accent on full display, "what is the meaning of this? Detective? Mr. Cooper?"

I smiled over my shoulder at the two men in question. Mac was on his knees, doing his best to dry the water he'd spilled on the carpet with one of my personalized linen napkins. Presley walked over to me, winding his way between my feet, and I scooped him up before speaking again. "Mac, would you mind getting the detective some refreshments?"

"Sure." He made a loud noise as he stood. "The kitchen is over here, Detective. You want, uh, some water . . . ?"

"I've been seeing a lot of you two as of late," Detective Hodgson said, making his way into the kitchen with his hands in his pockets. "Really looking forward to that changing as soon as possible."

"Hey, maybe today, eh?" was Mac's reply as the two of them disappeared into the other room.

I adjusted my hold on Presley until he was more comfortably situated in the crook of my arm. "I wanted to speak to you first, Mr. Sharpe. Before the others arrive."

"The others?" Mr. Sharpe shifted on his feet. "Miss Murphy, I am very busy. I have work—"

"Work, work, work. Yes. I know, you're a busy, important man. Thank you for taking the time out of your day to see me. I wanted to talk to you. I've been busy myself. Solving mysteries."

The corners of his lips twitched. "Mysteries. More than one?"

"Four, by my count. But I'm only going to tell you about one for now."

He waved his entire left arm as if to say *Go ahead*.

I tucked Presley under my chin. "It was the smallest mystery, so I thought about it the least, but my conversation with Henry this morning confirmed it."

The corners of his lips twitched again, this time in a tight, downward motion.

I grinned. Until this very moment, I hadn't been sure.

"Yes, Mr. Fox invited me for coffee this morning. We had much to discuss. But you see, after our conversation—he disappeared. He hadn't taken the elevator, or the service elevator, or the stairs. And I remembered when you disappeared on me in much the same way. I wondered, how would Henry know about the hidden passageways unless someone had told him? Why would someone tell him unless they were using it together?"

Mr. Sharpe bit his bottom lip between his teeth. "Miss Murphy," he whispered, "Evelyn. Please—"

"Don't worry, I'm not going to tell anyone. That's why I'm speaking to you alone. Henry is my dearest friend, and I would never risk hurting him. I won't let anyone else hurt him either."

Mr. Sharpe shook his head. "I shouldn't have snapped at you the way I did the other day. I acted out of fear. I'm sorry, Miss Murphy."

I accepted his apology, though it had taken him long enough. "It worked out, in the end. It helped me solve the other three mysteries."

"And . . . what were those, exactly?"

Wagging a finger, I said, "You'll have to wait and see, like everyone else."

I waited until the lot of them arrived, flittering to and fro and behaving like the proper hostess Nanny had always said I could be. They'd all come. Henry, both Count and Countess

Dreadful, Amelia and her parents, Florence the maid, Tilly Bourke, Poppy, and Mr. Burrows. No one was dressed as nicely as me, of course, except perhaps Mr. Sharpe, but that wasn't fair, since he always dressed well. And the countess, I suppose. Her brown hair curled to perfection, her dress short and a vibrant blue.

If only we were different people, we'd be best friends.

"Thank you all for coming. Detective? Would you come out, please?" I'd hidden him away in my bedroom, lest the suspect get suspicious and clear out early.

There was a general murmur of surprise from my guests at this rather dramatic reveal, but there was nothing to be done for it. "Please, lock the front door," I told him.

He murmured, "This better be worth it, Miss Marple."

"Everyone, everyone. Please. Take a seat. This will all be made clear in a moment."

My guests found places to sit. Most gathered on my white couch or pink chaise longue. Others sat on the dining room chairs Mac had brought over to the living room for this purpose.

I stood in front of the semicircle, adjusted my skirt around my legs. They were shaking. I took a breath, closed my eyes, and tried to find the feeling inside my body. What was it? Was I nervous? No, I wasn't nervous.

I was excited.

I said a quick prayer to Saint Anthony and opened my eyes.

"Ladies and gentlemen, thank you for coming. I'm sorry to say that one of you is both a thief and a murderer. And I have found you."

CHAPTER 49

"Absolutely preposterous," said the countess. "This child, marching us in here, *locking* us in here! To accuse us? The way she accused me! Assaulted me in the hallway!"

"I am sorry for that, Countess Drewry," I said. "I was wrong. You hadn't stolen that painting. Miss Bourke said you bought it fair and square. Though you were then attempting to sell it as if it was stolen, which is apparently not an arrestable offense?"

I looked over my shoulder at the detective.

He waved one hand at me, a dismissive gesture, as if to say, *What do you want from me? She's a bloody countess.*

"But, Countess," I continued, "not only do I owe you an apology, I owe you a debt of gratitude. If it wasn't for your money troubles and your desperate attempts to alleviate them yourself, I never would have figured it out."

She exclaimed, "I never!" while her husband sighed.

"You sell a stolen painting on the black market, you get paid twice, perhaps three times what it's worth," I said. "That's what Bell had been planning, you see."

Another murmur came up from my audience, and not all of it in English.

"Whatever do you mean, Miss Murphy?" Tilly Bourke asked. "Billie was planning something?"

The smile on my face stretched from ear to ear. This was delightful! "Yes. See, he was planning on selling his own paintings on the black market for more money than he would've gotten at an art show. Specifically, he was planning on selling the painting *stolen* at the art show on the black market. And since it had been stolen before the reveal, he could sell any number of paintings and say they were all the original one."

Henry scratched at his ear. "So who stole the painting, then?"

"Oh, darling, no one stole the painting. It didn't exist. It was a ruse thought up by Mr. Bell. He practically told me so himself before he was murdered, though I didn't put it together until after the countess tried to continue his plan."

Tilly's eyes shone behind her glasses. She sniffed, loud and wet. "Gracious!"

Amelia's mother took pity on her and handed her a handkerchief.

"Thank you." She dabbed at the tears on her cheeks. "I had no idea! I thought he'd lost his masterpiece. I was devastated by the theft. *Devastated.*"

"She fainted," Countess Dreadful said with a smile. "Poor dear."

The countess took a big sip of her champagne, and I titled my head to the side and watched her.

"I thought you might've been the murderer, Countess," I said. "What with your money problems. But why would you kill your golden goose? No, as much as I wanted it to be you, it wasn't."

She huffed. "Of course not. A knife in the back? If I was to kill anyone, it would be in the front." At that, she raised her eyebrows at her husband. The count clinked his glass against hers.

I did not understand their relationship. "Where were you two during the art show?"

The count asked, "What do you mean? We were observing the art."

"Yes, but after the theft, when Detective Hodgson was questioning us. He said the only people he didn't have alibis for during the reveal were me and Mac, Mr. Sharpe and Henry, and you and the countess. It doesn't matter now, I suppose, since there never was a piece of art stolen. But I am curious."

"Oh, that." Countess Drewry giggled. "We snuck off for a bit, didn't we, love? Found a comfortable little closet."

He giggled back. "We sure did."

I really did not understand their relationship. I shook off that mental image and turned back to my audience.

"I questioned Tilly after the murder. Do you remember, Miss Bourke?"

She nodded. "You were so kind to me."

"And you were so heartbroken. You even confessed to me how much you loved him. I had no choice but to strike you off my suspect list after that."

Mr. Burrows pushed his glasses up with his index finger. "But how would Bell sell it on the black market? Wouldn't he get caught selling his own stuff?"

"Billie Bell had multiple aliases," I said. "In fact, Bell was not his real name. He attended high school as Jack Westlake with our own Phil Hall."

Detective Hodgson grunted from behind me. "Even more evidence against him."

I ignored the detective. I wasn't done laying out my case yet. He'd come around. "Mr. Hall has a history of blackmail, unfortunately." I opened my clutch and pulled out my stolen note.

Mr. Sharpe inhaled loudly through his nose.

I flashed him an apologetic grimace and handed it over to the detective. "A few months ago, a maid stole some money from a guest's safe. When Hall figured it out, he tried to blackmail her into sharing the money. She refused, and Hall turned her over to Mr. Sharpe, who had reason to believe his longtime, trustworthy employee should continue to retain his trust."

"Looking worse and worse for your man," Detective Hodgson said, his eyes on the note. "Not great for you either, Mr. Sharpe."

He fixed his tie. "We handled it in house, in accordance with Pinnacle procedure."

I carried on with my case. "Hall realized that Bell was putting on an act. That, in fact, his entire career could be undone with the truth. He wasn't this foreign, eccentric artist. He was a regular boy from Brooklyn. He attempted to blackmail Bell. But Bell was killed before he had a chance to pay up. And the murderer knew about the blackmail and tried to frame Hall for the murder."

"Not tried," Mac added. "Succeeded."

Mac was right. Again. The real murderer had succeeded in getting Hall arrested.

But I wasn't done. "Yes. Gossip, as we all know, travels through this hotel faster than the common cold. Whoever killed Bell must've known about Hall's predisposition for blackmail.

They tried to get their hands on that note to further solidify their frame-up, first by breaking into Sharpe's office and then rummaging through my apartment, but I'd had it on my person the entire time."

Once again, I flashed Mr. Sharpe an apologetic look.

"The same day my apartment was torn through for that note, the brake lines in my car were cut, resulting in Mr. Cooper, Presley, and I getting into a car accident. That was no coincidence. Someone tried to kill me. I thought it was you, Mr. Burrows."

"Me?" The lenses of his glasses were foggy. "Why would I try to kill you?"

I shrugged a shoulder. "You were the only one who knew Mac and I were taking the car. You even fetched it for us. Perhaps you'd overheard Hall confront Bell and thought you'd try your hand at blackmail."

"And why would I do that?"

"Money, perhaps." I replied. "Or love. A man in love will do many a desperate thing. Your relationship with Miss Bourke had an unusual awkwardness about it, and the timing of your relationship with Miss Cooper was suspect."

He blushed but kept eye contact with me. "I didn't do it."

"Then I wondered if it had been Henry. My dear, sweet Henry."

He set his hand over his heart. "I would never. Evelyn!"

"You knew that the car was mine because I gave it to you. You also got into a very public fight with Mr. Bell during the art show. At the time, we had reason to think you caused a diversion on purpose so that the painting would be stolen. Or that you had gone into the Silver Room early and swiped it to ruin his supposed big reveal. But now we know that the painting was never stolen. I then found out that you knew Mr. Bell, that in fact you had a very contemptuous relationship with the man. Hated him. Maybe you were not motivated by money at all but simply revenge. And I was in the way."

"I can't believe you'd say such a thing, Evelyn."

I smiled at him. "I am sorry, Henry. I believe you innocent now, but I'm trying to explain my thought process and how I've come to my conclusion. Poirot *always* does this."

Mac chuckled. "You and your detective novels."

"For the longest time, I thought it was Mr. Sharpe," I said. "He was sneaking about. Being mean to me. He'd even hidden that very damning note. Then I wondered if perhaps Hall had killed Mr. Bell, and Mr. Sharpe was merely covering up the earlier blackmail to save his own hide.

"That's what you thought, isn't it, Mr. Sharpe?" I asked him. "That Hall had killed him?"

"Of course I thought so," Mr. Sharpe said. "I still do!"

"And that's why you hid the note."

He ran his fingers through his perfectly coiffed hair, messing it up. "I panicked. I'd been wrong about him all this time. I'd stuck my neck out for him, recommending him for promotions. Trusted him. I thought he was my friend."

"An employee murdering a guest will have an effect on management," I said. "Daddy will be looking for people to blame. He'll fire everyone he thinks will keep the hotel safe from legal recourse of the victim's family. As Miss Bourke shared with me, Mr. Bell did have family. A sister. Have you been able to contact her, Miss Bourke?"

She blew her nose into a handkerchief. "Yes," she said, "she was the one who approved the sale of the painting to the countess. But she didn't say anything about suing the hotel. She isn't that sort of person."

I licked my lips and weighed my words.

"I don't know how many of you are aware of this," I continued on, "but this hotel, in the hands of its former owners, was a hub of activity during Prohibition. There are false walls and hidden passages on every level."

Florence exclaimed, "The table! I *knew* there was something wrong!"

"The table, that's right. The hidden wall was behind that out-of-place table. Again, we have gossip to thank for our killer's plan. I realized this morning that they escaped me finding them by fleeing into one of these false passages. I found a bloody handprint on the wall in the hidden passage today, which Detective Hodgson has already processed."

I took a breath, looked around the room. All their attention, every set of eyes, all on me. I wasn't in the crowd, I was apart from it. Leading it. And loving every second.

"It was a left-hand print. With a line through the pinkie, like a scar."

"What does that have to do with anything?" Mr. Sharpe asked. The only left-handed person I'd ever known.

Poppy figured it out. "Because of the sketch!"

Everyone looked at her. I smiled and graciously allowed her to take the spotlight while I fetched the sketch out of my clutch.

"The sketch," she said. "One of Bell's sketches. It was done by a left-handed person."

I handed it over to Detective Hodgson. "I've tried to be careful with it," I told him quietly, "but I'm sure our prints are all over it still."

He glared at me, but there was no heat in it.

Henry guffawed. "What are the odds that the artist and his murderer are both left-handed?" He flexed his right hand as he said it, assuring everyone there was no blood on his dominant hand.

"Slim," I said. "Because Bell wasn't an artist."

Silence. Sheer, stunned silence filled my apartment. I reveled in it, grew taller in it. What would Dr. Sanders say about this? "Bell was the front. The face. The true artist was his left-handed killer. Someone who blends into the background of the hotel, who can slip in and out of rooms unnoticed, who has their ear to the ground when it comes to gossip. They heard about the hidden passages and Hall's past. They overheard my conversation with Mac about taking the car and rushed out ahead of Burrows to cut the brakes of the Rolls in an attempt to murder us before we uncovered the truth. His killer was the mastermind behind the art theft scheme."

They stared at me, stared at each other, back at me.

I smiled bigger than I ever had before in my life. "It was his assistant. Tilly Bourke."

CHAPTER 50

The silence broke. There was noise. Swear words in Italian, questions in French, disbelief in English. Amelia clapped her hands and grabbed Presley off Mac's lap. Detective Hodgson stood at my side. It took everything in me not to look at his face and gauge his reaction. Was he proud of me? Doubtful? Had I won him over?

Were we finally friends?

Tilly stared up at me, tears still streaming down her face. She was so small, so delicate. And she knew it.

"You led me to believe the two of you were in love," I said. "But that wasn't true. In fact, the first time you ever expressed a romantic interest in him was right before you murdered him, in order to establish an alibi. Lots of people will notice a couple behaving romantically around children. Then you gave him your key and sent him to your room, where you'd laid a trap. You were able to beat him there using the hidden passageways. And you surprised him with a knife in the back."

I shook my head. "Give it up, Tilly. They have your fingerprints. What I thought was a scar at first is the ring you wear on your pinkie finger. It's over."

The countess grabbed Tilly's left hand. "There's a stain! A smear of blood! I knew it! I should've gone to the police when I had the chance!"

That caught my attention. *Should have gone to the police?* Ah, of course. I gave the countess a knowing look. She hadn't purchased the painting fair and square. She'd threatened to reveal Bell's plan to the police if Tilly didn't give her the painting. That made sense. Bell was so proud of the plan, he'd even told me about it. But I wasn't a criminal, nor was I in money trouble, so I didn't take it to heart the way the countess must have when Bell bragged to her about it.

Tilly ripped her hand away from the countess, threw the handkerchief to the ground. "Fine," she snapped, and her British accent was gone, replaced with a thick southern American accent.

Kentucky, perhaps.

It shut every conversation in my apartment all the way down.

"Fine," she said again. "You've figured it out. I'm the artist. *Me.* I'm the genius! You know how many people buy works of art from a simple girl from Tennessee?"

Oh, so close!

"Almost none. You know how many idiots will buy that same art if a skinny man with a bizarre accent in a fancy suit says he created it?" At this, she glared at the countess. "Many."

The count, drunk on champagne, laughed until he burped.

"I was tired of being poor. I wanted success. And I found Westlake. A run-of-the-mill con artist. I teamed up with him, trained him. Together we made a small fortune. Then he went and got recognized. On the day we pulled off the art show heist? I had at least six buyers lined up for the stolen painting, all at three times what I could get at a show! Him getting made would've ruined everything.

"Besides, you know the one thing that sells for higher than a stolen painting on the black market? A stolen painting by a dead artist."

"One of your aliases," I said, "is Bell's sister and sole beneficiary. So when he died, you inherited his art. One way or another."

Detective Hodgson left my side. "And Phil Hall, with his monogrammed knife and his history with Bell, was an easy frame-up job." He pulled out his handcuffs. "Tilly Bourke," he said, "you are under arrest."

She snatched Presley out of Amelia's hands and jumped behind the couch. "I don't think so!" She threw open the sliding door of the balcony and ran outside.

Everyone yelled at her to stop.

My feet moved before my brain did, and I started running. Mac sprang to his feet and bolted ahead of me.

"Tilly," he said, his arm stretched toward her, "don't do this."

She dangled Presley off the railing with only two fingers under his collar. Presley kicked his legs, swinging back and forth. He couldn't breathe! I screamed his name and tried to push past Mac, but he wouldn't budge out of the way.

"Tilly, please!" I cried. Detective Hodgson grabbed both my shoulders and held me back. "He's innocent! Don't hurt him!"

"He's a *dog*. A stupid, worthless, dog. Come on, Detective," she taunted, "what's more important? Arresting me? You get close, I let him fall to his death."

I heard his gun click behind my back.

"Put him down," Mac begged. "Come on. Please put him down."

Tilly arched a perfect red brow. She said, "Okay, if that's what you want," and stretched her arm far over the railing. Presley rocked precariously on her fingertips.

"No!" I shouted. "No, please!"

"Miss Bourke," said Detective Hodgson, "set the dog safely on the ground, and we'll talk. Would you like that? You wanna talk? You can tell me all about how Bell deserved it."

"He did deserve it! He was an idiot! And that stupid, black-mailing security guard deserves to be in jail too."

I tried to wrangle my way onto the balcony, but Detective Hodgson's grip on my shoulder was too tight, Mac's strong arm locked across the open doorway. Why wouldn't they let me save my dog?

"Tilly!" I cried. "Take me!"

"What?"

"Leave Presley here," I said, "and take me! I've got money. I can get you on a flight out of the country!"

Both Detective Hodgson and Mac let out similar-sounding arguments against my very reasonable plan. I ignored them. "Please, Tilly, I'll take you anywhere you want to go. I'll give you anything you want. Please put Presley down. Please."

But seeing as how I couldn't get out of Hodgson's and Mac's grasp—and how the detective had a gun while Tilly had nothing and she wasn't a complete and total idiot—she ignored my plan, my pleading.

Tilly threw Presley.

Directly at Mac.

Presley yipped, we all screamed, and Tilly scaled down the fire escape.

Detective Hodgson crawled over Mac and me to follow after her, shouting orders to stop interspersed with swearing the whole way.

I scooped Presley up, held him close to my face. He licked my chin, his little heart beating so fast.

Mr. Sharpe and Burrows bolted out my suite door, no doubt attempting to cut Tilly off outside. Henry ran past us and followed the detective down the fire escape.

Fat tears rolled down my cheeks and wet Presley's fur. Mac enveloped the two of us in a hug, but I stomped on his toes.

"How dare you not let me go get him!"

He hopped up and down on one foot. "It was dangerous! What, you want me to let her throw you off the balcony?"

"If it would save Presley, yes!"

Amelia tugged on my dress. "Evelyn," she said, "I think we should play the elevator game again."

I wiped my face dry on top of Presley's head. "Yes, of course. Of course, you're right. Let's make sure these men don't bungle the arrest, shall we?"

She took the dog from me, who was all too happy to see her, and with Poppy and a limping Mac trailing behind, we went off in search of the other half of our party.

★   ★   ★

A crowd gathered around the scene. On the front steps of the Pinnacle, Detective Hodgson was cuffing Tilly's hands behind her back, both of them panting heavily. His hat was pushed up high on his sweating forehead, his tie loose around his neck. She'd lost her shoes somewhere on the way down, and the left sleeve of her silk blouse had torn.

Mr. Sharpe, Mr. Burrows, and Henry surrounded them, all struggling to catch their breath.

"I'm placing you under arrest for the murder of Billie Bell. Or whatever his name is."

He caught my eye over the crowd of people and gave a single nod.

That was it. He took her to his police car without another word. Were we . . . friends? Had I earned his respect? I'd solved the case for him! The least I could get was a smile. I wouldn't say no to a trophy either. Did they give trophies for solving murder cases?

No matter. I'd visit Judy and buy myself diamonds. Diamonds were better than trophies any day of the week.

"Come along, everyone," I said to my guests. "Let's open some more champagne. I think we've earned it, don't you?"

★ ★ ★

The party continued, surprisingly enough, even after Tilly's arrest. I think everyone was simply too shocked to move on. They needed to stay and eat and talk about what had happened. I was exhausted. The thrill of the reveal had filled me up, and then Presley's dangerous moment had emptied everything out of me.

What was left for me now that Bell's death had been solved? Now that the real killer was behind bars? The countess free to roam about my apartment, making snide comments over my decor?

I thought about filling the detective in on how I suspected the countess had come into possession of one of Bell's paintings but decided against it. She was a bloody countess. She'd have to do something very illegal for the police to get involved, and threatening a lying murderer wasn't it.

What I needed was a nap.

Mac, my sweet Mac, arrived with a cup of steaming coffee in his hand. He gave it to me with a kiss on the top of my head. "Evelyn Elizabeth Grace Murphy, detective-at-large."

I tilted my face up toward his, and he dropped a second kiss, this one on my lips.

"I'm proud of you, Evie. You found the truth like you find everything."

I raised my mug in a silent cheers and took a drink. Mr. Burrows and Poppy were eating chunks of bread dipped in cheese fondue and laughing as Florence made shrimp tails dance. Henry and Mr. Sharpe had coffees of their own and were sitting at the dining room table. Amelia and her parents fussed over Presley. The countess strolled around my apartment making rude comments. Her husband followed her around diligently, drinking champagne. I didn't know if the countess had been having an affair with Bell or if that had been a bit of gossip Tilly had used to make her lie sound more believable, and I didn't want to know.

"What I don't understand," Mac said, his arm around my shoulders, "is how you figured out the hidden passageway this morning."

I shook my head. "That was stupid of me. Mr. Sharpe disappeared in one earlier this week, but I didn't realize it until today when Henry did the same thing."

"Henry? And Mr. Sharpe? Were they in on the whole scheme?" He flashed me a wide smile. "Was I right all along?"

"No. They're completely innocent."

He shifted on his seat to look over at two men in question. "Then why were they sneaking around? What were they doing?"

"I suspect they were meeting each other." I sipped my coffee and didn't say anything else. Mac kept staring. Mr. Sharpe and Henry were still talking in low voices, leaning in close to each other.

"Oh," he said after a while. "*Oh!* Well. Guess I didn't need to be jealous of him all this time, did I?"

My head fit so perfectly on his shoulder. I settled in and smiled. "No, you really didn't."

"I owe you twenty dollars," he said. "You won the bet."

I nodded against his shoulder. "Give it to Poppy. Let her take an art class."

He kissed the top of my head, his mouth curling into a smile against my hair. "I love you, Evie."

"I love you too."

In my apartment, with all my friends—and a few enemies too—with my head on Mac's shoulder and my dog in the arms of a little girl I adored who adored him, it was the happiest I'd been in decades.

Everything I needed was right at the Pinnacle.

CHAPTER 51

We were in the middle of our two o'clock appointment when a shadow fell over us.

"Mr. Peters," I said, "you're blocking our sun."

The bartender stepped to the side so that Mac and I could continue tanning our legs. We rested side by side on recliners by the pool, Presley curled up at my feet. Mac had his sunglasses on, and from time to time he let out a little snore, though when nudged, he insisted in a groggy voice that he wasn't sleeping. I didn't know how either of them could sleep with all the noise. A large group of children were laughing and splashing each other. Their wealthy parents sat at the edge of the pool, soaking their feet while they drank and ignored their children.

The sun was warm, but a chlorine-tinted breeze chilled the air enough that I had to keep my floral cover-up on my shoulders.

"Miss Murphy," Mr. Peters said, rocking on the balls of his feet, "there's a phone call. Um. For you. From your father."

Hickory Dickory Death fell out of my hands and landed with a thump on the ground. Presley startled awake and jumped on top of Mac, who let out an exclamation of surprise.

So he had been sleeping after all.

"Daddy?" I repeated. "Daddy is calling? Whatever for?"

"Well, I don't know, Miss Murphy, but he's holding, and he hates to be on hold."

I was well aware of Daddy's hatred for waiting.

I took his phone call behind the bar, ignoring the guests waving me down for drinks like I was an employee.

"Daddy?" I said into the receiver. "How nice to hear from you! How are you, Daddy? Did you hear I solved the murder—"

Daddy had heard I'd solved the murder. He didn't care for it but was relieved it hadn't been an employee killing guests on the property. He then told me I'd been spending too much money.

"Too much money?" I repeated with a little laugh. "What—to what are you referring?"

He was referring to:

1. The car I'd bought for Henry
2. Tilly Bourke's hotel room stay
3. Dr. Smith's hotel room stay
4. The matching Tiffany's earrings, necklace, and bracelet I'd ordered only this morning

I cleared my throat. "Well, the diamonds . . . they were a treat, you see, for solving the murder, and—"

Daddy did not want excuses. He wanted me to learn the value of a dollar. He said I didn't know how much a dollar was even worth! That I spent money like it grew on trees.

"I don't understand, Daddy. Are we not rich anymore?"

He assured me that of course, we were still rich, but I was getting too old to be spending money like a child. He wanted me to grow up, and the best way to do that—he insisted—was for me to get a job.

Much like being put on hold, Daddy hated being guffawed at. He was not pleased at the sound that came out of my mouth and told me so.

"But Daddy, where will I work?"

At the Pinnacle, of course. He'd already spoken to Mr. Sharpe about it. I was to help plan parties, since I had such an eye for detail and a knack for handling the staff.

I looked over the bar. Presley had taken my spot on the empty lounger. Mac was fully awake, his sunglasses up on the top of his head, looking back at me. The sun draped over him like a blanket, dappled his tan skin and scruff-covered jaw. He waved and I waved back.

"Daddy, I will accept this job on one condition."

He mentioned that I was not in the place to negotiate, but he would listen to my request.

"I'll need a personal assistant."

Daddy seemed to take this condition as my desire to work so hard I'd need help to manage the workload.

Hardly.

I'd plan pretty parties, sure, but Mac needed to get paid, or he'd find a job and then I wouldn't get to see him nearly as much.

Daddy agreed and gave me a budget and hung up after a very brief, impersonal good-bye.

I gave the receiver back to Mr. Peters and ordered Mac and myself two strong drinks. With pineapple rings and little pink umbrellas, of course.

Mac grinned when I came back. He took the drink with a wink and a nod.

"Ah, thank you, Evie," he said. "You spoil me."

"Speaking of." I sat down next to him on his lounger, crossed my legs so my toes tickled his calf. "I have a proposition for you."

Mac let out a long-suffering sigh. "What do you need me to break into today?"

"No, no. Nothing like that. I want to hire you. As my personal assistant. You see, Daddy thinks, and I completely agree, that I should start doing a little more work around the hotel. I'll be planning parties for the foreseeable future, and I'll need an assistant to help me achieve my full potential. What was your salary when you were employed at the Pinnacle?"

He told me.

I laughed so hard I cried. It was such a small amount!

Once I'd managed to regain speech, I kissed his cheek. "Adorable. Well, let's triple that, shall we?"

"Triple!" He clutched his heart like he was near death. "Evie, baby! You're the ginchiest!"

"Of course! Just don't stab me in the back, lover."

Acknowledgments

Many, many thanks to my agent, Madelyn Burt, for believing in both me and Evelyn. This idea started with a tweet and you immediately responded, which gave me the gumption to get to work. Ev wouldn't be here without you and your timely use of a Judge Judy gif.

To Faith Black Ross, my editor. I can't thank you enough for believing in Evelyn, and for your invaluable insights and notes. I'm so grateful for this opportunity to work with you!

To my copyeditor, Rachel Keith. You're a lifesaver.

To Rebecca Nelson, Melissa Rechter, Madeline Rathle, Dulce Botello, Molly McLaughlin, Matt Martz, Holly Ingraham, and everyone at Crooked Lane for their hard work on this book.

To Kashmira Sarode for the beautiful cover.

To Ayesha, Ariel, Samantha, and Anni for their input on early drafts. And for reading those early drafts!

I am so lucky to have such an incredible group of family and friends around me, who encouraged me to keep going when I felt stuck, including (but not limited to!): Mom and Dad, who are both surprisingly cool with me writing about dead and/or absent parents. Doug, Kim, Stevie, and Reed. Rachel, José,

Fran, and Georgina. Billy and Angie. Joseph and Leilani. Catherine and the girls. And Joe and Ann too. Wish they were here to see this.

Miss Mercene, my favorite teacher, and the one who encouraged my writing.

Jordan, thank you for being the best friend and beta reader a person could have.

My amazing kids, Samuel, Avery, Eloise, Madeline, and Margaret. See? I really was working all those times I was on the computer! Well. A lot of the times, anyway. Thank you for letting me write. You're my best friends and I love, love, love you.

And, finally, to my husband, Paul. I always end up quoting Jane Austen when it comes to you, but it's true: if I loved you less, I might be able to talk about it more.

Read an excerpt from

THE SOCIALITE'S GUIDE TO DEATH AND DATING

the next

PINNACLE HOTEL MYSTERY

by S. K. GOLDEN

available soon in hardcover from
Crooked Lane Books

NEW YORK

Chapter 1

It isn't everyday a young woman wearing Little Red Riding Hood's cloak saunters into a busy kitchen, so why did none of the chefs stop what they were doing and look at me? With a huff, I slid off my hood and whistled.

Chef Marco, without looking away from the stove, managed to wag his massive eyebrows at me anyway. "No," he said.

"What do you mean, *no*? Please!" I stuck out my bottom lip. Nothing. "I'm sorry that more guests than we expected are showing up, but isn't that a good thing?"

Chef Marco did not look my way, but his tall white hat tilted to the side.

I batted my eyelashes, my fingers twisting around the hem of my red cloak. "It means more money for the mayor's campaign, after all. And everyone is so enjoying your food because you're simply the best chef in all of New York! Please?"

He picked up a pan only to drop it down on the same burner. "You told me. You said—you *promised*—Mr. Rockefeller would be here! And yet, he is not here."

"Right." I nodded. "Sure. We are all very disappointed that he's not here. But. Okay? But! The mayor is here. Hmm? The mayor? He's pretty good too."

"He has to be here," Marco said. "It's *his* fundraiser. What about your father? Will he at least be here?"

With a smile, I said, "He is supposed to be," because that was true. Did I know where Daddy was currently? No. But did I ever? Also no.

Daddy was the owner of the Pinnacle Hotel. But that didn't mean he stayed here often. He visited a few times a year, popped in to play golf with Manhattan politicians and New York City businessmen, and then left just as quickly.

"Why this?" Chef Marco waved a knife at my torso. "Why the red? What are you wearing?"

I looked down at my outfit. A white vest and black matador pants, covered by an exquisite red cloak that latched with a silver leaf brooch at the base of my throat. "It's a fancy dress party, Chef Marco. I'm Little Red Riding Hood!" I gave him a spin. "What do you think?"

"I think you're too skinny," he snapped. "I will—*fine*—I will make the extra plates. But you must promise to eat one yourself."

With a grin, I replied, "Promise. Thank you ever so."

He raised his knife-wielding hand up in the air. "Get out of here. Go! I have work to do!"

Skipping, I left the kitchen, heading for the service door that led to the Silver Room. I was working. Working meant taking the route every other employee took. Did I miss the descent from the top of the grand staircase into the party? Yes. A lot. But this was good too. Less glamorous, and no one was bothering to take a picture of me, but I found myself wishing I had a camera.

Mac and Poppy were in the hallway, fighting over a wolf head.

"It won't stay on like that," Poppy whisper-yelled.

"It was choking me!" Mac whisper-yelled back. "Is that what you want? Are you trying to kill me?"

"Oh, you are so dramatic! Just put on your costume like an adult!"

My giggling pulled the siblings apart.

Mac, frowning, snatched the wolf head out of Poppy's hands. She gasped. I laughed again.

"That's my project, mind you!" Poppy smacked her brother in the arm. "I need it back. I have to turn it in for a grade at my art school so I can graduate and become successful and move out of your tiny little apartment that smells like wet pants."

"You're welcome to move out at any time," Mac said. "Really. I'll help you pack." He smiled at me. "It doesn't really smell like wet pants, Ev. Cross my heart. You'll love it."

Mac was around my height—meaning, tall—with the broad shoulders, muscled arms, and tanned skin of someone who had spent a lot of time hauling luggage outside until a few weeks ago. Now, he was both my assistant and steady beau, and he'd helped me plan and organize this Halloween-themed fundraiser for the mayor's reelection campaign. His thick brown hair was slicked back and out of his soft gray eyes. Stubble covered his strong, square jaw and made the pronounced dip of his upper lip even more noticeable. I wondered if the butterflies that filled my stomach at the sight of him would ever go away. Or if I even wanted them to. He wore a blue sweater over a black, collared shirt, his dark-wash jeans rolled at the ankles to show off his new shoes, perfectly polished. He set the wolf head carefully on the top of his head, leaving the part that clipped under his chin undone.

We'd been planning for weeks for me to visit his apartment, but I still hadn't quite worked up the nerve. It was all the way in Yonkers, and really he could just as easily stay with me as I could with him.

Except it wasn't the same thing at all, and I knew that and I was working on it. I was!

Poppy fixed the silver leaf broach around my neck and straightened out the fabric of my red cloak. She gave a nod when she was satisfied with my looks. "I traded with Florence for the turndown service on the top floor so I could take Presley out."

"Oh, thank you ever so," I said. "That's so thoughtful." Presley is my perfect little Pomeranian mix who is normally with me everywhere I go, but I had to leave him in my penthouse suite for the evening since I was working.

"She ain't doing it to be thoughtful," Mac said. "It's all for tips."

She stuck her tongue out. "Not only tips! It's for cuddle time with Presley too. Be careful with my project, Malcolm! I'll see you later, and don't be confused—that's a threat! "

Mac offered me his arm, and I took it. "Did you get Marco settled down?"

"As settled as I could."

He pushed open the door, and we snuck inside the busy Silver Room. Adults in costumes ranging from a Night-Out-at-the-Opera to vampires to a white sheet with holes cut out for eyes filled the space and vied for time at the mayor's ear. The mayor was dressed like a politician and was pulling off the too-tight-tie look with practiced ease.

"Marco was disappointed Rockefeller didn't make it," I said.

The tables were set with large but respectable floral arrangements—silver, of course, this being the Silver Room after all. A dance floor was open before a small, raised stage that held a grand piano and a podium. Everything was lit by the shimmering chandeliers running down the middle of the high vaulted ceiling.

I hopped up on my tiptoes, but with all the different outfits it was impossible to tell for certain if he was here.

Mac kissed my cheek, the snout of the papier mâché wolf head wrinkling my hood. "Sorry, Ev," he said. "No word from your old man yet."

Sighing, I nodded. I don't know why I bothered looking.

"I'm gonna go in the kitchen and help with expediting." Mac squeezed my hand. "Holler if you need me."

I recognized my new personal care physician, Dr. Smith, among the guests. He was easy to spot as he dressed like a doctor, in a white jacket with a stethoscope around his neck. At least his ensemble hid his ugly tie, though his unsightly thick-soled shoes were easy to see. He'd been living at the Pinnacle for the last few weeks, and I was sure to invite him, but I was never sure he'd show up.

Introverted was a nice way of describing Dr. Smith.

Crotchety was more accurate.

He was speaking with a couple. The woman had luscious, dark curly hair and stylish red wing-tipped glasses, and was heavily pregnant. Her costume was nothing extraordinary: simple, gauze angel wings strapped over her bare, tawny shoulders. The man at her side had to be twenty years her senior. He wore an expensive suit tailored to his large form. His salt-and-pepper hair was trimmed short. And his gold Rolex watch on his thick, hairy wrist glinted in the light when he exchanged an empty glass for a full one, his fair cheeks already red from the wine.

He wasn't wearing a costume. Party pooper.

"Hello, Dr. Smith," I greeted, extending a hand. "Are you having a good time?"

He shook it, though he frowned when we touched. "Miss Murphy. Have you met Judge Baker? And his lovely wife, Elena."

"Oh!" I shook the judge's hand but brought Elena into a quick hug, kissing her on each cheek. "I didn't recognize you, Judge Baker." I hadn't seen him since his first wife died some years ago, and his hair had been more pepper than salt back then. "How are you doing? How are your boys?"

Judge Baker's sons from his first marriage were both in college. Harvard, to be exact, and could not be much younger than the second wife at his side now.

"They're both doing well," Judge Baker said. "Gordon is at the top of his class. On track to be valedictorian."

I grinned. "Takes after his father, does he?"

He bowed his head. "And your father? How is he?"

"Daddy is excellent, thank you ever so. And how are you, Mrs. Baker? You're positively glowing!"

She held her stomach with both hands, her massive diamond ring sparkling. "I'm so ready to have this little one here with us."

Dr. Smith snorted. "Should be shortly."

"From your lips to God's ears," she said, rubbing her stomach. She grimaced. "It's . . . very uncomfortable, Dr. Smith."

"Hmm. Are you in pain, Mrs. Baker?"

She swallowed hard. "A little. Every few minutes. Not so bad that I think the baby is coming, but enough that I . . ." She closed her dark eyes. "I'm sorry. I don't want to be a bother."

"It's not a bother at all," Judge Baker said. "You made it out here. You shook hands. Go home and get some rest." He kissed her temple. "If anything interesting happens, I'll tell you all about it when I get home."

I reached for the pendant of Saint Anthony I wore as a necklace, its familiar, cold metal soothing. The last thing I was fit to handle was a woman giving birth in the middle of the Silver Room. The *mayor* was here! "Please, Mrs. Baker. You're much more important than this stuffy party. Please excuse me for saying that—I am the one who planned it. If you're at all uncomfortable, I can call a car service for you."

She smiled at me, but her lashes were wet. "You don't mind? That would be most appreciated."

I clapped my hands. "It's settled then. I'll go and call for it myself."

Dr. Smith adjusted his ugly tie. He always wore ugly ties. It was almost as if he challenged himself every day to find the ugliest tie imaginable. This one was brown, like the inside of a used diaper, and covered in what looked to be liberal use of mustard. I wished he'd button up his white coat all the way so I wouldn't have to witness it. "I'll go with you, Mrs. Baker. I can give you an exam in the comfort of your home and make sure it's the usual late trimester discomfort."

"You're a good friend, Doc," Judge Baker said, offering the doctor his hand. "Thanks."

Dr. Smith shook it, the line between his eyebrows increasing drastically. "Nothing to it. Nothing at all."

"If you want to follow me," I said, "there's a back door to the kitchens. That way you won't have to climb up the steps."

"Wonderful. Thank you."

Elena Baker kissed her husband goodbye and then took Dr. Smith's elbow. I led the two of them through the crowded party, to the kitchen, and into the lobby. I waved down Mr. Burrows and told him to order a car, post haste, and put it on my account. Mr. Burrows pushed up his thick glasses with the back of his hand, stuttered some sort of reply, and ran out from behind the mail desk to get the car ordered. I did not see what Poppy saw in him, that much I was sure, but the two of them had been going steady now for a few weeks, and it didn't seem like she was in a hurry to end it.

Once the doctor and Mrs. Baker were on their way, I turned back toward the kitchens, but I never made it.

Mac swept me up in his arms and tugged me into a dark corner of the hallway. His wolf head was suspiciously missing.

I giggled. "What are you doing?"

"Nothing yet." Then he kissed me. "Now I'm gonna convince you to ditch this place."

"What?"

He set me on my feet. "Come home with me."

"I am home."

"To my home." Mac took my face in his hands and kissed my forehead. "Let's go to Yonkers. Come on. Let's do it. I'll be with you the whole way."

"But—" I pulled away from him to search his expression, to look for teasing. He was serious! "But I'm working!"

He shrugged a shoulder. "You planned the party. Party's almost over. Come on. Let's sneak away. I know you want to go, Evelyn. You said you would do it before the year is out."

"Yes. But it's only October!"

He kissed me again, wrapping his arms around my waist and holding me close. When he let me go, I was breathless.

"I promised Chef Marco I would eat," I tried. It hadn't been a *pinkie* promise, and everyone knows the only promise you can't break is a pinkie promise, but Mac didn't need all the details.

"I've got food in the refrigerator," he said.

"Where is your hat?"

"It's not a hat." Mac reached for the brooch around my neck, unclipping it and letting the hood fall on the floor. He picked it up, the red fabric draped over his forearms. "It's a travesty, that's what it is. Come on. What do you say?" He held out a hand. "Let's have an adventure. A perfectly safe adventure," he added.

Maybe he was right. Daddy hadn't made it and probably wouldn't make it. I'd gotten Chef Marco to make all the extra plates. The mayor had already given his speech. What was there left for me to do?

"I guess I . . ." I took his hand. "Yes. Okay. Let's do it."

Chapter 2

"Oh, I don't know, Mac," I said, pulse thrumming in my veins for reasons beyond being outside the Pinnacle's walls. We were still in its shadow, and he kept me boxed inside it, his strong, warm hands on my waist. He'd dropped my cloak off at the mail desk with a befuddled Mr. Burrows and zero explanation. "What about Presley?"

The air felt crisp, and even though it was dark outside, leaves shone brightly in yellows, oranges, and reds, illuminated by street lamps. Menacing smiles were carved into the pumpkins in the window of the Pinnacle's candy shop. I waved goodbye as the candles inside their carcasses flickered.

"We'll call the front desk. Chuck is working all night with Poppy. They'll take care of the ankle biter."

I swatted his chest, but my fingers got distracted by the soft, bluish-gray fabric of his sweater. The same color as his eyes. Toying my bottom lip between my teeth, I looked up at him under my lashes. "And you won't stay with me here, lover?"

He groaned and pressed his forehead to mine. Mac took a deep breath, and I rather got the impression he was breathing me in. He kissed me softly, lips barely parting. And then he pulled back much too quick, a wet kiss on my forehead my only consolation prize. "Nope! Come on, Ev. You've got a world to conquer. And it starts with Yonkers."

With his fingers laced through mine, Mac pulled me alongside him. His long legs meant long strides, but I was close to his height and was practically born in heels, so keeping up with him wasn't difficult. He grinned down at me and wrapped an arm around my back, his hand finding purchase on my waist again. "I'm chuffed. Wish I'd picked up the flat a bit and ran for some groceries, but it'll be hunky-dory with the lights off, Ev." He winked and my face flushed.

"Malcolm," I whispered, "I haven't got a change of clothes!"

"Why would you need clothes?"

I shot him an exasperated look under the streetlights. "Where are we going, anyway? Surely you don't mean to walk to Yonkers."

"Of course not." He chuckled. "The Pinnacle's parking garage is around the corner. I'm going to drive your Rolls. Make up for that—you know—hospital business a few weeks ago."

I did know. His first time driving my Rolls-Royce had landed us both in the hospital, though it was hardly his fault. "But what about my makeup? Or a toothbrush?"

"Evie, baby." He stopped walking long enough to pull me into another heart-stopping kiss. "I promise. You won't be thinking about brushing your teeth once we make it to my apartment." He held my hand in his and placed it over his heart. I was surprised to find I could feel it beating beneath my palm. At this point in our relationship, having been a steady item for a month—six weeks, to be exact, not that I'm counting every day that goes by with a little heart in my calendar—I worried he'd grow bored of me. Used to me. But the prospect of me in his apartment had him as flustered as my leaving the Pinnacle had me.

But I'd do anything for Mac.

Maybe he felt the same, though the very idea was foreign. I wasn't the sort of person that anyone stuck around long enough to feel that way about.

I nodded. "All right. Let's go get the Rolls." A wicked grin tugged at my mouth. "I trust you not to crash it for a second time."

He huffed, a smile on his face, nonetheless. "Come on then. No more stalling. The garage is after this left."

I've lived in the Pinnacle all my life. I used to come and go often, nowadays not as much. But even in my childhood, traveling to and from with Mom, or later with Nanny, I'd never been inside the garage. I was always dropped off and picked up on the steps of the hotel itself.

It was seven floors, not counting the empty roof, with no walls, only cars lined up to the edge of each floor. I stopped and stared at it, at the neon sign that spelled out "PARKING" in bright red letters along its side, at the metal stairs that curved around each floor.

"We aren't walking up those things, are we?" I asked Mac, unable to keep the shake out of my voice and hands. "They're likely to crumble in a good gust of wind!"

He made a rude noise with his lips and tongue. "We'll use the ramps inside," he said. "But those things aren't going anywhere. You think your dad wants a lawsuit from employees on his hands?"

My attention was stuck on the old, rickety staircase. "I suppose," I said. Daddy did hate to be tied up in court. But better safe than sorry. "Ramps inside, I think. But Mac—I don't have the keys!"

"No, the valet here has them." He smiled at me like I was a lost child. I didn't like it one bit and rolled back my shoulders so I might stand at my full height and remind him how grown I was. "Come on." He kissed my cheek. "We're almost there. Don't quit on me now."

He tugged me by the hand to the small booth outside the parking garage's entrance, shaded by a large umbrella striped in white and blue. Cars trickled in and out of the entrance, not quite a steady stream, but enough to make me wary of being run over. A Pinnacle employee, wearing the same uniform all the bellhops and lift boys wore—long sleeves, long slacks, green with gold buttons on the jacket, unshined black shoes—watched us before his eyes lit with recognition. "Cooper!" He greeted. "Miss Murphy! You two eloping?"

My cheeks burned and my heart skipped a beat. It was embarrassing to have a stranger describe your most precious dream out loud like that in front of your face. But I smiled at him all the same and hoped he didn't realize how well he knew me when I didn't even know his name.

"Ah, not quite," Mac said. "Taking the missus to Yonkers for a nightcap. You got the keys?"

Mrs. Evelyn Elizabeth Grace Cooper had a certain ring to it. Would Mac buy me a ring on his own, or would I be able to pick it out and help pay for it? There was always Mom's wedding ring, tucked away in a safe at the bank. Perhaps Daddy would let me use that when Mac and I exchanged our vows in front of a priest?

Mac would have to convert. Or we could find a priest who might look the other way if there was a hefty donation that followed the ceremony.

"Silver Cloud Rolls-Royce," the valet said, tossing Mac the keys. "Third floor. Can't miss it."

Mac dangled the keys in front of my face. "See? Easy as pie." He set his empty hand on the small of my back and started walking, his soft but insistent press making me leave the safety of the valet's podium and venture into the strange structure filled with parked cars.

"It's rather beautiful," I said. "In its own way."

Mac laughed as we walked up a sloped ramp. "That's one of the things I love about you, Ev. You can see beauty in a garage."

I tossed my hair over my shoulder. "Beauty always recognizes beauty."

He kissed my hand and kept walking. Some of the cars were in better shape than others, some more expensive. Each one backed into a little square and off, with no driver or passenger in sight.

"Only valets come in here?" I asked as we ascended, walking up the twisting ramps of concrete only cars normally drove on. One passed by us on its way down, a valet in green in the driver's seat, and Mac waved. "Or do people park their cars themselves?"

"Oh no—there'd be chaos," Mac said. "The valets on duty get to pick the spots. They keep track with little tickets. Here, see?" He held up the keys again, and I noticed a laminated keychain I hadn't seen before, with a number written in pen in the center: 321. "You get a forever spot because you're you."

I gave a little skip in acknowledgment.

"But if we let all the guests park their cars, valets would never be able to find them again. There'd be accidents. More than we got now, anyway. Scott let me in because he knows us. Granted, if you were some filly, he'd have got the car himself."

"Do you speak from experience, Malcolm?" I asked, giving him a look from the corner of my eye. "You take a lot of other girls here to this parking garage?"

"Evelyn, baby, I've never dated another girl with her own car before. You're the first filly I've ever taken into this beautiful garage."

We made it to the third level, two more valets driving customers' cars passing us on our hike, and I spotted my Silver Cloud Rolls-Royce toward the entrance, the number 321 painted in white near its trunk. The car was shining and undented, like the accident had never happened. "Let's keep it that way." I bopped him on the nose.

Mac pretended to bite my finger, and I giggled. He pushed me up against the passenger side of my car, his nose on my neck. "Of course," he whispered, "nobody says we gotta hurry outta here."

I relaxed into Mac's embrace, wrapping my arms around his back. "Lover, I might be the kind of girl you can talk into going to Yonkers, but I'm most certainly not the kind of girl who is up for a romp in the back seat of a car."

He kissed my neck. "Who said back seat?" He leaned back to grin at me. "Who said car at all?"

"Malcolm Cooper!" I giggled. "You're a terrible influence."

He nuzzled my hair before dipping his face to my shoulder, his nose grazing my cheek and the underside of my jaw. I giggled again at the tickling sensation. I glanced around us for the first time. Maybe there was something to his plan. We were all alone, and we'd hear a car approaching. The night was young and so are we.

Except . . .

A . . . shadow? In a driver's seat about four cars away. From a nearby pillar? But it was round, collapsed onto the steering wheel. And appeared much more solid than any shadow had the right.

"Is that a person?"

"No," Mac said without looking. "Valets aren't gonna be hanging around up here."

I pushed his chest to give myself more space to stretch my neck. There was a human-shaped something in the driver's side of the cherry-red Cadillac Coup de Ville four spots away from us.

"Mac," I said, removing myself from his arms with some difficulty. He even pinched my rear once I'd disengaged. "Something is wrong!"

He raked his fingers through his hair, wisps of his fallen pompadour brushing his eyelashes. Long and luscious, it was unfair for a man to have natural lashes like that. "All right. Let's go check out."

I tugged my vest down into its proper place, unsure of when exactly it'd been tugged askew. "Thank you."

"But it's nothing," he said, "and we're hopping in this car and going to Yonkers right after."

I cleared my throat. Yonkers. He had to live all the way in *Yonkers*. "Fine."

"Fine."

"I'll lead the way, shall I?"

He grinned. "Yes, you shall."

Mac had the annoying habit of being almost always right. So, if he thought the person-sized shadow in the Cadillac was nothing, it was probably nothing. But my nose wrinkled at the sight of it anyway, and I was compelled toward the driver's door, my shoes clacking against the rough concrete of the garage. My nose has a terrible habit of wrinkling whenever I'm deep in thought. I'm aware of it, and it does nothing for my appearance—only adds to the number of wrinkles I'll have to deal with as I age—but I cannot stop myself from wrinkling my nose.

It stayed wrinkled until I opened the door and cast light inside the Cadillac, revealing a dead body.